# Theater in Sierra Leone

# THEATER IN SIERRA LEONE

ങ്കഃ

## Five Popular Plays

Edited by
Iyunolu Osagie

**Africa World Press, Inc.**

P.O. Box 1892
Trenton, NJ 08607

P.O. Box 48
Asmara, ERITREA

Copyright © 2009 Iyunolu Osagie
First Printing 2009

All rights reserved. No part of this publication may be reproduced, stored in a retrieval system or transmitted in any form or by any means electronic, mechanical, photocopying, recording or otherwise without the prior written permission of the publisher.

Book design:     Saverance Publishing Services
Cover design:    Ashraful Haque

Library of Congress Cataloging-in-Publication Data

Theater in Sierra Leone : five popular plays / edited by Iyunolu Osagie.
    p. cm.
 ISBN 1-59221-682-X -- ISBN 1-59221-683-8 (pbk.)
 1. Sierra Leonean drama (English)   I. Osagie, Iyunolu Folayan, 1960-

PR9393.7T48 2009
822'.9140809664--dc22

                          2009001281

To the artists of Sierra Leone,

    Who bear witness…

        In life and in death

# CONTENTS

◊◆◊

| | |
|---|---|
| ACKNOWLEDGEMENTS | ix |
| FOREWORD Eustace Palmer | xi |
| INTRODUCTION Iyunolu Osagie | 1 |
| THE BLOOD OF A STRANGER<br>Dele Charley | 27 |
| LET ME DIE ALONE (Madam Yoko)<br>John Kolosa Kargbo | 83 |
| THE PATRIOT<br>Julius S. Spencer | 141 |
| THE POOL<br>Tonie French | 205 |
| NOT YOU TOO<br>Mohamed Sheriff | 259 |
| GLOSSARY | 305 |
| PLAYWRIGHTS' BIOGRAPHIES | 309 |

# ACKNOWLEDGEMENTS

◊◆◊

This project actually began in 1994, when I won grants from the Research and Graduate Studies Office in the College of the Liberal Arts and the Minority Faculty Development Office at the Pennsylvania State University to conduct research on the Amistad story in Sierra Leone. During my six-week field trip to Sierra Leone for the Amistad project, I used the opportunity to interview many theater practitioners of various stripes and to also collect plays for this current project. At the time, the civil war raging in other parts of the country was still a far off affair. The war eventually spread to Freetown in all its crude reality, causing the work on this second project to be stalled for many years after. I lost contact with many artists––some died during the war, and others fled the country. Significant sites, like the Sierra Leone Broadcasting Service (SLBS), with its archive of radio plays, had been completely destroyed. It was only after the war, when I revisited in 2006, that I saw the urgency of collecting many more plays to capture what little was left of our ravaged past. Reestablishing contacts with many artists became a challenge, and preserving some measure of a vibrant artistic past became an urgent task.

I want to thank the English department for its continued support of my research interest. In particular, I want to thank the undergraduate interns (Joanna Guldin, Marisa Cavanaugh, and Shalaina Parsell) the department provided to help me with computer support. Many thanks to Raymond Desouza George and Tom Cauurray who helped me in reestablishing contacts with artists in Freetown, and in locating some vital research material. I thank all contributing artists, or the relatives of deceased artists, in making this project a reality. Through Angela Ajayi (editor) and Sam Saverance (designer), Africa World Press has provided me with excellent partners to work with. I cannot thank them enough for their professionalism. Thanks to Eustace Palmer who graciously agreed to write the foreword. My thanks to my husband, Sylvester, for his infinite patience and support. Thanks also to my sister, Octavia Johnson, who is always there when I need her. My thanks to Almighty God who makes me see light where there is only darkness.

# FOREWORD

Sierra Leone is truly out of the literary doldrums. Within the last twenty years or so a tremendous number of writers have emerged like Syl Cheney-Coker, Lucilda Hunter, J. Sorie Conteh, Tibbie Kposowa, Delia Jarrett-Macauley, Sheikh Umarr Kamarah, Aminata Forna, Gibril Koroma and others who in prose and in verse have attested to the great creative spirit latent in that country. However, this astonishing literary renaissance was led by the dramatists, who, as from the 1960s onward, brought about a tremendous transformation in the cultural landscape of the country. Spearheaded by the efforts of Juliana Rowe and building on the achievements of earlier dramatists like Raymond Sarif Easmon and Yulisa Amadu Maddy, a new generation of dramatists like Dele Charley, John Kolosa Kargbo, Raymond De Souza George, Adeyemi Meheux, Clifford Garber, Akmid Bakarr, Julius Spencer and Bobson Kamara transformed the Sierra Leone theatrical scene by writing plays in the vernacular, greatly broadening the theater audience, and bringing the theater home to the citizens of Sierra Leone. They introduced professionalism into the theater, and made the citizens of Sierra Leone realize that the theater was not a distant middle class phenomenon, but something that dealt with issues they could relate to and in a language they could all understand. They utilized local situations, deployed the oral tradition, and also translated the works of dramatists from other nations and other epochs, like Shakespeare, into the local languages, thus showing that the issues dealt with by those dramatists were the common concerns of all humanity.

But some of these dramatists like Dele Charley and John Kolosa Kargbo also wrote and staged some compelling plays in English. The plays in the vernacular, though enormously popular in Sierra Leone, so popular and relevant in fact that at times the dramatists incurred the wrath of the then dictatorial government who therefore clamped down heavily on theatrical activity, did not reach the wider world audience that they deserved. The main reason for this was that publishers simply could not handle plays written in the Krio language. However, the plays written in English, though remarkably successful on the stage, were also not published and a wider world audience was therefore denied the opportunity of enjoying the creativity and versatility of these young writers. Scholars and teachers who wanted to make use of these plays for the purposes of scholarship or for inclusion in the school curriculum, so that the world and the younger generation would be made aware of the great relevance of these plays to society, bitterly complained that they were unavailable in print.

It is for this reason that the present collection of five plays in English by that astonishing generation of Sierra Leone dramatists is to be warmly commended. These plays, though manifesting different styles and differing degrees of theatrical expertise, all deal with issues central to African writing and the human condition: tradition versus change; colonialist arrogance, corruption, and exploitation; the condition of African womanhood and the changing roles of women; female circumcision; patriotism and resistance to oppression; and the degradation and corruption of contemporary African society.

Dele Charley's *Blood of a Stranger*, the Sierra Leone Entry to the African Festival of the Arts held in Lagos, Nigeria, in 1977, is undoubtedly that late dramatist's best play, though he also wrote several plays in Krio and Krio adaptations of some of the plays of Shakespeare. A compelling spectacle

## Foreword

on the stage, this play also makes compulsive reading in the study. It is about the fraudulent activities of a white colonialist exploiter who, showing tremendous disregard for the people's customs and traditions, wishes to corrupt them with petty gifts, seduce their women, and steal their diamond wealth. *Let Me Die Alone*, by the remarkable John Kolosa Kargbo, is surely one of the finest African plays ever written. John Kolosa Kargbo is one of those Sierra Leonean playwrights whose trenchant exploration of the then Sierra Leonean social and political situation in a play like *Poyotong Wahala* aroused the wrath of the then government and forced him into exile. *Let Me Die Alone* is based on historical material: the life and times of Madam Yoko, a legendary monarch of the Mende people. Making superb use of the English language, the play deals with issues that are at the forefront of the modern feminist movement: relations between husbands and wives, women forced into loveless marriages, brutal husbands, women forced into stereotypical roles, and the right of women to determine whether their femininity should consist solely in the ability to bear children. The play also portrays colonialist arrogance, blackmail, intrigue and murder, and the presentation of Madam Yoko, a truly tragic heroine, is one of the most memorable portrayals of a woman in the whole of African drama.

Like *Let Me Die Alone*, Julius Spencer's *The Patriot* is also based on history: the life and exploits of one of Sierra Leone's legendary heroes, Bai Bureh, who, in Sierra Leone at least, has, like Dedan Kimathi, become the symbol of resistance to exploitative and arrogant Western imperialism. A professional theater scholar with a Ph.D. in Drama, Spencer has been able to deploy some very interesting theatrical devices in this play such as the skilful use of a narrator, and to incorporate singing, dancing, and the oral tradition, which have become staples of African drama.

*The Pool* is the only play by a woman dramatist in this collection. It shows that women have also been in the forefront of dramatic activity in Sierra Leone as actors and dramatists. It is by Tonie French who, until her untimely death, was the leading female playwright working in Sierra Leone. Not surprisingly, it deals with the condition of African womanhood including male exploitation of African women, lack of opportunities for women, male irresponsibility and marital infidelity, and prostitution. Mohamed Sheriff's *Not You Too* also interestingly, for a male dramatist, explores the condition of African womanhood, concentrating on the controversial issue of female circumcision.

It is significant and unfortunate that three of these dramatists—Dele Charley, John Kolosa Kargbo, and Tonie French—are no longer with us. It is hoped that this collection will be seen not just as a fitting testament to the dramatic creativity of Sierra Leoneans, but in some measure, as a memorial and tribute to them.

Eustace Palmer
Department of English
Georgia College and State University

# INTRODUCTION

## Prelude

In the 1970s, Professor Eldred Durosimi Jones of the University of Sierra Leone edited a special collection for the journal *African Literature Today* titled "Drama in Africa," a much needed volume that rightly gauged the academic necessity to engage, intellectually, the prolific dramatic products emanating all over Africa. In his editorial commentary to this edition on drama, he astutely pointed out that the list of published plays in Africa belied the impressive productivity of theatrical material on the continent. In fact, he stressed that much popular theater is hardly scripted, and barely ever published. He also hinted that an African audience is more likely to watch "popular" theater, which is more grounded in their everyday life stories and in the "language" of the people, than be drawn to the more "sophisticated," Western-oriented production and technologically more challenging variety of the educated/published play. One would hesitate today to make such a clear distinction between African popular theater and Western style theater because many African artists have learnt, through the art of syncretism, to use both versions to their full advantage. It is however still true that more than three decades later the majority of playwrights, particularly in Sierra Leone, are yet to adopt the publishing tradition that prevails in most other parts of the world.

Several factors are responsible for this weak publication record in Sierra Leone. Firstly, lack of economic opportunity has made it all but impossible for most artists to take up the extra cost of publication; the amount of energy necessary to find patrons who would sponsor a major production most likely discourage artists from tapping those same sources for publication support. Secondly, these artists are in such intense competition with each other that most of their effort goes into producing the next new play so as to attract a good audience pool. Playwrights often feel immense pressure to come up with something new. Generally, the tradition of recycling plays (except for a few stock classics like *The Blood of a Stranger*) has not been appealing to the populace. Thirdly, the very high illiteracy rate in the country has made it difficult for artists to see past the financial assessment of textual production to the culturally rewarding goal of creating long-term historical memory. Indeed, this 30-year production dearth (plays were published in the 1960s and early 1970s) gravely reflects the economic and political downturn of a nation in decay. This decay, as we all now know, culminated in the civil war of the 1990s.

My interest in putting together a collection of plays from the 1970s, 80s, and 90s is partly born out of my memory of some of the excitement that began in the 1970s, when I witnessed and enjoyed the theater world as a participant in a play directed by Clifford Shafume Garber and as I attended many theater workshops hosted by the Sierra Leone Broadcasting Service (television). Back then, I was just one of many restless youth who hung out at Dele-Charley's house (he helped us realize our dream to start a social club) and followed the highly acclaimed John Kolosa Kargbo around. In 1994 when I visited Sierra Leone from the US, I had the opportunity to interview actors, directors, and playwrights, some of whom I had known in the past. I also had the good fortune of collecting some of their plays. At the time, I was quite unaware of

## Introduction

the devastating effects that the war, which had begun in other parts of the country but at this time had little effect on the capital city, Freetown, would have on the nation. Today, some of the artists I interviewed are dead, and others are scattered around the world as refugees. Also, my visit to Sierra Leone in the summer of 2006 (which confronted me with a new unrecognizable country, it seemed) impressed upon me the need to preserve the artistic past I knew so well from that very rich theatrical period. In fact, in an article titled "A Historical Background to the Contemporary Theatre in Sierra Leone," Dr Julius Spencer makes specific reference to the 1980s as a period characterized by a "theatre boom" in Sierra Leone. Indeed it was a period in which theater became "a viable entertainment enterprise" reaching all strata of the Sierra Leone community. It was also a compelling historic period because theater transformed itself from its very amateur status into a quasi-professional powerhouse.

At least three Sierra Leonean scholars, Eustace Palmer, Julius Spencer, and Mohamed Sheriff, in separate essays, have all traced the beginnings of theater in Sierra Leone. I will not retrace their steps here but will highlight some of the major observations in their essays; this will help contextualize theater at the end of the twentieth century that we are concerned with here. I should make it clear from the onset that formal theater as discussed by these artists only reflects theater development in Freetown, the capital city. As Sheriff states in an essay on Sierra Leone theater, "Western-style theatre never really made much impact outside Freetown. To date, there are just a handful of theatre groups doing western-style African theatre outside Freetown, but there are many cultural traditional performing groups all over the country, despite the devastation and instability caused by war" (Banham 2004). Indigenous theater predates formal literary theater and continues unabated in strength. In fact, the elements of the traditional (song, dance, ritual, proverbs, and cultural themes) have found their way into Western-style plays in Freetown and can rightly be pointed to as the essential factors that make Sierra Leone theater unique.

Nonetheless, today's formal theater, or modern theater, in Sierra Leone had its beginnings in European theatrical forms. Both Spencer and Sheriff agree that the different stages in the social and political development of the nation have shaped the kinds of plays that were written and produced.

Throughout the twentieth century, the social and political scene of power was significantly reflected on stage. The first quarter century produced small dramatic groups performing mostly European classics or plays written by members of the European community, such as *The Downfall of Zacharia Fee*, written and directed by Sir Arnold Hodson, the colonial governor in Sierra Leone (1934) at the time. Also, the small Sierra Leone elite, made up mostly of the Krio community (descendants of freed slaves) and other educated segments of the society, entertained themselves largely through school and church dramatization of Bible stories. These meetings, as Spencer points out, eventually blossomed into "Pleasant Sunday Afternoon Gatherings," popular as a leisurely diversion right through the 1950s. Although both Gladys Casely Hayford and N.J.G. Ballanta-Taylor had in the 1930s introduced Freetown audiences to African folklore through their plays (Hayford) and operas (Taylor), there is no record of any compelling attraction to this trend until the 1950s. The established practice was to do Biblical and European plays in English. Sheriff has identified this period as theater of the colonial era.

The anticipation of independence by the mid 1950s and its achievement by the turn of the decade saw an emergence of plays with more Sierra Leonean flavor. John Akar's plays, "Valley Without Echo" (1954) and "Cry Tamba" (1961), were clearly "African in outlook." Akar's first play, which premiered in London, was seen as "the first significant play about African village life" and his second play placed second in the Independence Play competition (Spencer 1988). Akar was unique in using indigenous songs and dances. Akar's nationalist vision also led him to set up the Sierra Leone National Dance Troupe, which became an icon of pride in the country. Also in this era of independence, the first published Sierra

## Introduction

Leonean playwright, Sarif Easmon, emerged with *Dear Parent and Ogre*, a play that won the Independence Play award in 1962. The play was later published in 1964. Although much criticized today for its decadent language and European sensibilities, the play was well received by audiences of its day. Easmon's second published play, *The New Patriots* (1965), also received favorable reviews from approving audiences. Nonetheless, like the first play, it also emulates Krio elitism, and by association European cultural superiority. Although Easmon wrote a third play that he never published, he had, with his two plays, ushered in a new era of publication history in drama. Pat Maddy, who later changed his name to Yulisa Amadu Maddy, also published several plays that he wrote mostly in the 1960s, in a collection called *Obasai and Other Plays* (1971). Maddy's plays focus on the disillusionment of a post independence society that has lost its political will. Whereas Easmon's plays display the admirable qualities of Western society, Maddy's plays exposes the underside of Krio elitism by using murderers, prostitutes, and truants to protest an ailing economy and a degenerate political system. The stark ideological differences between Easmon and Maddy, for example, have led to Eustace Palmer's observation of a clear pattern of artistic development in the nation's literary history. Like Spencer and Sheriff, Palmer's observations cannot be separated from the political fortunes of the nation itself.

In "The Development of Sierra Leone Writing," an essay Palmer wrote in 1975, he finds it puzzling that Sierra Leonean artists, a small crop of intellectual elite of the 1950s and 60s, did not display a strong sense of African consciousness, a trait he had discovered in the work and impulses of artists such as Chinua Achebe and Camara Laye. Because the Krio community identified more with the British colonizers (in their eyes their liberators from slavery) than with the indigenes of their new country, the community, not surprisingly, produced an artistry that reflected its sentiments. The pioneers of Sierra Leonean literature, among them Adelaide Casely-Hayford and her daughter Gladys Casely-Hayford, Crispin

George, Abioseh Nicol, Sarif Easmon, and Robert Wellesley-Cole, were all Krios. They constituted its intellectual elite and were leading "members of the establishment," the cream of the cream as Palmer describes them.

Palmer makes a distinction between "pioneers" such as the Hayfords and what he calls "the middle generation" of writers, such as Easmon and Nicol. The key factor to understand in Palmer's analysis is that a certain consciousness was beginning to develop, as in the work of Abioseh Nicol; Easmon attempts to address the bridge (or lack thereof) between the Krio and the indigenes but with disastrous results because Easmon esteems Krio civilization, a creative imitation of British culture, very highly and succeeds in killing the spark of African consciousness which his plays attempt to tease out. Palmer also makes a distinction between this middle generation, mostly of the 1960s, with what he calls the future generation—artists who wrote mostly in the late 60s, for example Gaston Bart-Williams, and the 1970s, for example the poets Syl Cheney-Coker and Lemuel Johnson, and novelist and playwright Yulisa Maddy. This later generation, with various levels of success, according to Palmer, mainstreamed Sierra Leonean literature because they critiqued racial and ethnic discrimination and seemed more aware of their cultural displacement.

## Context

Today, the Krio intellectuals who were at home with British culture (that Palmer describes in his 1975 essay) have largely disappeared. The next three decades brought with it a high sense of cultural awareness, especially as the political fortunes of the nation were securely established in the hands of provincial leaders. To begin with, the Krio community was always dwarfed by the indigenous communities and it was only a matter of time for the community's sense of superiority to dissipate as well. In short, Krios today have embraced a strong sense of nationhood and have, like the rest of the country,

# Introduction

embraced their national heroes. For example, a play like *The Patriots*, written by Spencer, a Krio, praises the exploits of Bai Bureh, a heroic fighter from an indigenous background. Like Palmer predicted, intellectuals of non-Krio heritage are also in the business of making art (Alusyne Bangura in fine art and John Kolosa Kargbo in drama, for example). Even in a genre like drama that throughout the 1980s continued to be dominated by Krio playwrights, such as Dele-Charley, and Clifford Shafume Garber, these artists' aesthetic sensibility is thoroughly steeped in a cultural sense of place.

Consequently, the plays in this collection have a strong cultural flavor. Beyond the names of characters and their geographical mapping, there is a certain authenticity in the adaptation of the English language to convey a deep cultural aura. The world the characters occupy is uniquely Sierra Leonean. By this I mean that although Krio is the major lingua franca, it is a language whose very legacy as a product of slavery has an enriched vocabulary from a variety of European and African languages. Its natural elasticity has also rendered it accessible to Sierra Leone's diverse population groups (Sierra Leone has at least 14 ethnic groups) and it continues to be a dynamic and growing language because phrases and expressions from the different indigenous languages so often become available registers in Krio. Playwrights have found this facility of adopting and adapting vocabulary in other languages with/in the Krio language enabling and powerfully effective, particularly in portraying a range of emotions on stage. It is also at the level of language that a lot of humor is communicated to the Sierra Leonean audience. Tonie French's play, *The Pool*, is a case in point. A mere reading of the play does not adequately convey the humor that is transmitted, whereas a full performance, with a series of Krio accents that indicate class, social upbringing, or attitude, keeps the audience laughing.

The popularity of Krio as the language of choice for the theater has not gone unnoticed. Eustace Palmer has discussed at length the role that vernacular drama has played in creating a taste for theater in the masses and for breaking down the line between art and life: "The dramatists exploited to the full all the resources of the indigenous spoken language and of the oral tradition: various idioms and turns of phrase, proverbs, riddles, songs, variations in tone and pitch and accompanying gestures, mannerisms and facial expressions. The people loved it; they flocked to the theatre in huge numbers and the plays in the vernacular became enormously popular" (Palmer & Porter 2008). It can be argued therefore that the Krio language as an effective tool in the hands of Sierra Leonean playwrights has become a blueprint for those playwrights who choose to render a play in English as well. It is in fact not uncommon to find a play first written in Krio (given its popularity with all audiences) and then translated by the same artist into English. We can conclude, then, that although most plays in Freetown are done in Krio, when playwrights decide to write plays in English, there is a natural carryover of a rich cultural vocabulary into such plays. The five plays in this collection reflect this rich tradition. However, this embrace of the cultural essence of language as reflective of the identity of the people is not the only common denominator among Sierra Leonean playwrights.

Another important pattern of development is the growing politicization of the theater. Ngugi wa Thiongo describes this type of tension between artists and their government as "a struggle between the power of performance in the arts and the performance of power by the state" (1998). As theater became more and more central to the social life of the people in the 1970s, theater artists began to use their artistic productions to criticize the Sierra Leonean government by highlighting the social malaise around them. The economic downturn in the 1970s through the mid 1980s forced many playwrights to turn from simple love stories to the more challenging issue of historical relevance and survival as a nation. John Kargbo and his theater group, Songhai Theatre, for example, were on the government's blacklist. In the 1970s Kargbo had written and directed a play in Krio called *Poyotogn Wahala*, detailing the failures of Siaka Steven's inept government and the rampant

## Introduction

abuse of human rights in Sierra Leone. Naturally, Siaka Stevens, then President of Sierra Leone, did not like the play and the extent of its popularity, especially in Freetown. While artists like Kargbo sought to awaken the audience's political consciousness, the government was doing all in its power to douse all political awareness. It was because of *Poyotogn Wahala* that President Stevens ordered the commission of a Censorship Board within the Ministry of Education, where all plays, whether Sierra Leonean or foreign in origin, had to meet the approval of the board before they were performed. The bureaucratic delays this Commission set in motion can only be imagined. Political apathy under Siaka Stevens's long-standing one party government, the All People's Congress, gave rise to pockets of political unrest in different segments of the population, most notably University student demonstrations throughout the 1970s and 80s and finally in 1992, under the leadership of President Joseph Momoh, a successful military coup by young underpaid soldiers. Through the many politically turbulent years that followed government oversight of artistic productions, theater artists continued to galvanize audiences to stand up politically for just causes.

Although Sierra Leone, given its latent colonial legacy, was not known for its nationalistic sense of identity in the first three decades after independence, it would be fair to say that theater has emerged as a significant player in helping create a sense of identification with the nation's destiny. In my book *The Amistad Revolt*, I expounded on the role Charlie Haffner's *Amistad Kata Kata* played in fostering a sense of political agency after the 1992 coup by the National Provisional Ruling Council (NPRC). Haffner's artistic articulation of the Amistad story (a story that had been lost to the Sierra Leonean people for over one hundred and fifty years) had, by chance, coincided with the successful execution of the military coup of 1992 and military leaders were quick to use the people's identification with the Amistad story to consolidate political power (Opala 1994; Osagie 2000). Such "enactments of power," as Ngugi would put it, highlight the significance of the Sierra Leonean theater in the everyday politics of the nation. Haffner's contribution was just one of several plays that were focused not just on entertainment but also on educating the public about its past. As early as 1976, Kargbo's play about Mammy Yoko, *Let Me Die Alone*, had begun to stir the community's conscience by evoking a great female leader from the past. Later, Spencer's play, *The Patriot*, whose title ironically comments on Easmon's *The New Patriot*, also evokes another great leader, Bai Bureh. Incidentally, both leaders, Mammy Yoko and Bai Bureh, have often been looked upon from an ironic distance by Sierra Leoneans.[1] Through such historical focus playwrights have tried to reorient the nation's uneasy reflection on itself. Other playwrights, such as Tonie French and Mohamed Sheriff, critique specific cultural and social ills in the society, challenging the people to think critically of different facets of their everyday lives. These theatrical objectives on the part of Sierra Leonean playwrights parallel the existing scholarship on African drama that highlights both entertainment and education as vital characteristics of African theater (Jeyifo 1985, 2000; Byam 1999; Kamlongera 1988; Mlama 1991).

The political and social relevance of the Sierra Leonean theater can also be measured by the outreach abilities of many local groups. Throughout the 1990s, theater groups were solicited and contracted by many different organizations, such as different units of the United Nations, the Sierra Leonean government, and many non-profit organizations, to do awareness programs in many communities across the country. By becoming a tool for development throughout the country, theater in Sierra Leone, much like theaters in other parts of Africa, has redefined the meaning of popular theater.[2] It is therefore not a surprise that when the intense phase of the civil war reached Freetown in 1999, it was a theater artist, Julius Spencer, who became the voice of the people's resistance against the invading rebel forces. The military arm of the West African economic community, ECOMOG, in conjunction with the Kabbah government in exile in Guinea, sought

# Introduction

the help of Spencer, a Professor of Theater at the University of Sierra Leone. Spencer, who was behind ECOMOG lines (a West African military force led by Nigeria) in an undisclosed location, was able to broadcast over the airwaves to the civilian population caught in the throes of war. Pointing out the many victories of the anti-rebel coalition, he forcefully and persuasively articulated the need to resist the advancing rebels. He became the conscience of the nation. After the war, many in Freetown attributed their sanity to that familiar voice on the radio. Today, the place of the artist as a major player in guiding the nation morally is well established.

Theater has indeed developed from its humble beginnings, when it merely mirrored Western plays, to a position where confident self-recognition as a player on the nation's stage is well articulated. Although there is plenty of room for maturity, there has been a healthy growth in the direction of professionalism. Charlie Haffner's theater group, Freetong Players, for example, has been credited with being the first group to hire full time artists. Spencer, who has left both his professorial position at the University of Sierra Leone and his post-Civil war office as Minister of Culture, runs his own professional company as an artistic consultant and a filmmaker. Apparently, the goal of most amateur groups today is to one day be a professional outfit.

## Critical Analysis

This volume contains five popular plays by some of the most recognized contributors to the climate of drama in Sierra Leone since the 1960s. The first play, *The Blood of a Stranger*, by Raymond Dele-Charley, is perhaps the most dramatized play in the last half century in Freetown. Dele-Charley himself remains the most celebrated artist in Sierra Leone and is seen as the father of modern theater in the country, because his theater group, the popular Tabule Theatre, birthed many of the artists who later founded notable groups, such as Shegureh Players, Kailondo Tiata, Ronko Theatre, Kakua Players, Freetong Players, and Spence Productions. In a competition organized by the Ministry of Tourism in 1975, Dele-Charley won the award for Best Play for *Blood of a Stranger*. The play was later selected to represent Sierra Leone at the Festival for the Arts (FESTAC) held in Nigeria in 1977. *Blood of a Stranger* is set in a fictional village in Sierra Leone in the early days of the colony and centers on the unavoidable conflict between traditional preservation and the modernizing presence of the British colonizers. The fraudulent activity of the British colonizers, represented by a white stranger, symbolically called Whitehead, is exposed in the play through the king's son, Kindo, who is the chief of the warriors and the next in line to the throne of Mando land. Kindo is an upright defender of Mando land; he is willing to defend his culture and his people even to his own hurt. Whitehead on the other hand is a crass, greedy dictator who arrogantly believes he can deceive the entire land into granting him access to its diamonds.

A further irony is that Whitehead both disregards the culture (he introduces the people to alcohol, tobacco, and hard core hallucinatory drugs) and manipulates the culture by seizing on key traditional beliefs that favor his ominous plot. For example, he seizes on the decree of death for anyone who kills in peacetime, so as to trap Kindo. He also describes diamonds as evil stones that should be handed over to him in a land purification ritual he dreams up. Whitehead's moral decadence is further exacerbated by his attempt to rape a country virgin, Kindo's woman, Wara. The attempted rape of this country virgin in the play symbolizes the rape of the country's natural resources that the Colonial government is essentially after. It is worth noting, however, that Whitehead's deft manipulation of Mando society is aided and abetted by the corrupt priest of the shrine, Soko, and the Chief assistant to the King, Maligu, who are hoping to gain personal wealth by assisting Whitehead. Their ignorance of Whitehead's true motive—he wants diamonds, whereas they think he is there

## Introduction

to grow tobacco—is reminiscent of the general exploitative track of colonial history in Africa. While beads, tobacco, and cloth were among the initial innocent exchange in a barter of goods for palm oil and other products between Europeans and Africans, it did not take long before Africans themselves became the battered goods of choice by Europeans, who used corrupt local leaders to accomplish their scheme.

Moreover, the tragic essence of the play rests mainly on the king's rigid adherence to tradition in the face of irrevocable change. It may seem a little odd, even disappointing, that the king would hastily banish his own son without regard for the motive behind Kindo's behavior, especially since Kindo remains morally impeccable throughout the play. Perhaps, one could chalk the king's cultural rigidity at this juncture in the play to the fact that Whitehead has introduced him to hallucinatory drugs, although the link between the two events is not convincingly made in the play. A more convincing explanation may lie in the playwright's consistent critique of the uncritical adherence to culture, as if cultures are static, not dynamic. That is to say, that while the play seems to esteem tradition, it also challenges the audience to examine the values behind traditional beliefs, especially where common sense changes are needed with the changing times. For instance, Kindo, like Maligu, knows that the priest does not honor the traditions of the land, even though he is supposed to be the protector of it. Soko has built a hut in the forest where he enjoys a comfortable bed instead of sleeping in the rustic shrine at night. Ignorant of this fact, the people of Mando land, including the king, hold the shrine in veneration. Maligu would of course use the knowledge of Soko's deception to blackmail him into "divining" the entrance of a white stranger into the land, thus further contravening the law of the land. The corrupt leadership of the priest of the sacred shrine and the Chief adviser to the King parodies the colonial legacy of political, social, and spiritual decadence in the country. Overall, as tragic as the play is (seemingly tragic for Kindo), there is moral retribution in the end when Whitehead is given a taste of his own recommendation—he is sacrificed rather than Wara. The play successfully demonstrates the evils of African colonial encounter with the West, without presenting the colonized as mere victims.

The second play, *Let me Die Alone* (1976), addresses the gender struggles of the famous Madam Yoko, who was the first notable female Paramount Chief over the Mende people in the Southern province of Sierra Leone. Although she was influential with the British, and was one of the most powerful rulers of the Kpaa Mende confederacy, her femaleness remained at the core of the many crises she encountered both within and without her chiefdom. Playwright John Kolosa Kargbo, fondly known as JK in the theater world, depicts the life of this celebrated female ruler. In his portrayal, Yoko is a beautiful, ambitious, and courageous woman who joins an all male secret society (the feared Poro society) and consequently loses her right to motherhood, though not to her sexuality. In becoming a male-female, Yoko is much feared by her male contemporaries, envied by women in her constituency, and doubly pliable in the hands of the British rulers. This popular play was in great demand with theater audiences. The play however angered both the government and some members of the Poro society in Freetown; this latter response sent Kargbo and other members of Songhai Theatre (later renamed African Heritage Workshop), temporarily into hiding.

Like Dele-Charley's *Blood of A Stranger*, JK's *Let me Die Alone* does critique both traditional culture and colonial arrogance. It critiques traditional culture that insists that women be confined to traditional female roles, in spite of the fact that there have been successful women leaders among the Mende people throughout recorded history. In his important work *The Mende of Sierra Leone*, Kenneth Little observes that a prevailing tension in male-female power sharing exists. Male and female roles in Mende society are clearly drawn out, but the society also allows women with exceptional qualities to cross gender lines as leaders in various capacities. This paradoxical, boundary-shifting identification often brings a lot of tension

## Introduction

between the sexes. History tells us that before Gbanya, Yoko's husband, died in 1878, he had asked Governor Rowe and some of his relatives to secure the throne for Yoko, his senior wife. However, Yoko did not secure the throne until Movee, Gbanya's successor, died in 1884. The colonial government then installed her as a "dependable ally" (Alie 1990). Seen by many of her subjects as a usurper and a friend of the colonial administration, she remained controversial throughout her reign until her death in 1906. In the play, this controversy is packaged as a defiance of the cultural norm that women should not bear rule during war times. Being a visionary who willingly gives up the privilege of childbearing for the leading chieftaincy title in all of Kpaa Mende, she is willing to disprove the myth of female inferiority. As historian Joe Alie reports, Yoko was even instrumental in the arrest of many chiefs who participated in the Hut Tax War, the subject of the next play by Julius Spencer. Greatly feared by many male chiefs, Yoko was able to gain oversight of their chiefdoms. Yoko also wielded tremendous influence with the colonial rulers, although in the end the colonialists betrayed her.

Kargbo has done a tremendous job of portraying Yoko as an impressive ruler of heroic proportions. Indeed, the historic Yoko was nothing short of heroic. Kargbo presents Yoko as a complex figure whose feminine comportment, sensuality, and beauty promoted her among women, but whose fearless soul and unrestrained ambition made her a competent and visionary leader among her male counterparts. Nevertheless, in *Let Me Die Alone*, Yoko does call into question a tradition that insists on her relinquishing motherhood for the crown of leadership, when she dotes on Jeneba, a much loved child in her kingdom, and when she openly laments the sacrifice of child bearing. Since leadership and motherhood are mutually exclusive, the Mende culture seemingly presents leadership as a male domain. Lamboi, Yoko's brother, exploits this flawed belief when he accuses his sister of sacrificing children (in this case Jeneba) to formulate powerful medicinal powers to keep her on the throne. By framing Yoko as a heartless female "who does not know the pain of childbirth," Lamboi essentially reconfigures her as male. By implication, her success as a leader cannot therefore be credited to her femaleness.

Overall the play is a feminist critique of a masculinist culture, at a time when feminism as a theme was still unpopular and rare among male playwrights in Africa. Kargbo deals with wife beating, male prejudice against female leadership, the problems of loveless marriages, and the tendency to measure masculine virility and sexual dominance against female oppression and sexual surrender. The play is particularly well crafted and the language is embedded with cultural nuances that adequately contextualize the play. Kargbo carefully intersperses the different acts with song and dance and pays particular attention to sound effects. Moments of comic relief also heighten the overall tragic nature of the play.

The third play, Julius Spencer's *The Patriot* (1988), also focuses on a major historical leader in Sierra Leone. This historical drama is based on the life of Bai Bureh of Kasseh, chief of the Karene district. Bai Bureh resisted the British government's attempts to impose a "hut" tax on the natives in the protectorate. The Frontier police sent to enforce the tax had used unnecessary force and violence. In response Bai Bureh and other chiefs refused to collect the tax and instead attacked some police stations and massacred many British subjects (mostly Creoles and some British and American missionaries). Bai Bureh's popular uprising against the British galvanized the Temnes and other ethnic groups in their resolve to defy this tax law, which they saw as diminishing their autonomy (Crooks 1903; Utting 1971). For months, Bai Bureh waged successful guerrilla warfare against the British. He was widely believed to have native powers that made him invisible and impenetrable to bullets. Nevertheless, he was captured by the British, imprisoned on treason charges, and exiled to the Gold Coast. Years later, he was pardoned and reinstated—a late reaction to the investigative report on the rebellion faulting the District commissioner and his high-handed tactics. In spite of Bai Bureh's tragic experiences,

# Introduction

Spencer urges a celebration of the courage and strong sense of justice that incited Bai Bureh to embark on what was, by all accounts, a suicide mission.

*The Patriot* was first performed at Njala College (another campus of the University of Sierra Leone) in March 1988. Its success at the College led to subsequent performances at the British Council in Freetown, in the month of August the same year. The play was later performed by Spence Productions (founded by Spencer) in 1991; it had a five day run at the British Council, playing to full houses each day. Spellbound audiences enjoyed the play's storytelling technique and strong audience participation strategy. The narrator emerges out of the audience and captures the attention of the audience through singing the popular Bai Bureh song. Throughout the rest of the play, the audience is encouraged to reexamine this well-known song by reflecting on the life of Bai Bureh and the choices he made during the Hut Tax rebellion. The play ends with the narrator and all the actors singing the song and mingling with the audience. Many interesting theatrical devices also keep the audience engaged throughout the play. The narrator plays several roles, swinging in and out of roles as the play requires. In Bretchian fashion, the other characters in the play also keep the audience consistently conscious of the fact that this is just a play; there is no attempt to pretend it is real. Actors come in with their own props and take the props with them as they exit the stage. This highly creative play even features similarities between Bai Bureh and the governor of Sierra Leone, Colonel Sir Frederic Cardew, when they perform the same poses at the same time at one point in the play. Indeed, Spencer deftly shows that the British colonial force meets its match in Bai Bureh and his guerilla fighters, because one party's war strategy is equally matched by the other group. Although poorly armed, Bai Bureh and his men show themselves equal in mental capacity and valor. In the end, however, Bai Bureh surrenders as he is out gunned, but it is evident that the playwright wants the audience to meditate on the justness of the cause and the overall sacrifice that was made on their behalf. Spencer's goal, essentially, is to instill pride in Sierra Leoneans about their past, by re-presenting their image of a failed past in its true color as justified resistance.

The only female playwright in the volume, Tonie French, has written two plays, *What A Life!* and *The Pool*, both performed in the 1990s. Already in her fifties when she wrote her plays, Tonie French's presence in the theater, after an exceptional public career (especially as a media personality), has helped to build a positive space for young female dramatists. Although she has been the most well known female artist writing in English in recent years, other female artists, such as the Casely Hayfords, mother and daughter mentioned earlier in this essay, should be acknowledged for their artistic output from the 1930s to the 1950s. Another notable female writer was Juliana John (now Juliana Rowe) who wrote the first truly successful plays in Krio—*Na Mami Bohn Am* in 1968 and *I Dey I Noh Du* in 1969. As I mention in the essay, "The Significance of Tonie French as a Female Artist in Sierra Leone Theater," women have been significant in all walks of life in Sierra Leone and their role in the theater is no less so (Palmer & Porter 2008).

In her important contribution to women's rights in Sierra Leone, French emphasizes the tragic consequences of a second-class education for women in both her plays. In *The Pool* (1994), she uses the lack of quality education for women to explore prostitution as a trap that many women fall into. Khaday, the main character, becomes a prostitute when she attends a job interview conducted by James Macauley, a so-called respectable civil servant of the government. Thereafter Khaday plunges downhill, morally, servicing men to meet the needs of her family. The audience meets Khaday when she decides to enroll at Mrs. Coker's Typing Institute, through the help of her friend, Mabel. At the Institute, she comes face to face with Marion, James's daughter, who is also a student at the typing pool. Khaday's disdain for Marion stems from her realization that James's exploitation of her is not just about gender but also about class. James has jealously guarded his daughter's virginity, while exploiting other young girls who hail from poor homes.

Against the James-Marion-and-Khaday debacle, French also demonstrates the ideal love encounter in the relationship between Aina Jones and Joseph Buckle. The effaceable Aina is played by French herself. She also uses her husband's first name—Joseph—for the Buckle character, played by Randy Wright, a seasoned actor in Freetown. Although the dialogue between Buckle and Aina sometimes comes across as stilted, both characters constitute the core comic element in the play. Mr. Buckle is a 40-year old bachelor who is guileless and bumbling. Aina is a widow with four children who, after her husband's death, is trying for the first time to enter the workforce by preparing for the Pitman exam at the Institute. Aina's innocence and Buckle's blusters give the other characters in the play and the audience plenty of laughs.

This comic relief is tastefully embedded into the main plot, which deals with the tragic condition of the African woman in a male dominated world. French demonstrates in her play that as a second-class citizen, the African woman is vulnerable to sexual and psychological abuse, among other things. For instance, Khaday is not too thrilled with Aina's claims that her husband spoilt her when he was alive. Khaday reads Aina's helpless condition (as a home-bound babysitter) as a form of abuse. However, Khaday's self conscious critique of the African woman's condition is not often fully explored in the play and the other female characters do not discuss Khaday's hints or reflect on Khaday's concerns. Ironically, unlike Khaday, they all seem particularly concerned with meeting societal expectations.

Alice is another example of a form of female psychological abuse in the play. As James's wife, she has all the amenities of modern life because her husband can afford it. However, she is secluded in her privilege and has neither voice to protest her husband's infidelities nor even a female arena where she can vent her frustrations. The so-called privilege that some women may enjoy as part of the middle class is also portrayed as a weapon that men can use to divide and conquer all women. Because Alice is friendless and voiceless, she even loses society's sympathy as she comes across as proud, cold, and loveless. For example, Jusu, James's friend, refers to her as a problem and Khaday calls her a puppet. The complexity of Alice's position introduces controversy in the play. Is it Alice Macauley's fault that her husband is adulterous? Marion will eventually answer the question at the end of the play when she finally claims to understand her mother's coldness: it is her father's fault.

However, French does leave the impression that women are sometimes to blame for their own victimization. When I watched the play in 1994, I remember that the audience was incensed at Mrs. Macauley's unresponsiveness to her husband's overtures. Another disturbing factor in the play is that Marion and Khaday bicker throughout the play over Marion's father, yet Khaday willingly goes into James's arms during their afternoon rendezvous. In short, Khaday's anger is directed against another woman rather than against the man who is exploiting her. The play does end with a revelation of the irresponsibility of men, but this knowledge does not lead to any possible reconciliation between Marion and Khaday. Thus, while French offers important social commentary on the plight of the black woman in Sierra Leone, she merely raises audience awareness but does not suggest a solution.

Another playwright that would take up the issue of female dispossession is Mohamed Sheriff in his comedy *Not You Too* (1996). The play begins with Gulama trying to drag his daughter to the Bundu bush so that he can marry her off to the man of his choice after she undergoes female circumcision. Gina already has a boyfriend, Borbor, of whom her father disapproves. Going through with the circumcision not only means physical injury that could be life threatening, it also means marrying the aged Chief Jaia, whom she does not lov,e and aborting her education. Gina is in a bind, and her mother and grandmother cannot agree on how to deliver her. She and Borbor come up with a scheme, but it is her aunts,

# Introduction

Kate and Kula, visiting from abroad, that eventually come up with a workable plan of escape.

Unlike French's bewildering ending in *The Pool*, Sheriff's play lays emphasis on what can be done in spite of a constricted social system. The play suggests that women can work together to combat abuse as a first step to ultimate liberation. The play also suggests that the war against institutional sexism is a long one; thus it does not offer a redemptive closure at the end of the play. Nonetheless, Sheriff has produced a truly feminist play on the rejection of female circumcision by the new generation of women in Sierra Leonean and the domestic clash that arises when a father insists on having the ritual performed on his daughter against the wishes of the female members of his household. Like French, Sheriff is dealing with the displacement of women in Sierra Leone culture. In particular, Sheriff deals with the issue of forced marriage, the premature end to a woman's educational ambition, the controversial female circumcision, selfish fathers who sell their daughters, and husbands who beat their wives. Sheriff further broadens the social space for this discussion on cultural displacement by offering a comparative analysis of the situation for women in Africa with the situation of our sisters (white and black) in Western countries.

In fact the play's title, "Not You Too," is a reference to Christie's admission that she too, like her African sisters Kula, Kate, and Mary, lived through an abusive marriage in America. Christie, Mary's white friend, is an American volunteer who has come to Sierra Leone to help during the Civil war. By tilting the play in reference to Christie's narrative of terror, Sheriff deftly shifts the gaze back on the West. Without diminishing the significance of the issue, Sheriff shows that female circumcision is not the hallmark of sexism and victimization in the world. It is just one such trail that needs to be dismantled.

Sheriff's play also attempts to maintain respect for the custom through Granny, Mary's mother, who insists that changing the ritualistic and cultural context of female circumcision is mutilation—in response to Borbor's suggestion that the process take place in a hospital under "humane and hygienic conditions," rather than in the Bundu bush. This fervent belief by Granny, however, is counteracted by Gulama's feigned love for custom and tradition. The only reason he bullies his daughter into the ritual is because he intends to hand Gina over in marriage to the powerful Chief Jaia, from whom he has already received many gifts. Chief Jaia will only marry a circumcised woman. Like Dele-Charley and John Kolosa Kargbo, Sheriff also demonstrates the internal corruption of tradition by those who claim to be protecting it.

*Not You Too* was written in 1996 and first performed in September 2000 by the National Performing Arts Troupe. Julius Spencer directed the play. The play had been selected as Sierra Leone's winning entry to the Accra Festival of Arts and Culture (ACUFEST) to be held in Accra, Ghana, the following month of October. ACUFEST was, for a variety of reasons, cancelled that year. Nevertheless, the publicity the play garnered as an ACUFEST entry brought huge crowds to the theater. Its premiere at the British Council had amongst its most distinguished guests the Head of State, President Kabbah, as well as many local and foreign dignitaries. It was performed to full houses and had many more performances beyond its original scheduled run.

## Closing Thoughts

I have selected these five plays as representative of plays from three decades of prolific theater history in Sierra Leone and by authors that are instantly recognizable to the Sierra Leonean people. Almost all of these playwrights have received a measure of international recognition by performing their plays abroad or winning some notable award for their effort at home. All five plays in this collection bring awareness to Sierra Leonean and world audiences about the challenges and legacies of the colonial encounter, the exploitation of African

## Introduction

womanhood, the advantages and pitfalls of traditional practices, and the need for national pride and self elevation. The social commentary each play offers is an important building block in the collective memory of the nation and in the production of national identity. The plays also trace the political, social, and cultural challenges the country faces. Indeed, the plays are markers of the growth of Sierra Leone's theater over the course of three decades of its history. Although only a small slice of that history can be recorded here, I hope that the plays selected succeed in conveying the earnestness with which Sierra Leonean playwrights have both embraced the nation's destiny as their own and have stimulated the consciousness of the nation by making theater immediately relevant to the dreams and hopes of its people. In honor of the many truly talented artists who have died, so often leaving unrecorded the artistic pieces they labored on, I hope that this publication of a few representative plays will be a salutation to them all. It is telling that three of the five playwrights in this volume, Raymond Dele-Charley, John Kolosa Kargbo and Tonie French have all joined the ancestors. Their dreams however live on.

> Iyunolu Osagie
> Department of English
> Penn State University

## Notes

1. For my discussion of the lack of a patriotic history evident in cultural representations of the country's past, see Osagie, *The Amistad Revolt*, Chapter Five.
2. For a meaningful discussion of theater for development see, Kamlogera, *Theatre for Development in Africa with Case Studies from Malawi and Zambia*. Also Byam, *Community in Motion*, offers a fresh and different perspective on the issue.

## Works Cited

Alie, Joe. *A New History of Sierra Leone*. NY: St. Martin's P, 1990.

Byam, L. Dale. *Community in Motion: Theatre for Development in Africa*. Westport, CT: Bergin & Garvey, 1999.

Crooks, J.J. *A History of the Colony of Sierra Leone: Western Africa*. London: Frank Cass, 1903.

Jeyifo, Biodun. *The Truthful Lie: Essays in a Sociology of African Drama*. London: New Beacon, 1985.

Jones. Eldred Durosimi, "Drama in Africa." *African Literature Today*. 8 (1976).

Kamlongera, Christopher. *Theatre for Development in Africa with Case Studies from Malawi and Zambia*. Bonn, Germany: Education, Science, and Documentation Centre, 1988.

Little, Kenneth. *The Mende of Sierra Leone: A West African People in Transition*. NY: Routledge and K. Paul, 1951.

Mlama, Penina Muhando. "Women's Participation in 'Communication for Development': The Popular Alternative in Africa." *Research in African Literatures* 22.3 (1991): 41-53.

Muana, Patrick and Chris Corcoran. ed. *Representations of Violence: Art about the Sierra Leone Civil War*. Porter Butts Gallery Exhibition and Conference Proceedings. Madison: Wisconsin Humanities Council, 2003.

Ngugi wa Thiongo. "Enactments of Power: The Politics of Performance Space." *Penpoints, Gunpoints, and Dreams: Towards a Critical Theory of the Arts and the State in Africa*. Oxford: Clarendon, 1998. 37-69.

# Introduction

Opala, Joseph A. *"Ecstatic Renovations!" Street Art Celebrating Sierra Leone's 1992 Revolution.* Freetown: Ro-Marong Industries, Ltd., 1994.

Osagie, Iyunolu. *The Amistad Revolt: Memory, Slavery, and the Politics of Identity in the United States and Sierra Leone.* Athens: U of Georgia P, 2000.

_____. " The Significance of Tonie French as a Female Artist in Sierra Leone Theater." *Knowledge is More than Mere Words: A Critical Introduction to Sierra Leonean Literature.* Edited Eustace Palmer and Abioseh Michael Porter. Trenton, NJ: Africa World P. 2008. 137-150.

Palmer, Eustace and Abioseh Michael Porter (eds). *Knowledge is More than Mere Words: A Critical Introduction to Sierra Leonean Literature.* Trenton, NJ: Africa World P. 2008. 1-33.

_____. "The Development of Sierra Leone Writing." *A Celebration of Black and African Writing.* Edited by Bruce King and Kolawole Ogungbesan. Ahmadu Bello UP and Oxford UP, 1975. 245-257.

Sheriff, Mohamed. *A History of Theatre in Africa.* Edited by Martin Banham. UK: Cambridge UP, 2004.

Spencer, Julius. "A Historical Background to the Contemporary Theatre in Sierra Leone." *International Journal of Sierra Leone Studies.* 1 (1988).

Utting, Francis. *The Story of Sierra Leone.* Freeport, NY: Books for Libraries P, 1971.

# THE BLOOD OF A STRANGER

## A PLAY IN THREE ACTS

BY

DELE CHARLEY

*Dele Charley*

# CHARACTERS

| | |
|---|---|
| MALIGU | Chief Adviser to the King |
| SOKO | The Priest of the Shrine |
| WARA | Kindo's Woman |
| KINDO | The King's Son; Chief of the Warriors |
| SANTIGI MANDO V | King of Mando Land |
| SIMA | Warrior |
| BOKO | Warrior |
| PARKER | Whitehead's Assistant |
| WHITEHEAD | The White Stranger |

Palace Guards, Warriors, Dancers, Drummers, Attendants, Townspeople

# ACT ONE

◆

# Scene One

(*The space in front of the Priest's cave. It is night. Drumming and the sounds of nocturnal insects can be heard in the background. Maligu suddenly appears, looking furtively over his shoulder. He goes over to the entrance of the Priest's cave and calls*)

MALIGU: Soko! Soko! It's me, Maligu. Soko! (*He goes in and as he comes out again, he almost bumps into Soko*) You frightened me. Do you have to move so quietly like a stalking leopard? You know my heart is getting old.

SOKO: I did not call you here.

MALIGU: Where have you been?

SOKO: What are you doing here?

MALIGU: I want to talk to you. Let us go....

SOKO: Talk to me here. You know that I do not sleep in the cave. Why did you come to see me here?

MALIGU: I thought you would come here and leave very late when all the people have gone to their huts.

SOKO: You have been watching my movements.

MALIGU: I am not the only one. Kindo, too, watches your movements. He watches me. I watch you and you watch me... Why are you so worried? Nobody saw me...

SOKO: I saw you leave the palace and I followed you.

MALIGU: As stealthily as the leopard. Why did you not call me?

SOKO: I wanted to be certain no one was following you. I wanted to find out where you were going.

MALIGU: Who would follow…?

SOKO: Kindo trusts no one. He fears darkness. His men are everywhere. He does not like you.

MALIGU: Do I like him? He is brave but he is brash.

SOKO: Maligu, the Priest must sleep, though the people believe that he does not sleep. The night grows old. What do you want?

MALIGU: My brother sent a letter today. *(Brings it out)*

SOKO: Why do you come to me? You know that I cannot….

MALIGU: The letter says a stranger is coming here.

SOKO: Have you told the King?

MALIGU: No. Not yet.

SOKO: Why do you come to me then? I am not the King.

MALIGU: The stranger is a white man.

SOKO: What? Another *Baliha*?

MALIGU: A *Baliha* is not a white man.

SOKO: And he is not a black man. What is he then? I have never seen a white man.

MALIGU: Neither have I, but I have seen pictures of them in my books. The white man has magic, which I would not be able to explain. He is not an ordinary man.

SOKO: It is good to be able to read books. That is why you have so much wisdom.

MALIGU: Your wisdom overshadows mine in many ways, Soko.

SOKO: But I have never seen pictures of a white man.

MALIGU: Pictures of white men are not the only things in books, Soko.

SOKO: Maligu, the night does not stop growing to give us more time to talk. Tell me about this letter.

MALIGU: Would you like to become rich, Soko?

SOKO: Is that what the letter says?

MALIGU: No. I have a plan Soko.

SOKO: Yes you have a plan! Always you have a plan, Maligu. Always you have a plan! And always you carry trouble on your head.

MALIGU: Do you want to die a poor man? A servant to the King?

SOKO: The Priest has great honor. He is not a servant.

MALIGU: The Priest lives on the sacrifices we make to the spirits of our forebears.

SOKO: It is the custom.

MALIGU: The Priest is hunted like prey by the Chief of the warriors. Is that honor? The Priest will starve if there are no sacrifices. Is that honor?

SOKO: It is my destiny, Maligu.

MALIGU: Ha! You play with words.

SOKO: That is the way the Priest should live. That was the way my father and his father before him and his grandfather lived. That is how we have always lived.

MALIGU: It is now a dying breed, Soko. You have no son.

SOKO: I have a....

MALIGU: The custom demands a Priest, Soko. There has never been a Priestess. When you die, the Priesthood dies.

SOKO: My Chief Attendant will...

MALIGU: The custom does not change, Soko. Your blood is not in your Chief Attendant.

SOKO: I cannot change my destiny, Maligu.

MALIGU: Is your destiny to die poor and unhappy?

SOKO: I am not dying, Maligu, and the Priest does not seek happiness for himself. His happiness is the happiness of the people.

MALIGU: Then why do you not sleep in the cave? Why do you have a nice warm hut in the bush? Why do you deceive the people? Why do you break the custom?

SOKO: You are shouting.

MALIGU: If I go anywhere, Kindo is watching me. He is watching you. He is even watching the King. If a man sleeps with his wife Kindo will know. Tell me, are the people happy? Are you happy?

SOKO: The Priest is never happy.

MALIGU: I know that the Priest is never happy. I know that his attendants revel in performing the Harvest Harmony rite, which empowers them to steal food and animals.

SOKO: It is the custom.

MALIGU: It is the custom, too, for the Priest to sleep in the cave.

SOKO: His attendants sleep in fine huts in the Palace compound, but the Priest must sleep on the cold hard floor of the cave as atonement for the sins of his people.

MALIGU: It is the custom, but you do not keep it.

SOKO: No priest has ever sincerely kept the custom.

MALIGU: You do not have to tell me your secrets. Hey, but we squabble over nothing. The white man has traveled from his country. He is coming to live with us and he is…

SOKO: To live with us?

MALIGU: My brother's letter says so.

SOKO: Why should he come here?

MALIGU: He is a farmer.

SOKO: (*Shocked*) A farmer?

MALIGU: Yes.

SOKO: Do we not have enough farmers?

MALIGU: He will plant tobacco only.

SOKO: What do we want to do with tobacco? You are the only one who smokes a pipe or is he coming to plant it for your pipe?

MALIGU: He will sell the tobacco outside.

SOKO: Will he keep the money…?

MALIGU: Some of it. He will pay the people who work on his tobacco farm.

SOKO: How shall I become rich then?

MALIGU: My brother's letter says…?

SOKO: Your brother's letter says many things.

MALIGU: It is a long letter. It says if I find someone to assist the white man, we shall both become rich.

SOKO: Everyone has a farm or a boat or animal traps. Who will agree to work for the white man?

MALIGU: That is part of my plan.

SOKO: Since our neighbors stopped making war on us and made peace with us no stranger has come here. Will the people...?

MALIGU: That is part of my plan, Soko. The white man is no ordinary stranger.

SOKO: You seem to know him though you have not met him yet.

MALIGU: When you can read, you know many things, Soko. Kindo will refuse to let us admit the stranger.

SOKO: The King, too, will refuse.

MALIGU: The King has no voice or will of his own.

SOKO: But your voice and Kindo's strength give him a rigid support.

MALIGU: Soko, you put too many obstacles in the way.

SOKO: The obstacles have been in the way all the time. I only warn you so that you do not fall over them in your blindness.

MALIGU: The people expect you to help them challenge their obstacles but you are afraid to challenge your own obstacles.

SOKO: What should I do?

MALIGU: Talk to the King. Talk to the people. Your voice is the voice of unearthly wisdom. It is the voice of the spirits of our forefathers. You divine the fate of the land. The people kneel with hope in obeisance when you perform your weird incantations and rites. They believe everything that you say and do. Where is that voice, Soko? Where is that wisdom? You are not...

SOKO: You raise your voice.

MALIGU: You irritate me. You cower like a cornered animal. You waste time. Tomorrow, you will summon the people and tell them that you see a stranger approaching and that he must be received because the spirits of our forefathers say that harm will befall us if we drive him away. Leave the rest to me.

SOKO: My attendants are always present when I look into the future. They help me perform the divination rites. It is the custom.

MALIGU: It is the custom. It is the custom. The crops are dying. This year, the harvest will not be good. You will starve to death if the offerings are small. The priest is not allowed to have a farm. It is the custom. Is it the custom for the Priest to starve to death? I want to hear the drums before morning. The spirits can also appear to you in a dream, can they not? Or do the attendants also share your dreams?

*(Maligu goes out. Soko remains standing for a few moments before he goes into the cave. There is drumming in the background. Kindo enters dragging Wara behind him)*

WARA: Let me rest, Kindo. You have dragged me all the way. You should have carried me.

KINDO: Rest? We have reached the place.

WARA: Here? Let us go back. I am afraid, Kindo.

KINDO: What are you afraid of?

WARA: I have never come here at night.

KINDO: You are with me.

WARA: Kindo, you know that only the Priest and his attendants should come here.

KINDO: That is why I have brought you here. Nobody else will come. The Priest has...

WARA: I tell you, the Priest is in the cave. Look, there is a light.

KINDO: Wara, I tell you that Soko does not sleep in the cave.

WARA: How can you say that, Kindo? You must not anger the spirits.

KINDO: What spirits?

WARA: (*In a fierce whisper*) Be quiet, Kindo! You talk like Maligu who is drunk with his books.

KINDO: There is wisdom in some of the things he says.

WARA: Let us go back, Kindo.

KINDO: Have we come this far for nothing?

WARA: We shall go into the forest when it is light.

KINDO: The farmers will see us. I have to go hunting with the men. No, Wara, I cannot wait. Now!

WARA: Let us find another place.

KINDO: What other place can we find? My men are everywhere with their women. They are at the stream. They are at the marketplace. And we cannot go to the palace; the guards will see us.

WARA: Let us go into the forest, away from here.

KINDO: I do not have my *jonga* or my hunting knife with me. Look, I can show you that Soko is not in the cave. Come with...

WARA: No! No! (*Restraining him*) Do not go in there, Kindo. You know it is forbidden to go there.

KINDO: It is just an ordinary cave in which the people believe that Soko sleeps.

WARA: No Kindo, do not talk like that! Do not bring the wrath of the spirits on us.

KINDO: Wara, do you believe that I too can read and write?

WARA: No, I have not seen you do it.

KINDO: It is my secret. Before the wars started, my mother was a singer and when she traveled with her dancing girls she took me with her. At one time, she was away for five harvests. I went to school in a big town and learned to read and write. As we continued to travel, I met more people who taught me many things.

WARA: I do not believe you, Kindo.

KINDO: I know. You believe Maligu. You believe Soko.

WARA: The King himself calls Maligu "the wise one." Soko is the Priest.

KINDO: Soko is false. The Priests are false.

WARA: Did you read that in your own books? They must be different from those that Maligu reads.

KINDO: Wara, I do not beat a woman. Do not let me beat you.

WARA: Beat me if you want. I am your woman. Do anything you want with me.

KINDO: I do not trust Maligu.

WARA: You do not trust anyone. You do not trust the King, your own father.

KINDO: I think of the welfare of the people.

WARA: And yet you want to bring a curse from the spirits upon them by mouthing such strange things.

KINDO: There is truth in what I say. Soko is not in the cave! (*He moves forward, but Wara holds him back*)

WARA: Kill me before you go into the cave, Kindo, because if you go inside, I will never be your woman again.

KINDO: Then you will be free to go to Maligu. Do you think I do not know that he wants you? I see the way he rolls his eyes and licks his mouth when you are dancing.

WARA: But do I want him? Do I tell him to roll his eyes and lick his mouth? You talk like a little boy, Kindo. I do not have eyes for other men. When I dance, I dance for you only.

KINDO: I feel something strange in the air, Wara. The hunter sees with his eyes and ears and nose. He sees with his whole body. I smell trouble, Wara. It makes me restless. It makes me distrust everybody.

WARA: Is it because you distrust me that you do not take me to your room in the palace? Is that why you have not yet made me your wife?

KINDO: Wara, our custom demands that the Chief of the Warriors will only marry when the woman is with child for him.

WARA: The King will not…

KINDO: No, Wara. The custom is the custom. The King cannot break the custom.

WARA: You were going to break the custom.

KINDO: To show you that the Priest breaks it.

WARA: What is this strange thing you speak of, Kindo?

KINDO: I do not know. The hunter senses something. He does not know what it is. He stops and listens. He hears the sound of breaking bush and suddenly a leopard leaps at him. Only then does he decide what to do. If he is slow, he will die. If he does not sense the leopard before it attacks him, then death is on top of him before he can even raise his arm to throw his *jonga*.

WARA: I hope there will not be another war. A war would snatch you from me.

KINDO: I shall come back to you. The enemy warrior who would kill Kindo has not been born yet. Wara, the night slips away stealthily while we talk. Let us go over there. The ground is flat. You can spread your *lappa*.

WARA: There is someone in the cave.

KINDO: Quick! Come with me! (*He drags her into the shadows. Soko comes out of the cave with a gong, which he starts to beat. When he goes off, Kindo and Wara come out of hiding*) You were right, Wara. He was in the cave.

WARA: Did he see us?

KINDO: No. He did not.

WARA: Why is he summoning the people? We have performed the Hunting and Fishing rituals and it is not yet time for Harvest.

KINDO: Something has happened. That is why he was at the cave this night. He never sleeps there.

WARA: Stop saying those things again, Kindo! How do you know that he never sleeps there?

KINDO: Many times I have watched him come out of the cave late in the night and go to sleep in a hut in the bush. He always returns to the cave very early in the morning.

WARA: Do the attendants know?

KINDO: I do not think they know. They all live in the palace.

WARA: Have you told anyone?

KINDO: Only you. That secret is a *jonga*, which I can use when the time comes.

WARA: I am afraid, Kindo…

KINDO: We go there into the bush.

WARA: No, Kindo. Please, please, let us go back.

KINDO: No! We go into the bush! If you do not want to go, I shall carry you. (*He lifts her and goes offstage with her, ignoring her cries of protest and desperate struggle. In the background, the big drums pick up Soko's call and pass it around. Lights out*)

## Scene Two

(*Full lights on stage. People of the land anxiously wait to learn the reason for the summons. Four men enter, carrying the Priest aloft. He is laid in front of the sacrifice-stone. A round of drumming greets the King as he enters, followed by Maligu and Kindo. The people prostrate in greeting until the King sits down*)

SANTIGI: The ceremonies begin, Soko. (*Soko gets up and leads a dance as greetings to the spirits, "protectors of the land." At the end, he takes a horn, which has been carried all this time by an attendant, and drinks from it*)

SOKO: The monkey is wise. The leopard is strong. Their blood is for Kings and great warriors. (*He gives the horn to the King who drinks from it and passes it to Maligu. Maligu drinks from it and passes it to Kindo, who refuses to drink*)

## The Blood of a Stranger

KINDO: The King and his servants do not drink from the same horn.

MALIGU: You are too humble, Kindo. The King and his son may drink from the same horn.

KINDO: I am not the King's son now. I am his royal servant. (*He moves to stand somewhere else. Soko takes the horn and gives it back to the attendant. Then he moves to the sacrifice-stone*)

SOKO: Spirits of our forefathers! Protectors of the land! You were kings! You were warriors! You are still with us. You still guide us. You protect us. You talk to us. You will protect our children, and their children and grandchildren after them. The dog dies with its dream in its belly. I will not die with my dream. My dreams are your words. Are they not? Spirits on the mountain! Even Soko cannot understand what you say. I call on you to help me understand my dream. (*He gets up and takes a sword from an attendant and gives it to the King. The King gets up and moves towards the sacrifice-stone. The attendant with the horn also moves towards the stone*)

SANTIGI: Spirits of kings! Spirits of warriors! Spirits on the mountain! Your blood flowed to give us life. Your blood flows through our bodies. Your blood flowed to give us peace. We give you blood so that you can give us more peace. Accept this sacrifice! (*Soko hands over a sword to the attendant and collects some of the blood with the horn. He smears some on the King's forehead and his own forehead. The drumming starts again and Soko starts an incantation. He starts to dance and the attendants join him. At the end, he assumes a trance-like pose*)

SOKO: Here are the words of our forefathers. (*Everyone prostrates. Soko speaks in a strange voice*) We gave our blood for peace. We gave our lives for our children. But peace is like the moon. It stays not forever. The sun drives it away. A stranger comes to the land. If you want peace, treat him well. If you want peace throw more blood. The blood of a virgin, born in another place (*Soko sinks exhausted to the ground. The attendants carry him off. The rest go out. The King, Maligu, and Kindo remain*)

SANTIGI: Maligu, prepare to receive the stranger.

MALIGU: Yes, my Lord.

SANTIGI: Kindo, get your warriors.

KINDO: My lord, we must not receive the stranger. We have not received strangers since the wars. They bring bad luck and sickness.

MALIGU: The Priest said…

KINDO: I know the Priest said we must receive the stranger but is it wise to do so?

SANTIGI: Kindo, do you doubt the wisdom of the spirits?

KINDO: I do not, my lord.

MALIGU: The Priest's voice is the voice of the spirits. Do you perhaps doubt the Priest?

KINDO: The spirits have also warned us through the mouth of the Priest that we must not allow strangers on the land.

MALIGU: (*Growing impatient*) The spirits now warn us that more blood will flow if we do not welcome the stranger.

KINDO: My lord, will you offer the blood of…?

MALIGU: That was what the Priest…

KINDO: I speak to the King! My lord, will you offer the sacrifice?

SANTIGI: I cannot choose, Kindo. I cannot go against what the spirits demand.

## ॐ The Blood of a Stranger ॐ

KINDO: My lord, I wish also for peace and happiness in the land. Strangers have always brought us ill luck.

MALIGU: The spirits said we must receive...

KINDO: The spirits say; the spirits demand; it was Soko who said...

MALIGU: Do you question Soko's power to commune with the spirits?

KINDO: I question your eagerness to advise the King to receive the stranger.

MALIGU: It is my duty to advise the King.

KINDO: Maligu, you talk and talk. You make plans. You look into the future with eyes different from Soko's eyes and when trouble comes, it is Kindo the King calls.

MALIGU: I did not tell the stranger to come here.

KINDO: No, but you are very willing to receive him and yet you do not even know who he is.

MALIGU: I am very willing to execute the command of the spirits. In time, we shall know who the stranger is.

KINDO: My lord, I...

SANTIGI: (*Raising his hand*) Kindo, you will make the necessary preparation to receive the stranger. Maligu, you will tell Soko to offer a sacrifice of appeasement to the spirits, on behalf of my impetuous son. Kindo, you will send out some of your men to go and find out what this stranger looks like. They should return here before he arrives here.

MALIGU: My lord, the spirits would not like that. I think I... I... I know what kind of man is coming.

SANTIGI: You know?

KINDO: Soko did not say...

MALIGU: Soko does not know. My brother in the city sent a letter to me. The letter says that a stranger is coming here.

SANTIGI: When did you get the letter?

MALIGU: Yesterday morning, my lord.

SANTIGI: You did not tell me.

MALIGU: I did not think there was any need to tell you. The stranger in my letter may not be the same stranger the spirits have warned us about. (*Kindo attempts to talk*)

SANTIGI: Who is the stranger in your letter?

MALIGU: A white man who…

KINDO: A white man? Before Government men go anywhere, a messenger travels before them.

MALIGU: He is not a Government man. He is a farmer.

SANTIGI: A white farmer? Is this a joke? I have told you that the white men do everything for themselves. They are extraordinary people. They have great powers. They can…

KINDO: What is a white farmer coming to do here?

MALIGU: He is coming to plant tobacco, which he will sell outside according to the letter. The village will become rich.

KINDO: According to the letter, who invited him here?

MALIGU: I do not know. He must have found out that we have very good soil.

SANTIGI: It is what the spirits have willed.

KINDO: Can we trust this white man?

MALIGU: I can trust any white man.

KINDO: I know you can.

SANTIGI: (*Cutting him short*) The spirits command us to receive him. Kindo, I have spoken. Let us not anger the spirits by wasting time.

KINDO: My lord, we do not know whether the white man is the same stranger in Maligu's letter. May I see the letter, Maligu?

MALIGU: The letter? What do you want to do with it? Can you read?

KINDO: Will you believe if I tell you that I can read?

MALIGU: No. I have never seen…

SANTIGI: He can read, Maligu.

MALIGU: Is that true, my lord? Do you believe him?

SANTIGI: He is my son. What he says is true.

MALIGU: You have never told me…

SANTIGI: It does not matter.

KINDO: It is good to have secret weapons to surprise the enemy.

MALIGU: I… I… I cannot give you my letter. There are other things…

SANTIGI: Very well, Maligu. Kindo, go and make preparations. Maligu, get the women ready. (*Maligu turns to go but Kindo lingers*)

KINDO: My lord, I carry out your command unwillingly.

MALIGU: I do not see why you should be unwilling.

KINDO: You do not see! There is dust in your eyes. Whenever you say "yes" to something or you are very willing to carry out an order, I smell something.

MALIGU: You must be a dog with an eager nose.

KINDO: (*Acidly*) Yes, to smell out untrustworthy cats like you.

SANTIGI: (*Getting up*) That will do! Come with me, Kindo (*They go out, leaving Maligu fuming. Soko enters*)

SOKO: Why did you talk about the letter? Kindo may smell something.

MALIGU: So you have returned from the land of the spirits?

SOKO: Was it necessary to tell the King about your letter?

MALIGU: Why did you talk about a virgin-sacrifice? Your grandfather was the last Priest to offer a virgin as sacrifice.

SOKO: To make it sound sweet.

MALIGU: Will it sound sweet if the king orders the sacrifice?

SOKO: I have thought of that. I shall sacrifice Wara.

MALIGU: Wara? Even a fool will not play with fire. Why did you choose Wara?

SOKO: She was not born here. Her mother was taken prisoner by one of our warriors during the war. Her mother ran away after giving birth to the child and…

MALIGU: I know all about her mother but why did you choose her?

SOKO: Should I not have chosen her? I chose her because she is Kindo's woman.

MALIGU: That is why you should not have chosen her. Kindo is fire and he will burn you if you touch Wara.

## The Blood of a Stranger

SOKO: It is your task to help execute the command of the spirits. If the spirits say we should sacrifice a young girl, they will also guide our hand in choosing the sacrifice.

MALIGU: Soko, you are a very sincere liar. I shall soon start to believe that the spirits really said so. Will you sacrifice the girl?

SOKO: No, I shall tell her that the spirits have guided my knife to her heart but I am willing to let her escape.

MALIGU: She will tell Kindo.

SOKO: If she does that, she will have to remain here and if she lives here, the spirit will demand her blood so she will have to run away without telling Kindo.

MALIGU: The King has to see the ritual. The attendants have to be present.

SOKO: None of them goes near the sacrifice-stone. They will not know that the sacrifice is not Wara.

MALIGU: Who will it be?

SOKO: Leave everything to me. You ask too many questions.

MALIGU: You are greedier than I thought. If you make a mistake, do not call my name in it.

SOKO: The King ordered you to go and help make preparations to receive the white man. You waste time.

(*Maligu goes out. Soko too, goes out. A short while later, Kindo comes in and sits down. He is deep in thought when Wara comes in. Kindo senses her presence*)

KINDO: What are you doing here?

WARA: I have been waiting for you. I saw you leave your father...

KINDO: The King!

WARA: I saw you leave the King and come here.

KINDO: The King's wives do not follow him everywhere he goes.

WARA: The King does not choose his wives so they will not die out of worry for him. They are given to him. He uses them to get his food and to bear him children. They go to other men when they get the chance.

KINDO: You are talking about the King!

WARA: Don't you feel anything, Kindo? Don't you feel cold when rain is falling? Don't you feel angry when Maligu irritates you? Don't you feel happy when you are with a woman?

KINDO: I do. I do.

WARA: You don't. You do not feel for yourself. You feel the pain of the people. You feel their hunger. You feel their joy. You feel like a hen protecting its children; but you are not the King. The people do not feel the same for you.

KINDO: The King is old. He will die soon. The people will not die yet.

WARA: And you will become Santigi Mando the Sixth. The mothers of the tribe will leave their daughters in front of the palace gates. But there will be none like Wara. *(Pause)* Don't you feel anything for me, Kindo?

KINDO: I feel my heart breathing fast. I feel something like drumming in my head.

WARA: For me?

KINDO: For the safety of our people—innocent people and children. I sense trouble. I sense disaster.

WARA: You are always saying that. You mean your heart beats faster for the safety of the people than it beats for me. You mean you are still thinking about the words of the spirits. You mean you do not trust Maligu and you want to know where the trouble will come from?

KINDO: Wara, you are one of the people. If the people are in danger, you are also in danger. If I stay close to you, that will not help you. If there is trouble and we run away, and many people die, how would you feel? (*Pause*) You do not answer?

WARA: Do you think there will be fighting?

KINDO: I do not know. (*Pause*) Do you not already know why we were summoned?

WARA: I know. My grandfather told me.

KINDO: Why did you not go home with your grandfather?

WARA: My grandfather is not Kindo. That is why I am here.

KINDO: Strangers are not allowed in the shrine.

WARA: I am ready to risk anything to be with you, Kindo.

KINDO: Risk anything, but strangers are not allowed in the shrine.

WARA: Why don't you stop calling me a stranger, Kindo?

KINDO: Are you not a stranger?

WARA: My father was a man from these parts.

KINDO: You were not born here. Your mother...

WARA: No, Kindo, no! People say too many bad things about my mother. She was not born a slave. She did not...

KINDO: All right, Wara, I am sorry. People talk so much about it that...

WARA: Am I a stranger to you, Kindo?

KINDO: I did not say that. (*Pause*) Wara, I tell you again, something evil is about to happen. I can feel it.

WARA: Kindo, you are not the Priest. You are only Chief-of-the-Warriors. You are making your life full of misery and I share that misery with you. I want to be your woman, I want to live in your hut and bear you children. Kindo, are you listening?

KINDO: My destiny seems not to care about Kindo-who-is-Wara's-man, but Kindo-the-Chief-of-the-Warriors. You will always be my woman, Wara. My destiny will one day give its permission.

WARA: Will the Priest perform the virgin-sacrifice?

KINDO: I do not know, although the King may order it. Wara, you must try not to be weak. You must not follow me wherever I go. I am a warrior.

WARA: You are also a man!

KINDO: Do not shout!

WARA: Do you love me, Kindo?

KINDO: You are my only woman. (*Maligu enters*)

MALIGU: Kindo, the King will not be pleased to learn that you bring a woman, a stranger, into the shrine.

KINDO: Maligu, when night comes, all the men in the village stay near their women or find *mampama* to drink. Wara, let us go into the forest. (*He lifts her and goes out, stopping halfway*) Even the Chief of the Warriors sometimes feels like a man. (*Kindo and Wara exit. Soko enters*)

SOKO: Why do you come here?

MALIGU: Kindo will make trouble for us if we are not careful.

SOKO: Maligu, people call you "the wise one." You should be able to make bigger trouble for Kindo.

MALIGU: Kindo is as wily as a monkey.

SOKO: Then you must be the hunter who catches that monkey.

MALIGU: You jest with something very serious.

SOKO: I do not jest. I just laugh at your cowardice. Kindo brought the girl into the shrine, did he not? I saw them. You saw them. We shall carry out our plan soon. Without the girl, Kindo will be weak.

MALIGU: Then you do not know Kindo. He is very ambitious. He does not allow his woman business to interfere with the security of the people. Do you know that he can read and write? I wonder how many secrets he has.

SOKO: Enough, Maligu. Go, now. We must not be seen together too many times. Have you given instructions to the men?

MALIGU: Yes. They know what to do. (*He exits. Lights out*)

# ACT TWO

◊◆◊

## Scene One

(*The Palace. A few days later. The people await the arrival of the stranger. Meanwhile there is drumming. The drummers and dancers greet the King as he enters. With him are Soko and Kindo. The people have brought presents and the dances symbolize the sources of the presents—their occupations: hunting, farming and fishing. The King acknowledges the greeting and the presents, dancing a few steps with the dancers. The dancing stops as he sits down*)

SANTIGI: Kindo, have you seen the white man? What is he like?

KINDO: I did not see him well, my Lord. He covers his face from the sun and he has the same kind of hammock like the Government man.

SANTIGI: Is he coming now?

KINDO: Maligu went to tell him that we are ready. He has not come back yet.

SANTIGI: You do not like Maligu.

KINDO: Father, I do not like men who see everything and say everything they see. I do not like men who have no backbone.

SANTIGI: One day, you too will become an old man and you will have no backbone, like Maligu.

KINDO: I shall die a warrior-king, father. I shall always have my backbone. I shall always fight for truth, father.

SANTIGI: There are times when a warrior has to fight with his head and times when he has to fight with his mouth, Kindo. Only when you can do that would you be able to rule well. You are too impatient.

KINDO: I think Maligu is the only one with whom I am impatient.

SANTIGI: Why?

KINDO: I do not trust him, father. I do not know why. Perhaps, it is my warrior instinct.

SANTIGI: You need a woman, Kindo.

KINDO: I have a woman, father.

SANTIGI: A woman according to the custom, Kindo; a woman who will live with you and give you children. Then perhaps, you will not think so much about… ah, here comes Maligu. He looks confused.

KINDO: He always looks confused, my Lord (*Maligu enters*)

MALIGU: My Lord the white man cannot come today. He says he will come tomorrow.

SANTIGI: Did you speak to him?

MALIGU: No, my Lord, I spoke to a black man who says he is the right hand man of the white man.

KINDO: Did he say why the white man cannot come today? (*Maligu does not answer*)

SANTIGI: Answer the question, Maligu.

MALIGU: The right hand man said he is tired after his long journey and he has to rest.

KINDO: He has been here for two days now. Is that not enough time to rest? What is he? A sick man? An old woman?

MALIGU: He has said he will come tomorrow.

KINDO: (*Mimicking him*) "He has said he will come tomorrow." And you take that as an answer, which you bring to the King like a dog running with its tail between its legs.

MALIGU: If the white man cannot come today, am I to blame? Did I tell him not to come?

SANTIGI: I do not understand what is wrong with the two of you. You are both working for the welfare of the people, but you are always growling and tearing at each other like two hungry dogs who see a piece of meat at the same time. What will happen when I die and you become King, Kindo? Now, what are you going to do about the white stranger who has not come to pay his respects to me?

KINDO: He will soon come, my Lord.

MALIGU: My Lord, do not allow him to do anything rash. The white man is resting. He has been toiling in the sun. He will come tomorrow as he has said. Do not let him be forced to return.

KINDO: Did we call him here?

MALIGU: My Lord, the white man has plans that will make the tribe rich. We must not…

KINDO: You are always talking about poverty and making the tribe rich! We are not poor. We are not starving. Our forefathers tried to make the tribe rich by making war on weaker tribes. Did they succeed? The weaker tribes united and defeated them. Out forefathers tried to live at peace with the surrounding tribes. They left their doors open to them. Did the tribe become rich? Our neighbors came, took what they wanted, ate and drank, pissed and left their excrement on our doorstep. I want our children to live like children in other places. I want the best things for our people, but there is a price we have to pay for those things—the price of peace. We must learn to know peace among ourselves before we can live at peace with strangers. We must be patient. We have been at war for too many years. We do not know whom to trust.

SANTIGI: (*Pleased*) Those are not the words of a warrior, Kindo. Those are the words of a wise elder.

KINDO: Sima! Boko! (*Two guards come in*)

SIMA: Yes, Chief, we are here.

BOKO:

KINDO: Bring the white man here!

MALIGU: My Lord, tell him to be patient.

KINDO: Take some men with you. Drag him if he resists.

MALIGU: My Lord, I shall go with them. The white man must be handled with care.

KINDO: My Lord, if Maligu makes the stranger think that we are begging him, I shall order my men to seize him as a traitor.

SOKO: My Lord, Kindo is going too far. You must…

KINDO: So the Priest speaks again. But I shall pretend that I did not hear. What are you waiting for? Go! (*The guards hurry out, followed by Maligu*) Soko, the white stranger appears to be a troublemaker. What do you think?

SOKO: The spirits said, "Treat him well."

KINDO: You must commune with the spirits again and ask whether we should give the white man the right to dishonor our custom.

SOKO: He does not know the custom.

SANTIGI: You, Maligu, and the other councilors are upholders of the custom and you make excuses for the man?

SOKO: The spirits said that he is not an ordinary stranger. (*Kindo moves off in irritation to talk to Wara*)

WARA: What are you going to do when they bring the white man?

KINDO: You will see.

WARA: Kindo, do not do anything which will anger the spirits.

KINDO: Wara, you have always looked up to me as a woman should look up to a man. You have never doubted my word. You have never asked many questions. Don't do so now. I tell you that I sense something evil in the air...

WARA: Don't begin to talk like that Priest, Kindo.

KINDO: This is very serious, Wara. I am very young but I fought in my first war when I was only a boy. It is this strange thing, which I always feel, that has helped me to return from five wars! Ah, here they come.

WARA: Don't do anything rash, Kindo.

(*Two guards enter with the white man's right hand man in front of them and four others bring in a stool on which the white man appears to be sleeping. Maligu follows immediately after. At a signal from Maligu, the stool is put down. Kindo talks to the right hand man*)

KINDO: What is your name?

PARKER: Andrew Samuel Stevenson Thomson-Parker, Esquire.

KINDO: That is too heavy for my mouth. I shall just call you Parker. Are you the white man's servant?

## ᚛ The Blood of a Stranger ᚜

PARKER: I am not his servant. I am his Secretary, Assistant, Interpreter, Adviser… I am his right hand man. Are you the King or Chief or what?

KINDO: Is your father still living?

PARKER: Yes. Why do you ask?

KINDO: If you go to visit him in his house, would you not first look for him and greet him before you ask for water to wash? (*Pause*) You do not answer?

PARKER: It is a strange question.

KINDO: It is not a strange question, but do not answer if you wish. You are not a white man. You have been here for two days and you have not come to pay your respect to the King.

PARKER: The white man was…

KINDO: I do not want to hear anything more about the white man! He comes from a far place. You brought him here. He should not tell you what to do.

PARKER: I am also a stranger. I was not born in these parts.

KINDO: You are a black man and I know that black men everywhere should greet the owner of the hut when they go into his hut. That is what we teach our children. Parker, let us stop fooling. If I talk to you, the King talks to you. You will be treated the way we treat our children who do not respect the elders. Guards, bring whips! (*Two men come forward with whips. The guards strip him*)

PARKER: Mr. Whitehead! (*Frantically*) Mr. Whitehead! Wake up! Please! They are going to assault me!

KINDO: Whitehead will soon wake up. (*The men strip Parker, leaving only his under-vest and pants. Kindo strides over to the stool and throws Whitehead off. He blinks his eyes open and tries to sit up. He is obviously half drunk)*

MALIGU: My Lord, you must stop him!

SOKO: Remember the words of the spirits! His actions will bring a curse on all of us.

SANTIGI: I am going to the shrine. Come with me Soko. Kindo is in charge.

MALIGU: My Lord, will you not tell him to stop?

SANTIGI: I speak only because I am not yet dead, Maligu. I sit on the throne for that same reason and because custom demands that. Kindo is almost your King. I am tired. Let us go, Soko (*They go out*)

WHITEHEAD: What's going on here? How did I get here? You! You!

KINDO: Call me Kindo.

WHITEHEAD: What are you doing to my man?

KINDO: Whitehead, you are drunk.

WHITEHEAD: Call me Mister Whitehead! Who says I am drunk? Who are you, anyway? Are you the King?

MALIGU: No. Whitehead, the King is not here. Please do not get angry with Kindo. He is the King's son, but he is...

KINDO: Whitehead, you came here two days ago, and refused to come here to pay your respect to the King.

WHITEHEAD: I sent my man to say that I was tired.

KINDO: Your man did not come, so I am going to let him taste what we give to our children who disrespect the elders.

WHITEHEAD: Are you going to beat him?

## ଓଃ The Blood of a Stranger ଞ

KINDO: How did you know? That means you are not drunk. Guards! Do your work. Parker, what is your age?

WHITEHEAD: This is an outrage! You are a savage! (*He takes a step forward but is seized by the guards as two others start to beat Parker*) Take your hands off me! (*His struggles against the two guards are feeble*)

KINDO: Parker, what is your age? If you do not tell me, the men will beat you until you…

PARKER: My age is forty-two!

KINDO: Guards! Forty-two!

MALIGU: Kindo, I hope you know what you are doing. It is not good to anger the spirits.

KINDO: Maligu, I ceased to respect you when you ceased to respect yourself. I will not hesitate to give my men the order to beat you and lock you up if you try to stand in my way. (*To Wara*) Wara, if you want to remain my woman, do not twist your face when I am doing my duty! Guards, stop! He makes too much noise. He has no liver. Let him sit on the ground. Whitehead, my men will not whip you. You are a stranger. You will only have to kiss the ground in front of my feet.

WHITEHEAD: I… will do… what?

KINDO: Do you want an interpreter? I said, kiss the ground in front of my feet.

WHITEHEAD: I… you must be… you can't let me… I… (*The guards seize him and are about to force him down, Kindo signals and they release him*)

KINDO: Whitehead, let me ask you a question. Don't you kiss the ground in front of your King?

WHITEHEAD: I do not kiss the ground. I bow. (*Demonstrating*)

KINDO: Here, it's different. You will kiss the ground in front of my feet. You saw what they did to Parker. I will not tell you to kiss the ground again. Guards! Whip him! (*Whitehead hurriedly kneels and bows down*) Your forehead should touch the ground! (*Whitehead does so and Kindo stamps his face into the ground with his foot. Wara lets out a suppressed gasp and Maligu begins a prayer*)

MALIGU: O, Spirits of our forefathers, Spirits of our forefathers! Have mercy on us.

KINDO: Do not pray for us, Maligu. Pray for yourself. Pray for greed and ambition not to destroy you. Whitehead, the King will come here again tomorrow morning. You will come and present yourself or you will go back where you came from. You will talk like a man who is sorry. (*He turns to go and stops halfway*) You will kiss the ground in front of his feet as I have taught you. (*He strides out. Wara and the guards follow. Maligu and Parker help Whitehead up and frantically dust his clothes*)

MALIGU: Mister Whitehead, please do not be angry with us. I do not know what has come over Kindo. He is stubborn but he is not always like this.

WHITEHEAD: You promised to take care of him.

MALIGU: I am trying, Mister Whitehead, I am trying.

WHITEHEAD: You had better try harder. I will not be insulted like this again.

MALIGU: Be patient, Mister Whitehead. Be patient. We shall succeed. Soko has agreed.

WHITEHEAD: I do not trust that funny witchdoctor. Are you sure I can depend on him?

MALIGU: You can trust Soko, Mister Whitehead. Soko is a man I like.

## The Blood of a Stranger

WHITEHEAD: I do not care whether you like him! Is he a man to trust?

MALIGU: Yes, Mister Whitehead.

WHITEHEAD: Have you picked the men you want?

MALIGU: Yes, Mister Whitehead. (*Whitehead gives him some money*)

WHITEHEAD: Buy something that they need with it. Do they drink?

MALIGU: They drink *mampama*, Mister Whitehead, but they do not buy it.

WHITEHEAD: Go to the big village and buy something better than your *mampama*. Buy some clothes for their women. Say they are presents from Mister Whitehead. And Maligu?

MALIGU: Yes, Mister Whitehead?

WHITEHEAD: Buy as many pipes as you can.

MALIGU: (*Surprised*) Pipes, Mister Whitehead?

WHITEHEAD: That was what I said. You hear well, don't you?

MALIGU: Yes, Mister Whitehead. (*Whitehead goes out followed by Parker*) Mister Whitehead, the Spirits bless you. The Spirits bless your children. (*He keeps the money and goes out. Lights out*)

## Scene Two

(*Singing, dancing, and drinking in the background, Soko, Maligu, and some girls are gathered around Whitehead*)

MALIGU: I told you everything would be alright, Mister Whitehead.

WHITEHEAD: Everything is not alright yet.

MALIGU: The men are ready to start work tomorrow.

WHITEHEAD: What about Kindo? I am sure he only pretended to be happy. The way it happened was too easy.

SOKO: Mister Whitehead, when Kindo smiles, things are not bad. Kindo smiled this morning.

WHITEHEAD: I want things to be good. I do not just want things to be "not bad."

SOKO: Mister Whitehead, you worry too much.

WHITEHEAD: I should worry, shouldn't I? I'm spending my money, am I not?

SOKO: Y…y…yes, Mister Whitehead.

(*A group of men moves down stage singing, dancing, and drinking*)

1st MAN: Mista Whitehead. Hey, hey, Mista Whitehead.

OTHERS: *Dorobe*

1st MAN: Mista Whitehead. Hey, hey, Mista Whitehead.

OTHERS: *Dorobe*. Mista Whitehead, number one, *dorobe*.

1st MAN: Mista Whitehead *na wi* man. Mista Whitehead "get" money.

OTHERS: Mista Whitehead, hey, hey. Mista Whitehead, *dorobe, dorobe, dorobe*.

MALIGU: They are paying their respect to you, Mister Whitehead. They are very happy.

WHITEHEAD: They should be. I paid for the gin they are drinking and the things they are wearing. Maligu, I want to see the girl who was with Kindo yesterday. Bring her to my place.

MALIGU: Er… Er… that would be difficult, Mister Whitehead.

WHITEHEAD: Why should it be difficult?

MALIGU: She is Kindo's woman, Mister Whitehead, and Kindo is trouble.

WHITEHEAD: Maligu, I have given you much money…

MALIGU: Yes, Mister Whitehead.

WHITEHEAD: I must be able to get anything I want or I shall demand my money back.

MALIGU: Please, Mister Whitehead, I shall try. Give me some more time. It should be done carefully.

WHITEHEAD: I want her tonight at my place.

MALIGU: It will be difficult, Mister Whitehead. I don't even know where she is now.

WHITEHEAD: Find her. She must be somewhere. Bring her tonight! (*Kindo enters*) Ah, Kindo, I thought you would not come. Come on, you are still not angry, are you? We both agreed to bury the hatchet. Why did you not come with Wara?

KINDO: A man does not walk together with a woman. The woman walks behind him.

WHITEHEAD: Ha! Ha! Ha! That was good. I think we are going to be friends, Kindo.

KINDO: What made you come here, Whitehead?

WHITEHEAD: Would you like something to drink, Kindo?

KINDO: Answer my question. Why have you come here?

WHITEHEAD: Do you not believe that I have come here to plant tobacco?

KINDO: Why did you come here to plant tobacco? Why did you not go to another place?

WHITEHEAD: You have good soil, very good soil for planting tobacco. You will see when I begin to plant.

KINDO: I see that everybody is drinking the white man's gin. From where did they get it?

WHITEHEAD: I sent some men to buy it from the big village.

KINDO: We do not buy anything from those people.

WHITEHEAD: How would I know? The men did not tell me. Does it matter? After all, I hope to sell some of my tobacco to them. Wara has not come yet. Where is she?

(*Kindo does not answer. He goes over to a man lying face down on the ground. He turns him over with his foot. He is clutching a bottle to his chest. He starts to mumble*)

TOWNSMAN: (*Drunkenly*) Leave my botchul, Kindo. Don't come near me. Leave my botchul. Chell him, Mista Waiched. He won cho chake my botchul. (*He staggers to his feet and starts to dance*) Mista Waiched, *dorobe*, Misita Waiched, number one. (*He dances off into a corner*)

KINDO: Whitehead, these people have never behaved like this before. If the King hears…

WHITEHEAD: Will you tell him?

(*KINDO has moved over to a group of people lying in a state of stupor*)

KINDO: Did you give them pipes?

WHITEHEAD: I gave them the money. I also gave them clothes. Surely your custom does not prohibit smoking in the village? Maligu smokes a pipe. Tobacco is very good for resting tired nerves and making them fresh. (*Kindo has picked up a pipe and is sniffing it*)

KINDO: This is not tobacco, Whitehead.

WHITEHEAD: Do you smoke a pipe?

KINDO: Did you give it to any of my men?

WHITEHEAD: I don't know. It was Maligu who…

KINDO: (*In a rage*) Did you give the tobacco to my men?

WHITEHEAD: It is not the tobacco, I tell you.

KINDO: Where is Maligu?

WHITEHEAD: He has gone to his compound. He says he is tired.

KINDO: Whitehead, I am going to look for him. If these people do not get up and go to their huts before I return there is going to be trouble for you.

(*He dashes out. Maligu comes in with Soko following*)

WHITEHEAD: Do you have the girl?

MALIGU: Yes, Mister Whitehead. She is in your compound.

SOKO: But we have some trouble, Mister Whitehead.

WHITEHEAD: What sort of trouble?

SOKO: She fought and shouted; so we had to fight her and tie her hands and cover her eyes and put a cloth in her mouth.

WHITEHEAD: Did she see your faces?

SOKO: No, Mister Whitehead. I kept saying that she was the choice of the spirits of our forefathers. Er... er... you would not understand our customs, Mister Whitehead. The spirits have...

WHITEHEAD: I do not want to understand your customs. I want the girl. Why did you leave her at my compound? There is no-one...

MALIGU: Parker is there, Mister Whitehead.

WHITEHEAD: Good. I must go at once. Come back later and take her away. (*He takes a swig from his bottle and hands it over to Maligu. Then he staggers out*)

MALIGU: I told you everything would be easy. (*He takes a swig*)

SOKO: Don't finish that. It is better than *mampama*. (*Maligu hands over the bottle*)

MALIGU: When Mister Whitehead is finished with the girl, we take her to the cave and tell her about the wish of the spirits to have her as the sacrifice. She will run away tonight and you perform the sacrifice tomorrow.

SOKO: And Kindo won't have this woman again. (*He starts to sing*) Mister Whitehead, *dorobe*.

MALIGU: Mister Maligu.

SOKO: *Dorobe*. Mister Soko.

MALIGU: *Dorobe, dorobe, dorobe* (*Kindo rushes in*)

KINDO: Maligu, why did you give gin to my men?

MALIGU: They did not say "no" when I gave it to them.

KINDO: Why did you bring gin here, in the first place?

MALIGU: Mister Whitehead sent me to buy it. He wanted to make the people happy.

## The Blood of a Stranger

KINDO: Whitehead is a stranger. He does not know the custom.

SOKO: It is only this once, Kindo. It will not happen again.

KINDO: Whitehead seems to be here to make trouble. You stand by and let him break the custom.

SOKO: The spirits said…

KINDO: The spirits said, the spirits said! Because Whitehead is a big stranger, he must break the custom? The spirits said! Whitehead insults the King. Whitehead buys gin from outside and gives it to the people. The spirits said! Where did you get that strange smelling tobacco which you gave the people?

SOKO: Mister Whitehead gave it to us to give to them.

KINDO: It is not ordinary tobacco.

SOKO: Yes, this was what Mister Whitehead said. It is a very strong tobacco, but it is good for making tired nerves fresh.

KINDO: It is not tobacco. It makes animals of the people. Their eyes are red. The women are giving themselves to the men everywhere: in the market place, at the *barre*, and at the stream. They are running about naked, like children.

SOKO: That is the result of the gin they have drunk.

KINDO: Gin does not do that to people, The whole place smells of that evil tobacco. You have brought evil into this place. Whitehead is evil. What will the King do if he hears the noise the people are making and he comes out, and sees them?

MALIGU: The King is sleeping.

KINDO: Yes. The King is sleeping. Do you know anything about the evil tobacco? The people will ask for more tomorrow. If you cannot give it to them there will be trouble.

MALIGU: Mister Whitehead has plenty of it. He wants to keep the people happy.

KINDO: The people were happy without gin and that evil-smelling tobacco. Have you seen Wara? She was not in her grandfather's compound and she was not here when I came the first time.

SOKO: We… we have not seen her.

KINDO: Did you give her the evil tobacco?

SOKO: No. She did not come here.

MALIGU: Perhaps she is also looking for you somewhere else. Perhaps near the shrine. (*Kindo goes out. Parker comes in running, almost out of breath*)

PARKER: Mister Whitehead calls you. The girl got away.

MALIGU: The girl got away? How did that happen?

SOKO: We tied her hands and feet and put a cloth in her mouth.

PARKER: Mister Whitehead took her into his room, untied her and took the cloth out of her mouth. She started fighting and running around the room. Mister Whitehead called me to help him. He forced her to swallow some gin and smoke some of his tobacco in his pipe. She smoked it and she became quiet. I went out again and left the two of them in the room. Suddenly, I heard a scream and before I could do anything, the girl came running out, knocking me down. I went into Mister Whitehead's room and found him holding his jaw where the girl had bitten him. He was bleeding.

MALIGU: Which way did the girl go?

PARKER: I don't know.

## ॐ The Blood of a Stranger ॐ

MALIGU: Soko, you stay here. Parker, you go that way. I shall go towards the forest. Take her to the shrine if you find her. Parker, you know the way to the shrine?

PARKER: Call me "Mister Parker."

MALIGU: Mister Parker, if we do not find the girl before Kindo finds her and learns what has happened, we shall all be in trouble. Do you understand, Mister Parker?

(*Parker and Maligu go out in different directions. Soko still has the bottle and he takes a swig from it. Wara comes in*)

SOKO: Wara, why are you running? Come my child. Do not be frightened. I am Soko, the priest.

WARA: Soko?

SOKO: Yes.

WARA: My head feels heavy and my heart is beating fast.

SOKO: It is because you have been running.

WARA: No, Soko, it is not because of that. The white man is evil. He sent two men to take me to his compound. They were saying strange things to me. The white man took me into his room. The man called Parker helped him. They gave me something strong to drink and a pipe to smoke. The white man wanted to take me. I bit him on his face and ran away. Have you seen Kindo?

SOKO: Do not look for Kindo, my child.

WARA: Why, Soko?

SOKO: It is the will of the spirits. You must not be foolish. Do not waste your life. I have never performed the human sacrifice ceremony. You shall have to leave tonight. I shall tell Kindo and he will come to meet you. He will bring you back many days after the sacrifice.

WARA: Will everything be all right?

SOKO: Yes, my child. Just leave at once. I shall tell your grandfather. Don't bother to go back.

WARA: Thank you very much Soko. My grandfather has a wife in the next village. I shall go to her.

SOKO: Be very careful, my child. Do not waste any time. Go now (*She runs off. Soko takes another sip from the bottle just as Maligu enters*)

MALIGU: I could not find her. Did she come this way? (*Soko shakes his head*) Then she is not in town.

SOKO: Why did you want me to take her to the cave? We agreed to tell her to run away.

MALIGU: Soko, if she runs away, she will talk about what Mister Whitehead did to her. Kindo will force us to talk. He will drive Mister Whitehead out and we shall not get any more money. (*Whitehead has come in unseen*)

WHITEHEAD: Oh yes, you will get all the money you want if you do what I say. If the girl has run away, Soko will offer a goat instead. Then we shall have to get rid of Kindo before he drives me out. Come to my compound very early in the morning and I shall tell you my plan. (*He goes off*)

SOKO: I do not like this, Maligu. It could be dangerous.

MALIGU: Getting money is dangerous.

SOKO: I am not interested in getting money if there are too many dangers.

MALIGU: You can tell Mister Whitehead that in the morning.

SOKO: I do not trust him. He seems to be an evil man.

MALIGU: He does not trust you too. You are a coward.

SOKO: Maligu, I smell evil. Let us stop before it is too late.

MALIGU: It is too late already. You have lied to the people so that Mister Whitehead can come into the town. You have helped Mister Whitehead make his plans. You believe in the power of the spirits. If you give up now, they will still come after you.

SOKO: They will come after you too.

MALIGU: I am not the Priest. I do not believe in them.

SOKO: I am not going to Mister Whitehead in the morning. It is finished for me. (*He walks out*)

MALIGU: Coward with no liver! (*He spits on the ground. Parker enters*)

PARKER: She did not pass by, Maligu, and I am tired.

MALIGU: I am tired too. Mister Whitehead has gone back to the compound. He has a plan, which he will tell us about in the morning.

PARKER: I don't trust you, Maligu.

MALIGU: Why?

PARKER: You would do anything for money.

MALIGU: Mister Whitehead has not told me that he does not trust me. (*Hisses and goes out. Lights out*)

# ACT THREE

◊◆◊

## Scene One

*(The Palace. The next morning. Whitehead and Parker are seated awaiting the King. Shortly, he enters with Soko. Whitehead and Parker prostrate)*

SANTIGI: Soko, you perform the sacrifice tonight. Have you got the girl?

SOKO: Yes, my Lord. We have prepared her. Everything is ready.

SANTIGI: I hope you slept well, Whitehead?

WHITEHEAD: The spirits would not mind if you offered an animal instead.

SANTIGI: Whitehead, you are a stranger. You do not understand our custom. We have been at war with other tribes for many years. We want peace and the spirits say to get that peace for which many lives have been lost, we must shed the blood of a stranger—just one life, not the blood of a goat.

WHITEHEAD: My man and I are strangers. Why did you not choose one of us?

SANTIGI: The spirits demand the blood of a virgin. Whitehead, do not question our customs if you want to live with us.

WHITEHEAD: I am sorry, my Lord. It is just that where we come from, we do not perform virgin sacrifices.

## The Blood of a Stranger

SANTIGI: When do you want to start to plant, Whitehead?

WHITEHEAD: Tomorrow, my Lord.

SANTIGI: And the people will be able to look after their own farms? We cannot eat tobacco, you know.

WHITEHEAD: They will work on my farms only in the morning. Then they can go and work on their own farms.

SANTIGI: Maligu has told me that you will build a school for us and find some good teachers for us.

WHITEHEAD: My man and I will teach there also, my Lord.

SANTIGI: Ha! Then our children will be able to read and write like the white man himself.

WHITEHEAD: I just want your people to understand what I am going to do for them so that they work very hard, my Lord. No tobacco, no money. No money, no school.

SANTIGI: I shall talk to them. That is why I have called them to the *barre* this morning. Have they come, Maligu?

MALIGU: They are waiting, my Lord.

SANTIGI: I have not seen Kindo this morning.

MALIGU: Perhaps he is at the *barre*.

SANTIGI: I should not keep the people waiting. Wait here, Whitehead. (*He gets up and goes out. Soko goes with him*)

WHITEHEAD: You can go, Parker. I want to talk to Maligu. (*Parker goes out glaring with hatred at Maligu*) Maligu, I am telling you this part of my plan because I trust you and I need you. Have you ever heard about diamonds?

MALIGU: I have read about them, Mister Whitehead, but…

WHITEHEAD: You will have to try to forget about this "Mister" business, simply call me Whitehead if we are going to be friends.

MALIGU: I have never seen diamonds.

WHITEHEAD: You have them here.

MALIGU: We have them here?

WHITEHEAD: Yes. That is why I am here.

MALIGU: But you are here to plant tobacco.

WHITEHEAD: This is what everyone has been made to believe. There are diamonds in the stream and in the place near the tobacco farm. The people have never seen a diamond, so you will tell them before they begin to dig that there are many devil stones in that place. Each one they find must be put into a special jug which we shall take away everyday to the shrine, so as to kill the devils before we throw the stones away into the river.

MALIGU: But Soko will be at the shrine all the time. He will demand to know what we are doing. Kindo will go to the farms to see the work and if it is true that he can read as well as I can, he might have read about diamonds.

WHITEHEAD: You know that diamonds can fetch a lot of money?

MALIGU: I know, Mister… I know, Whitehead.

WHITEHEAD: Then if you want some of that money, you must work for it. Listen carefully. How do you punish a man who kills another man when it is peacetime?

MALIGU: He is banished from the land.

WHITEHEAD: Kindo will find the girl and bring her back. She will have told him about what I tried to do to her. If the King hears that, he will be angry. We shall wait for Kindo to come back. He will go straight to Soko and Soko will tell him about our plan. I shall send Parker to kill Soko. Are you a coward? Are you afraid of blood? Getting money can be very dangerous.

MALIGU: Kindo will kill him if…

WHITEHEAD: That is what I want to happen. Parker is of no use to me any longer. After Kindo has killed him, you urge the King to banish him. (*Pause*) There is one problem, however. Will the King do it?

MALIGU: Santigi Mando is an upright man. He lives by the law. I want to ask a question, Whitehead.

WHITEHEAD: Yes?

MALIGU: Will you kill me when you do not need me again?

WHITEHEAD: For as long as I am here, I shall always need you, Maligu.

MALIGU: Then I shall have to kill you when I think you no longer need me.

WHITEHEAD: I like you Maligu. We shall be friends.

MALIGU: Who will perform the sacrifice then?

WHITEHEAD: There will be no need for the sacrifice if you can force Kindo to go straight to the shrine where he will meet Parker and kill him.

MALIGU: Suppose he does not kill him?

WHITEHEAD: He will. I shall tell Parker to kill anyone who meets him in the shrine.

MALIGU: If Parker is afraid to go?

WHITEHEAD: I shall have to kill him and we shall put the blame on Kindo. But he will go. I think the King is coming back (*The King enters alone*)

SANTIGI: The people are very happy, Whitehead. They danced and sang your name. They are all prepared to work for you. But their eyes are red and they are singing: "We want more tobacco, *dorobe*." This I do not understand.

WHITEHEAD: I gave them some tobacco of the kind we are going to plant.

SANTIGI: Did they smoke it?

WHITEHEAD: Smoking tobacco is not a bad thing, my Lord. I smoke a pipe. Parker smokes a pipe. Maligu smokes a pipe. Tobacco is good for the brain. It refreshes the brain, my Lord. It makes you feel young again. Here, my Lord, try some.

SANTIGI: I have never smoked a pipe.

WHITEHEAD: It is better than snuff, my Lord. Try it.

SANTIGI: If the white man says so, then I must try it. (*Whitehead lights the pipe for him*)

WHITEHEAD: Draw the smoke into your head, my Lord. Slowly. Draw again. Keep the smoke in your head. Close your eyes. Do you feel anything?

SANTIGI: Yes, I feel. I cannot say how I feel. I feel… I feel as if… (*He draws on the pipe again*)

WHITEHEAD: Do you see anything?

SANTIGI: Yes! I see… women… many of them… they are washing in the stream. They are… calling to me… and their men are laughing (*He draws on the pipe again and, getting up slowly, he walks out, calling one of his wives*) Sirah! Sirah!

WHITEHEAD: Here, Maligu. Give this pouch to Sirah. It contains more tobacco. She must put more in the King's pipe when it is empty. She must stay with the King until it is time for the sacrifice. If she is tired, she must call another of his young wives to take her place. Go quickly and meet me at the compound. (*The big drum sounds in the distance*) Ah, Soko is getting ready for the sacrifice. You must give the people more tobacco and gin because you may have to perform the sacrifice.

MALIGU: Perform the sacrifice.

WHITEHEAD: Yes. They will not know who is wearing the mask. They will believe that the power of the spirits is in Soko and his voice has changed. We must be ready with another plan in case we cannot go on with the first one. You understand, don't you?

MALIGU: Yes, Whitehead.

WHITEHEAD: You must not make a mistake. You must not let me down. If you fail, there will be no diamonds. There will be no money if there are no diamonds. If you fail, Kindo will have you banished from the land in disgrace. (*He exits. Lights out*)

## Scene Two

(*The Shrine. Evening. The King is seated, with a confused-looking Whitehead near him*)

SANTIGI: You look worried, Whitehead. Are you afraid of blood?

WHITEHEAD: I have never seen a human sacrifice, my Lord. I have fought in a war and I have killed people.

SANTIGI: Then you would not be afraid. We are ready.

(*The drummers start to drum. The girls start to dance. The attendants bring in the Priest, who is actually Maligu wearing the special mask. They put him down and he starts to dance*)

KINDO: My Lord, the sacrifice cannot go on! You must stop it!

SANTIGI: Kindo, you must not bring a curse from the spirits on us simply because the girl chosen for the virgin sacrifice is your woman.

KINDO: She is not a virgin, my Lord.

SANTIGI: You cannot say such things in the shrine, Kindo. Are you mad?

KINDO: The body on the stone is not a girl, my Lord. It is Parker's dead body. Parker killed Soko. Here comes Soko's dead body. (*Two warriors enter with Soko's body and put it down in front of the King*) I killed Parker. Now we shall know…

WHITEHEAD: Then you must be banished from the land.

KINDO: Did you hear that, my Lord? Whitehead is breaking our customs.

SANTIGI: You should not have killed a man, Kindo.

KINDO: My Lord, you do not ask why Parker killed Soko. You do not ask why Maligu is wearing the Priest's mask. You do not ask why he was going to kill Parker a second time. Don't you want to know their plan?

SANTIGI: You have killed a man, Kindo.

KINDO: Yes, my Lord. I have killed a man.

SANTIGI: Our customs forbid you to kill a man during peacetime.

KINDO: You were going to kill a girl, my Lord.

SANTIGI: Do you still question the will of the spirits?

KINDO: It is all false, my Lord. The people are being fooled. The spirits did not…

MALIGU: (*Tearing off the mask*) This is enough, my Lord. Kindo must be dealt with as custom demands, even though he is your son. HE KILLED A MAN!

SANTIGI: My son is not above the customs of our forefathers, Maligu. No one is above the law.

KINDO: My Lord, there is evil in this place. These two men have an evil plan. You must listen to me.

SANTIGI: You killed a man.

KINDO: Then you must banish me before you learn the truth?

SANTIGI: It is the custom.

KINDO: It is not strange that the greatest protector of the custom should now be punished by the custom? Punish me, my Lord, but first listen to what I have to say. Mando land is in danger.

MALIGU: Parker who killed Soko is now dead. You killed Parker and you are still standing. There has never been so much bloodshed since the wars ended. The spirits will be angry.

KINDO: My Lord, you do not even ask what happened to the girl that should be sacrificed. You do not even ask why Parker killed Soko.

SANTIGI: I shall ask later, but you must leave immediately. Maligu will perform the rituals to purge the town of the foul deed you have committed.

KINDO: My Lord, what has happened to you? My Lord there is something evil going on between Maligu and Whitehead. Soko spoke to me before he died. Parker spoke before I killed him! You must listen to me.

SANTIGI: You must leave at once, Kindo! It is the will of the spirits.

KINDO: Very well, my Lord, I shall leave, but you cannot shut my mouth. I shall speak before I leave.

SANTIGI: I shall not listen to you. You have shamed me. You broke the law.

KINDO: I speak to the people. You are old. You will die soon. You will not live to eat of Maligu's fruits of evil.

My people, I have always fought to protect you. I have been a warrior since I was a small boy, while many of you worked on your farms. You were afraid of war. You were afraid to defend your land. You are all powerless to plead for me now. The custom says so. Whitehead has killed your priest. The spirits say that Whitehead is a big stranger. The spirits did not say so. They did not say anything! It was false! It was a plan between Maligu and Soko with the hand of Whitehead directing it! Whitehead will kill the King and you will let him go away because you cannot kill him. The custom says you must not kill in peacetime! I have killed. I killed to save you from the greed and selfish ambitions of one of our brothers who is now hiding behind the law of the land and power. I killed to prevent your children from knowing such an evil man. I leave now, but I know that you will tell it to the children that one of their heroes was banished because he defied the will of the spirits, because he defied the custom. There are two men of evil here. Both of them will kill the King. I have been banished because I killed a man. I think it will be just if I kill another man. Guards!

SANTIGI: Kindo!

KINDO: (*Maligu backs against the stone, Whitehead runs towards the exit. The King stands up. The two men are stopped by Kindo's men*) I will not kill you, Maligu. You will confess your plot to the King and live the rest of your days in disgrace.

WHITEHEAD: My Lord, he is mad! You must stop him! Loyal guards.

KINDO: All the guards are loyal to me first, then to the King. They will leave with me as custom states. My Lord, if you try to stop me, my warriors will seize you. Guards, take him to the stone. (*Whitehead is taken to the stone*) Spirits of our forefather! Spirits on the mountain look down from your home up there and receive the blood, which you asked for through the mouth of your priest. There is no virgin in the land who is a stranger so receive the blood of a stranger who brought evil to the land. You may strike me after I have killed him, but I will not let him live to plant more evil among the people.

WHITEHEAD: My Lord, you must stop them. Maligu, you must stop him! He is mad.

MALIGU: I cannot stop him, Whitehead. I am sorry. Thank you for the diamonds.

WHITEHEAD: You are a man of evil. You are greedy. (*He spits in Maligu's face. Kindo advances. Whitehead hurls himself at him, impaling himself upon the spear in Kindo's hands. He totters towards Maligu and he falls down on top of Parker's body*)

KINDO: I go now my people, but I shall come back. The King will soon die and you will make Maligu king. Then I shall come back with my warriors to take the crown, which belongs to me. There will never be true peace for you with a man like him as your king. If I do not come back, tell the story to your children. Give me your blessing, father.

SANTIGI: Don't come near me! You reek of blood! You are unclean! You are no longer my son.

KINDO: Then may you have peace and rest among the spirits. I go my people. (*He walks out slowly. His men follow him. The people move aside to let them pass*)

## LIGHTS OUT

# LET ME DIE ALONE

### MADAM YOKO

BY
JOHN KOLOSA KARGBO

*John Kolosa Kargbo*

# CHARACTERS

| | |
|---|---|
| YOKO | Ruler of Mende Chiefdom |
| GBANYA | Yoko's Husband. Ruler of Mende Chiefdom |
| GUARD | Palace guard |
| MUSA | Seer and Medicine Man |
| LAMBOI | Yoko's Brother |
| JENEBA | Ndapi's daughter |
| NDAPI | Chief Warrior |
| ROWE | British Colonial Representative |
| JILO | Ndapi's wife |
| LANSANA | Jilo's lover |
| LAVALIE | Warrior |
| FANNEH | Yoko's maid |
| MUSU | Yoko's maid |
| MESSENGER | Black Representative of British Colonial government |
| GIRL | Sande dancer |
| 2nd GUARD | Another palace guard |
| CROWD SCENE | Sande Dancers |

# ACT ONE

## Scene One

(*Gbanya's bedroom. Singing and "Sande" drumming offstage. Only a kerosene lamp lights the stage. There is a bed covered with "contri" cloth at one end of the stage. Various fighting paraphernalia: spears, machetes, and raffia skirts hang on the walls. On the other side of the stage is a shrine made with palm leaves, etc., on top of a small box. Gbanya enters pulling a shouting Yoko*)

YOKO: My lord wait, wait! I cannot leave the girls. They need me.

GBANYA: (*Pulling her into the room*) Your girls may need you, but your husband needs you now. Of what better use is a woman to a man?

YOKO: But my lord, can't you wait till the dancing is over?

GBANYA: When the loins of a husband catch fire, that fire must be quenched instantly. (*He steers Yoko to the bed*)

YOKO: But my lord, my lord! Please, let me dismiss my dancers.

GBANYA: Let them dance, and if they drop dead dancing... (*He forces her to the bed. Yoko's protests gradually change to ecstatic and sensual moans. They are interrupted by violent knocking offstage*) Who is that?

GUARD: (*Offstage*) The bodyguard, your Highness.

GBANYA: (*Gets up and adjusts his robes*) Stay here Yoko. (*To guard*) What do you want?

GUARD: (*Enters and prostrates*) A messenger has just arrived. He says the governor will be here tomorrow.

GBANYA: The Governor? He has never visited us. What else did the messenger say?

GUARD: He said no more, your Highness.

GBANYA: (*Pauses*) Tell Lamboi, Ndapi, Lavalie, and the others that we meet in the *barre* at sunrise.

YOKO: (*Rises*) Guard, tell the girls to stop dancing. (*Guard exits*) My Lord…

GBANYA: Go back to bed, Yoko, you are a woman. Your brain was made for music, your feet for dancing, steps that will fire the loins of any man, and your body for that bed. Not for the important affairs of the chiefdom. Go back now.

YOKO: He says the governor is coming? It must be important (*Drumming stops*)

GBANYA: This might have something to do with the boys I hired out to John Caulker to fight against his brother, George. A runner came two days ago and spoke of the governor and his soldiers. (*He goes back to bed*)

YOKO: My lord, you are troubled.

GBANYA: Woman, I'm unwell. I even fear to sleep at night. My mind, Yoko, my mind.

YOKO: When the mind is sick, the body too is sick. But why, my lord, what is this sickness that plagues my husband's mind? Sharing it with a wife will surely help.

GBANYA: (*To himself*) And now everything seems to be happening with such rapidity. I lost my best fighters in the Ashanti and Caulker campaigns. Just as in the dream of last night the Governor himself now comes to humiliate me in the eyes of my people.

YOKO: My lord?

GBANYA: Now what is it? Can't I have …

YOKO: When the bleeding heart yearns for love, the tongue, hands, feet, and lips are never still. My lord, forgive me. My love for you leads me to nagging.

GBANYA: Never did I fail to honor the rich memory of my ancestors. So they have visited me in my sleep several times these past nights from across the rivers, some riding on the high wings of red eagles and holding in their hands white cocks. They implore me to join them.

YOKO: Gods! Gods!

GBANYA: And last night my dead father came. I saw his face again and that beard resting on his strong chest bedecked with those same powerful charms. He said "Gbanya" and I answered. "Come." He said again, "come over." I must go. Yes, I must go very soon. But how will I enter the land of my brave forefathers?

YOKO: My lord, the dream is bad. Let us make sacrifices and hope that your journey starts in peace.

GBANYA: Peace? Peace? What is peace, woman, to the man who commands the finest, most courageous band of fighters in Mende land? What is peace? Where can we find it? I will tell you, Yoko. Peace is only found in the eyes on the head of the sacrificial lamb, long after that head has been severed from its agony-wracked body; peace is found in the limp body of the dead cock, when its feathers are being plucked out…Yoko, there is no peace in this world. But now, why should I who sent so many enemies on their quest for such peace be afraid to die? No, I'm not. My fear rests in the manner of dying. I would gladly have the sharp edge of an enemy's spear wedged in this rich heart that has loved you, this proud heart that has savored and enjoyed the sweet fruits of power, than die a dishonorable death.

YOKO: But a chief never dies without honor, my lord.

GBANYA: (*Laughs*) But I will. I know it. But I will let my enemy the Governor know my power. I will present him with the greatest of gifts. He will see the most dazzling and gracious of *Sande* dancers Mende land can boast of, the richest wine and the biggest cattle. Let my murderer know my power before he snuffs out my life. (*Yoko attempts to leave*)

GBANYA: Woman, where are you going?

YOKO: To get Ndapi, *Keke* Lamboi, and Lavalie.

GBANYA: Why? We don't need them.

YOKO: We do my lord. Remember you made a promise a long time ago that at the time of your death the chiefdom passes into my hands.

GBANYA: Yoko, of all my thirty-seven wives, you know I cherish you most. At the time of making that promise, I never knew that war would be ravaging this our land. Enemies, Yoko, too many enemies, are bent on wiping out my people.

YOKO: But, your promise.

GBANYA: Look, woman, if Senehun is to survive, a man must lead her. Come now, there are other riches you will outlive me to enjoy. Come, let me once again enjoy the spring in those steps, steps that will thrill me no more when I am gone to the land of my noble ancestors. Dance, Yoko, dance. (*Soft drumming commences*)

YOKO: No!

GBANYA: You won't dance?

YOKO: The chiefdom. I want the chiefdom.

GBANYA: No, you cannot have that. Take all the cattle, all the huts, take anything, but I cannot give you, a woman, the land of my ancestors.

YOKO: Then my lord, your love for me all these years has been prompted by this body. Remember you told me to bear no children as the *Poro* might need me. And now, on the verge of old age, you leave me, to remain alone in distress. What is the value of old age without children? Now I know all my sacrifices these past years have been in vain.

GBANYA: No, they have not been in vain. Have I not expressed my love to you? Have I not put you above my thirty-six other wives?

YOKO: Well, to whom will you leave the chiefdom?

GBANYA: It will go to Ndapi. The lot of a leader is not to be envied. Think of the fears, the suspicions, the doubts of knowing that the whitest set of teeth is accompanied by the most evil plotting mind. A chief must be ruthless; he must never be seen to be weak. Now dance.

YOKO: No, I won't.

GBANYA: (*Moves over to her*) Look Yoko, you can't force me. You know you can't. You are important to me; that you know. But I cannot grant you this wish.

YOKO: I knew all along that I have been stupid. I would rather die than share a bed with Ndapi when you are gone.

GBANYA: Why? He's the best warrior in Mende land.

YOKO: Even if he were the best bedfellow on earth, I'd rather die than share a bed with that heartless man.

GBANYA: I know I cannot convince you, Yoko. But if you say you cannot dance for my pleasure there is another use for a woman.

YOKO: And what might that be, my lord!

GBANYA: The bed, woman, the bed.

YOKO: But my lord, do you think I'm a calabash, a cooking pot or an axe to be used so indiscriminately? No my lord, I am a woman but I'm also human. You say you cannot leave the chiefdom in my hands because I am a woman, but are there not other women who have been ruling chiefdoms successfully for many years? Take Yoya, Kema of Galu, Fangawa of Wando, Kpanda Gbello of Leppiama, Woki of Tunkia or Nancy Caulker in Sherbro land. Are they not all good rulers?

GBANYA: Yes, they are good rulers. Indeed they are. And they are also good lovers in bed. So show me what you can do. (*He drags her to bed again. Yoko screams and kicks out. Lights out*)

## Scene Two

(*Spotlight on Musa, the "Totogbemui," gradually brightens to cover entire stage*)

MUSA: No, I cannot do what you have asked, Lamboi; that's totally beyond my powers. I am not a giver of life so I cannot take it. I cannot.

LAMBOI: (*Enters*) Look Musa, this is not just for my sake, it is for the sake of the people. The people, Musa. Think of the people.

MUSA: I don't have his *Ngafo*, so how do I do it? No, I cannot. It can't be done. You are a *Poro* man, I'm a *Poro* man, and he's also a *Poro* man. How then can I do that to him? Have you also forgotten the allegiance, the oath we took in that bush many years ago?

LAMBOI: If I have forgotten that oath, then let elephantiasis cling to my legs the way mud clings to the legs of farmers in the swamps. The man who forgets the oath taken in that bush should never...!

MUSA: Don't shout, don't shout, Lamboi.

LAMBOI: But you taunted me, I can never forget the...

MUSA: Enough now! Enough Lamboi. Why do you think it necessary that he should die now?

LAMBOI: I fear that woman, Yoko. If he lives longer, she might be able to convince him to pass the chiefdom to her. And with war threatening each passing moment, with enemies surrounding us, it is necessary that a man should succeed Gbanya, not a soft woman who has music in her ears, itchy dancing feet, and legs wide open for a man.

MUSA: And what makes you so convinced that Chief Gbanya will hand over his staff to Yoko?

LAMBOI: He loves that woman more than the very eyes on his head. I saw the chief tremble and weep when she fell ill. I saw him kill a slave with his bare hands because the poor boy wandered into Yoko's room when the woman was naked. And she likes to be naked. That woman is really ruling Senehun now.

MUSA: Yes, go on, Lamboi, my ears are with you.

LAMBOI: I advised Gbanya that we must not undertake the Caulker Campaign. Yoko told him she needed more slaves to work on the farms he'd given her, so we had to go to war—a war which was not our own. Many of our finest fighters, young men, died just to satisfy the wants of a woman.

MUSA: Ah *ndake*, no, I don't believe that.

LAMBOI: (*Takes out a palm leaf, ties it around his wrist*) Ah *Ngewo*! If I'm lying let the *Poro* Devil...

MUSA: Don't swear, Lamboi, I believe you now.

LAMBOI: So, would you sit back, wait for the machetes of our enemies to pierce your heart?

MUSA: Me? Lamboi, I'm old and ripe for the journey across the river to meet my ancestors. Anytime death knocks at my door, I will welcome it.

LAMBOI: Now think, think, *Ngo* Musa, of your children and grand children. Would your spirit in the land of our ancestors ever know peace if Senehun is attacked and all of them are either killed or dragged into slavery?

MUSA: (*Pause*) It will not.

LAMBOI: Then?

MUSA: Lamboi, the task you are asking me to perform is impossible. Give me time. Let me sleep on it. My brain is old but I can still think. Give me a little more time.

LAMBOI: (*Grabs him*) Look *Ngo* Musa, our lives are at stake. This is just a little job that even a child can do.

MUSA: Then go and find that child. I will not kill the Chief.

LAMBOI: You will, *Ngo* Musa.

MUSA: Lamboi, are you deaf? I say I will not. And if you continue to play monkey games with me, I will tell chief Gbanya of your intention to kill him. I don't want power and I'm not prepared to kill anybody to get it or keep it. I have never killed a man, neither in war nor in peace, and I don't want to start doing so now. I have never killed a man and I will not start doing so for...

LAMBOI: *Ngo* Musa, if you have never killed a man, here, swear: let the *Poro* Devil spit on your nose and rot it; let it eat your fingers and make you a leper; let the *Gbeni* shout deafen you ears and blind you; let the *Gbeni's* whip beat elephantiasis into your legs... Go on swear, you wicked, crafty old goat. Swear! You don't? Of course you won't. A mad man may eat his own shit, but will never play with fire.

MUSA: Why should I swear to *Poro*? If you believe me, you believe me. If you don't then I am not the drummer to drum for you. Find another, I must go.

LAMBOI: *Ngo* Musa, our elders say, only the guilty are afraid. If you know your hands are clean, I dare you to swear.

MUSA: My hands are clean, I wash them everyday in the river.

LAMBOI: Yes indeed, in the river of blood, rich and hot human blood.

MUSA: Is this some joke? Lamboi, what are you talking about?

LAMBOI: That when you wash your hands, you wash them in blood, precious to the people of Senehun because its their blood, the blood of their children and...

MUSA: Lamboi, they often say power makes men drunk. Some say power makes men crazy, but you are already crazy, *ndake*, and power has not yet come your way.

LAMBOI: The blood of Yattah's son and Mama Kadi's daughter. Those you slaughtered and whose fat you used for your *bofima*. You want me to name what charms you made with their private parts? Or do you want me to lead Gbanya, whom you want to protect, to their shallow graves out there in the bush?

MUSA: Lamboi! *Ndake*, what are you getting angry for? I was just trying to make sure you are serious. You know I will do anything you say. After all, we are both working for the good of the chiefdom.

LAMBOI: All I want you to do is to kill the chief and help me to prevent the chiefdom from falling into the hands of a woman.

MUSA: But how do I do it? I don't have the...

JENEBA: (*Prostrates and greets them*) *Keke* Lamboi *Biwua, Ngo* Musa *bi sie.*

LAMBOI: My little wife Jeneba, *bi sie. Ka hu i ye na?*

JENEBA: *Ka hi ngewo ma.*

MUSA: How is your mother, Jilo. Did she send you?

JENEBA: No, papa says they are waiting for you at the meeting in the *barre*.

MUSA: Ah, we have forgotten about that. All right, Jenneh, when next I go into the bush to get some herbs I will bring some plums and berries for you. Now run along, good girl, and tell your father we are on our way. (*Jeneba skips out playfully*)

LAMBOI: Girls of her type stand to die in the hands of the enemies of Senehun.

MUSA: All right, Lamboi. The Governor is coming today. He has been causing a lot of trouble.

LAMBOI: The Governor?

MUSA: Yes, he is making his first visit to Senehun with his soldiers.

LAMBOI: Then there is going to be trouble. The warriors who fought in the Caulker Campaign crossed the frontier. Now look, whatever happens Gbanya may need your help. I don't know how you will do it but you must. And if you reveal this plot (*brings out a dagger*) I will plant this firmly into your chest and lead the people to those graves.

MUSA: Heh! Lamboi, I'll tell nobody, I know exactly what we need. After the Governor's visit, Gbanya will surely want to go to the *Poro* bush and drink from that bottle, the medicine that could kill him instantly. It is the gall of the Alligator. Just a drop will do the trick. Let's go now. Maybe when you become chief we shall go to war against our enemies and I shall have enough human fat for my *bofima*. Heh, heh, heh.(*They exit. Lights out*)

## Scene Three

(*"Sande" drumming offstage. The chief's barre. Horn blower enters signaling the arrival of the chief and his train, including Yoko, Jeneba, Lavalie, Ndapi, Lamboi, and Musa*)

GBANYA: Ndapi, go and tell the women to stop the music. Get runners along the path leading to the chiefdom so we can know when the Governor arrives. Lavalie, you go tell my wives to put on their best clothes. Tell them that each of them should be prepared to give a fitting present to the Governor. Yoko, are your *Sande* dancers ready?

YOKO: They are ready, my lord.

GBANYA: Lamboi!

LAMBOI: Your Highness.

GBANYA: Let them take five fat cows out to the corral, five fat rams and sheep.

LAMBOI: But why, your Highness?

GBANYA: They are presents for the Governor.

LAMBOI: I think it is too much, your Highness. Why should we give him all that just because he is the Governor?

GBANYA: Lamboi, you do not understand. Get the cattle and the rams.

LAMBOI: Your word is my command, your Highness. (*He exits*)

MUSA: Your Highness you have been neglecting the *Poro* bush these few days.

GBANYA: *Ngo* Musa, can a man ever forget the source of his strength? Unless a child can think of carrying the head of the elephant after the hunt. The moment the Governor leaves, I will go to the bush.

YOKO: My lord!

GBANYA: Yes, Yoko.

YOKO: I'm confused. Something tells me that a great ill will befall this household today. You should have prepared for war on the Governor's visit.

GBANYA: (*Laughs*) That's why I maintain that you are just a woman. Can our *chakabulas* and spears, or machetes and slings withstand the guns of the Governor and his frontier soldiers?

YOKO: (*Insistent*) You could ambush them. It's still not too late. Take them by surprise. My mind tells me that…

GBANYA: Don't worry, woman.

LAVALIE: (*Enters and prostrates*) Your wives are getting ready, your Highness.

GBANYA: Good.

NDAPI: (*Enters and prostrates*) May it please the chief. The warriors are stationed along the paths.

GBANYA: Very well. (*Lamboi enters, nods and takes his seat*) Now, you all will be wondering why I have decided to welcome the Governor in this grand manner. Yoko here suggested that we should ambush him because he is carrying something evil with him to this land. (*Lamboi gets up in protest, but Gbanya silences him with a gesture of his hand*) But suppose we kill the Governor, do you know how many soldiers will be sent from his country far across the seas to wipe us out? Do you know how many of us will die? Do you...

GUARD: (*Runs in and prostrates*) The Governor is on his way, your Highness. (*Yoko whispers to Jeneba and the child skips out. Soon "Sande" music starts and six girls enter dancing. Governor Rowe, in white, plumed helmet, badges and monocle, is brought in on a hammock. In one gloved hand is a pipe and in the other a short baton. He regards the dancers who, at a signal from Yoko, stop and exit*)

GBANYA: My master, Governor, I welcome you to Senehun. (*He moves to embrace Rowe*)

ROWE: Don't put those filthy paws on me, you savage! Call in the soldiers. (*One of the hammock bearers exits*) Now tell me, you brute, why did you send you war boys to fight on John Caulker's side against his brother?

GBANYA: I did not send anybody to fight in that war.

ROWE: You did.

GBANYA: Governor I did not...

ROWE: Shut up! (*Soldiers enter with guns*) When people like us leave our civilized society to come and bring both the light and the word to you out here in the bush, we expect you to conform. You, Gbanya, you have the effrontery, the audacity, to participate in a revolt even when I, Dr. Samuel Rowe, the sole representative of her Imperial Majesty, have commanded that there should be no more fighting.

GBANYA: Governor, my boys did not fight.

ROWE: If you annoy me, Gbanya, I will cut out that lying tongue. Soldiers! (*The soldiers move forward and drag Gbanya from his seat. He struggles. Lavalie, Ndapi, and Lamboi move forward. Rowe whips out a pistol and fires a shot in the air*) If anyone makes just one false move, I will pump him full of hot lead. (*The soldiers stretch Gbanya out on the ground*) And now, this will teach you never again to go against the command of her Imperial Majesty in whose service I am proud to be. It will teach you to confine your war boys at home. (*Signals to another soldier who brings out a whip with which Gbanya is beaten*) Stop! Now you dog, get up! You will pay a fine of fifty pounds in the equivalent of cattle and rice. And the next time you disobey my orders, you will be arrested and locked up in jail in the colony. By the time I get to the next chiefdom to deal with another brute of your type, I want the cattle and rice, or you will be taught the lesson of your life. (*He goes back into the hammock and as he and his soldiers exit, all on stage rush to aid their chief*)

LAMBOI: Lavalie, you block that door. Ndapi, block the other. No one must come in and see the chief in this disgraceful state. Woman, don't just stand there crying, get some water.

MUSA: Oh my ancestors, what curse did you put on my head that I should have lived to see this deed? Your Highness, up, up.

LAVALIE: The people want to come in. They are asking if the chief is dead.

LAMBOI: Go back. They must be stopped at all cost. Tell them the chief is alive and will be speaking to them shortly.

YOKO: *Ngo Musa.* (*She hands the calabash containing water to him*)

MUSA: Now woman, hurry. Get some hot water to calm the wounds on his back. Let me first apply something on them to stop the bleeding. (*Yoko goes out again*)

LAMBOI: Now, we are alone with him. You must not be afraid, *Ngo* Musa.

MUSA: Leave everything to me. *From the folds of his robes, he takes out the bottle containing the poison and adds a single drop to the water*) My lord, drink this, it will ease the pain.

GBANYA: I... I... I knew it, Musa. I knew that this was why the Governor came to us. I had known it....

LAMBOI: Hush, my lord, you must be still.

GBANYA: Where... where... where is Yoko?

LAMBOI: She has gone to fetch some hot water to wash the blood off your wounds.

GBANYA: I... I must... I must see... Yoko... I must see...

MUSA: All right, my lord, she will be here soon. Please drink. This medicine in the water will kill the pain. (*Puts the calabash to Gbanya's lips. The latter drinks*)

GBANYA: I must see Yoko.

LAMBOI: Relax, Your Highness, she will be here soon.

GBANYA: (*Clutches his stomach*) My stomach is on fire. My tongue is burning. Musa, Lamboi, what did you put in that calabash?

MUSA: Some medicine to stop the pain, your Highness.

GBANYA: (*Rising to his feet clutching his stomach*) Musa you have poisoned me. That is the alligator's gall. Why did you do it? Why?

LAMBOI: We had to, your Highness. We cannot sit idly by and watch you pass the chiefdom to a woman.

MUSA: With our enemies fully armed standing on our doorsteps, only a man can save Senehun.

GBANYA: But can a *Poro* man do this to a fellow *Poro* man? Ah.... ALLIEEUU! My stomach. Yoko! I must see Yoko. (*He attempts to exit but Lamboi moves and blocks his path*) Get out of my way, you murderer.

LAMBOI: No, you cannot leave this *barre* alive. (*Pulls out a dagger and raises it*)

MUSA: No, Lamboi, don't. Anytime now he will know the full effect of the alligator's gall.

LAMBOI: He wants to be stubborn.

MUSA: Not against the alligator's gall. It's foolproof and there is no remedy.

GBANYA: May the *Poro* Devil himself avenge this my death. May ALLIEEUU! May... (*Yoko Enters*)

YOKO: The water is.... my lord? What happened, *Ngo* Musa?

MUSA: He says he wants to see his wife and I think he means you.

YOKO: Did he drink the water?

LAMBOI: No, he did not.

YOKO: My lord, my lord.........It's me your wife, Yoko, my lord.

GBANYA: (*Raises his head*) Yo.. Yo... Yoko. The chiefdom. Take... take... take chargeeee of... of.... chief... (*He slumps dead*)

YOKO: Yeiyoooo!! (*She gets up and runs off crying*)

MUSA: (*Moves over and feels for Gbanya's pulse*) I told you the alligator's gall never fails.

LAMBOI: We cannot waste time now, *Ngo* Musa, there is still a lot to be done.

MUSA: Lamboi, do you think anybody will want to fight you for the chiefdom now?

LAMBOI: *Ndake*, nothing is impossible. We must try to assume a position of strength. We cannot afford to take any risks. First of all I will have to announce to the people that the Chief is dead... No, you will have to do that and tell them that I'm the new Chief. Warn them sternly that any attempts at subversion will meet with instant death.

YOKO: (*Comes in machete in hand*) And indeed, any attempts at subversion will meet with instant death from me... I don't know the manner of my husband's death, but you heard him when he said I should take charge, and I'm going to do exactly that.

MUSA: Yoko, you cannot.

YOKO: Then try to stop me, Musa. Your head and that of any other man who attempts to stop me will soon be rolling in the dust... Lamboi, how did my husband die?

LAMBOI: I don't know.

YOKO: *Ngo* Musa?

MUSA: I don't know either.

YOKO: *Ngo* Lavalie, Ndapi. (*Both rush in*) The chief is dead.(*They are both shocked and speechless for a moment. Lavalie recovers first*)

LAVALIE: Ah *Ngewo*! A finer man never ruled in Mende land, a braver man never walked this earth. May the hands of our forefathers grant him...

YOKO: Lavalie, tributes can wait. You are the speaker. Before he died, he told me to take charge of the ...

LAMBOI: That's a lie.

YOKO: Then swear to the *Poro* Devil if you did not hear his words.

MUSA: Don't blaspheme, woman, don't blaspheme!

YOKO: I am in charge.

NDAPI: How did the chief die?

YOKO: I don't know. But I have my suspicions.

NDAPI: Now that my master is gone, I lay down my spear.

YOKO: Ndapi, *Hindo*! Take your spear and let this my hand be the source of your power and my wants the cause of your actions.

NDAPI: I thank you, Madam.

YOKO: Take the corpse in the inner room. Lavalie, inform the people of the developments. Then assemble the warriors. When you are through with that I will be in the royal hut.

MUSA: You cannot enter that as a chief unless you join the *Poro*.

YOKO: I will be ready and willing at sunset.

LAMBOI: Do you know what that means? You will never bear children.

YOKO: I am ready. Go prepare for the ceremony. Leave me now. Leave me and let me mourn for the man who taught me the virtues and qualities of undying love. The man who made Senehun into a great chiefdom—the finest and most courageous chief in all Mende land. Leave me now and let me mourn for my husband's death alone. (*They exit*) Gbanya! Gbanya I have started feeling it—the suspicions, the doubts, fears, and uncertainties. There will indeed be many plotters, but let your brave spirit fill this my body. Let your strong powers guide me. Minds will this minute be plotting against me. I know it, but Gbanya, may your brave spirit know this, Yoko is ready, for pain and pleasure, for honor and distress, for loyalty and treachery, for peace and war. Yoko is ready! (*Lights out*)

# ACT TWO

## Scene One

(*There is a single bench downstage. Jilo emerges with a calabash, singing a tune softly. She sits down and starts peeling some cassava. Enter Lansana, one of the warriors. They exchange greetings*)

LANSANA: Jilo, *Nyande, bia-na?*

JILO: *Ngo Lansana bisie; o bi gahu?*

LANSANA: *Ka ye ngewo ma Nyande*, I'm hungry.

JILO: I am in trouble. I spent a long time at the market today and my husband might return home to find nothing to eat.

LANSANA: Well, you told me to come. Where is your husband? Jilo, I hate to leave a broom lying on the ground and sweep a hot fireplace with my fingers.

JILO: (*Laughs*) *Ngo* Lansana, it is dangerous. Ndapi could kill you if he finds you here.

LANSANA: Look, we will not waste too much time. We could go in at once.

JILO: No, *Ngo* Lansana, it's dangerous. Let's wait some other time.

LANSANA: Oh Jilo, you always tell me to wait. Wait, wait, wait. When will this long wait be over? You know I have always loved you. There is nothing you can...

JILO: But I'm married.

LANSANA: And me?

JILO: Then go to your wife.

LANSANA: (*Laughs*) *Nyande, Nyande*, for how long can a man go on eating *sakitomboi*? From time to time he should taste *jolabete*. (*Pause*) *Nyande*, you understand these things, you know...

JILO: *Ngo* Lansana, there are many *jolabetes* in Senehun. If you are tired of *saki* go and find what you want.

LANSANA: Let's not quarrel over this. It will not take too long. Once. Just once.

JILO: No!

LANSANA: (*Laughs*) Look at your body, *Nyande*. See how smooth it is—as smooth as the back of a bridal calabash. Look at your waistline, slim like that of a pet monkey. Look at your buttocks, round, shapely. Their movements remind me of the grace with which our madam used to move. Jilo, whenever I see you walking to the market or to the river, I long to hold these buttocks, to squeeze them and...

JILO: (*Jumps up screaming and rubbing her sore rump*) *Ngo* Lansana, stop this nonsense, or I'll tell Ndapi on his return.

LANSANA: Ndapi should not know, he will not know. This is just between the two of us (*laughs*)

JILO: No!

LANSANA: (*Pause*) Jilo, that cassava you are peeling, what will you do with it?

JILO: (*Surprised*) What do you mean?

LANSANA: Exactly what I said, my goddess, my queen. How will you prepare that cassava?

JILO: I'll boil it.

LANSANA: And if you don't boil it?

JILO: Why, I'll roast it. (*Pause*) Well?

LANSANA: Forgive me. I was only thinking. Look at it this way. I've tried to convince you with words and if I fail there is another way of getting what I want. If you don't roast the cassava, you boil it. So, if I can't get you with words, force will do. (*Grabs her*)

JILO: No! No! No! *Ngo* Lansana, stop. Stop it. *Nya ndengaa a wa o* Lansana, I'll scream! I'll bite! (*Lansana gags her with his hand and drags her into the hut. Enter Ndapi and Lavalie from opposite ends*)

NDAPI: *Keke* Lavalie, *bisie*.

LAVALIE: Ah! Ndapi, just the man I have been looking for. *Bia na ndake?* Senehun will have to go to war.

NDAPI: Why, we don't need more slaves, do we?

LAVALIE: No! But Madam is afraid of our neighbors. She was telling me only yesterday that we must attack them before they regroup and attack us.

NDAPI: Suppose the Governor calls again?

LAVALIE: He won't. Why he came to Senehun was because you crossed the frontier and attacked the people under his protection. Gbanya should have made his instructions clearer to you.

NDAPI: *Keke* Lavalie, the way our old chief died still worries me.

LAVALIE: Me too. But both of us were outside that day, shortly after the Governor had gone. And there was something unusual about the funeral. Did you see the color of the dead chief's skin? It was as black as charcoal. I demanded an explanation from *Ngo* Musa but he only mumbled that he was tired. Even Madam herself considers her life threatened these days. She doesn't even trust her brother, Lamboi.

NDAPI: So, when do we go to war?

LAVALIE: She says within the next three days. She's sent runners to the surrounding villages to tell the chiefs that they either give up their chiefdoms to her or be prepared to defend them with their lives. The runners will be arriving tomorrow and if the chiefs concerned decide to fight to hold their lands, we will spend the next day performing war ceremonies. Ndapi, there is something I want to discuss with you, something that's been worrying me for a long time.

NDAPI: But *Keke* Lavalie, you're the speaker. Can't you advise Madam to forget about war? We shall defeat the smaller chiefdoms, but I'd rather as a warrior fight to protect my people than engage in a battle to meet the greedy ends of Madam!

LAVALIE: Don't shout! Don't be so loud now, Ndapi! Come, there is still a way to stop her. Let's discuss what I have in mind. (*They exit. Lansana emerges trembling. Jilo follows adjusting her lappa*)

JILO: (*Excited*) Well, you see what I've been telling you? Had Ndapi found you here he would have killed you.

LANSANA: *Nyande*, after what you gave me in there, I would gladly have opened my hands to welcome my death. Jilo we must arrange to meet again at a safer place where we can spend...

JILO: (*Showing him out*) *Ngo* Lansana, stop chattering like an old monkey. Ndapi will be back soon and if he finds you here, there will be no teeth left in that mouth of yours to chew even an over-boiled potato.

LANSANA: (*Laughs*) Jilo, I'm prepared to risk my life, to drive my wife away, and steal you from your own...

JILO: You want my husband to kill me? You've got what you wanted. Go!

LANSANA: (*Fighting to restrain himself*) Don't push me like that, don't Jilo. Come on now, let's talk about the next meeting place. By the forest path? By the riverbank at sunset? Behind the... (*His voice trails off and Jilo returns to her cooking. Ndapi enters*)

JILO: (*Courtesies*) *Ngo bisie.*

NDAPI: *Bisie.* Where have you been?

JILO: I... I had to take... Jeneba to *Ngo* Musa, the *totogbemoi*. She was crying in her sleep last night.

NDAPI: So when the daughter is sick, the father must find no food in the house. So when the daughter is sick, the husband must starve! Eh? (*Steps on her toe*)

JILO: Yeiiayoo! *Ngo* you will crush my toe!

NDAPI: (*Slaps her*) You lazy woman, you're always finding excuses. Why are you shouting? Have I touched you?

JILO: *Ngo* please, you're crushing my big toe.

GUARD: (*Enters and prostrates*) *Hindo*! I've told you not to go on beating this woman everyday. If she gets used to the weight of your hands, whenever you become angry, your anger will sound like good, rich *Sande* music to her ears.

NDAPI: (*Laughs*) But *Hindo*, I've not touched her.

JILO: (*To guard*) Please tell him to stop. He's stepping on my toe!

GUARD: (*Pushing Ndapi away*) You rascal! You could crush her toe. (*Laughs*) You're eating raw cassava? Have you just married another woman?

NDAPI: Well you see, *Hindo*. This is the cause of the palaver. I never find cooked food whenever I return to this house. (*Slaps Jilo again*) I think I married a goat instead of a woman. (*Picking up a piece of raw cassava again and serving guard*) Come, what brings you here?

GUARD: Bad news. War. Have you...

NDAPI: *Keke* Lavalie told me about it a while ago. (*Shaking his head sadly*) Many heads will roll in the dust again this year.

GUARD: But *Hindo*, why? Is it necessary? We could avert this one, can't we?

NDAPI: Look, my brother, reasoning with a woman like Yoko is like telling a charging ram in mid-flight to hold its peace. It's impossible. I don't hate our Queen, but what puts my heart on fire is the way she fights to please the *pumui*. Everyday she's sending some message to the Governor or the district Commissioner. I'd not be surprised if either of them visits Senehun and spends the night in her room.

GUARD: (*Alarmed*) She is a *Maboye*, a *Poro* woman!

NDAPI: *Kpoo*, so what? *Poro* or no *Poro*, she's still a woman, requiring a man like any of them. All that aside, she's greedy, insolent, and power-drunk—very, very ambitious. Tell me, my brother, why do we need to expand the chiefdom?

GUARD: Are you not on speaking terms with the Queen? *Kpoo*! Why ask me? I have not asked you to go to war.

NDAPI: (*Pause*) I wish chief Gbanya were still alive. At least the wars he made us fight were honorable, brave ventures. I gladly slaughtered whole villages, dragged others into slavery for the sake of Senehun's survival. Now a woman leads us into vain warfare, the provocative type.

GUARD: She is putting her palm kernels into the fire and using our own fingers to pull them out of the flames.

(*Pause*) But she's your Queen and if she says fight, you fight. Come, *Hindo*. Don't be so despondent. Let's go find some palm wine while your wife is still cooking; it's good for the appetite. (*They start to leave*) Yoko should be in bed behind a virile man, not on the throne of Senehun.

NDAPI: (*To Jilo*) Jilo! Jilo!

JILO: Yes, my lord.

NDAPI: If I come back and find this house without cooked food, I'll beat you until you crawl back to your parents in Moyamba. (*Jilo mumbles to herself*) What did you say? What did you... (*Attempts to slap her*)

GUARD: (*Intervenes*) All right Ndapi. You can't go on beating her forever. You have such a hot temper.

NDAPI: But why should she grumble? Can't she tell me things to my face? *Hindo*, when a woman under your roof starts grumbling, the next thing she will think of doing is to poison your food.

JILO: (*In tears*) I did not grumble, my Lord. I was about to say that Madam hinted yesterday that we might be moving to Moyamba in the hot season.

GUARD: We? Who?

JILO: Everybody in the chiefdom.

NDAPI: When did she tell you that?

JILO: When I went to see her this morning.

GUARD: This is serious. Why does she want us to move to Moyamba?

NDAPI: How should I know? Power is making this woman crazy. It's making her drunk.

GUARD: This news has brought confusion to my head. It's not steady. Let's go and find this palmwine. (*They Exit. Lights out*)

## Scene Two

(*Lights on at the "barre" reflect significant changes since the death of Gbanya. "Barre" should reflect the fact that Madam Yoko has moved her chiefdom from Senehun to Moyamba. Madam Yoko is seated with her ladies-in-waiting in attendance. Fanneh, the older of the two ladies, is plaiting her hair, while Musu tends to her toes*)

YOKO: How are you finding things in Moyamba?

FANNEH: Madam I like it here better than Senehun, but the journey was long.

MUSU: The Chiefdom has expanded even more, Madam. All the surrounding chiefdoms are coming under your control.

YOKO: Hmm! There are times when I sit and think of my husband. Thoughts of him sadden me.

MUSU: Your husband, the late chief, is now in the land of our forefathers, and his spirit is guiding you.

FANNEH: That is true Madam. His spirit definitely guides you each passing day. Here in Moyamba we have found peace and the Governor himself is happy.

YOKO: I am always suspicious of this kind of quiet in the land. Evil men plot their nefarious deeds in the middle of the night. I feel uneasy. There are even times when I feel lonesome. I would have very much liked to have my own children. Children to hold, to love...

MUSU: (*Alarmed*) Madam!

FANNEH: Madam, you cannot say such things. The gods would be annoyed.

YOKO: I know, I know, but somehow... wait, Fanneh. You don't understand.

FANNEH: I do, Madam.

YOKO: You don't.

MUSU: Well, Madam, what would you prefer? Being queen over this vast chiefdom or a mother with a number of kids to care for?

YOKO: Would you like to change places with me, Fanneh? (*Pause*) You Musu?

MUSU: Madam, I don't know. I think I will be willing to do that.

YOKO: Will you? Do you know the pressures I undergo? The fear that someday someone will think of creeping into my room with a dagger to kill me?

FANNEH: May the gods forbid. How could you think of such things, Madam?

YOKO: A ruler should think of anything. Anything could happen at anytime. I know that not everybody is pleased over the fact that I am a chief of the Kpa-Mende tribe, especially my brother, Lamboi. I fear that man. He is cunning. *Ngo* Musa is another man I do not trust. He is like a chameleon. He changes easily. I think he killed my husband.

FANNEH AND MUSU: Madam!

YOKO: It's a fact. But let's not talk of such things. You must hurry. I am summoning a meeting of elders soon to discuss an urgent matter. Fanneh?

FANNEH: Yes, Madam.

YOKO: Where is Jenneh?

MUSU: Her mother brought her this morning while she was going to the market.

YOKO: Did you feed her well?

FANNEH: We did Madam.

YOKO: Musu, go and bring the child. There are times when I want to feel like a real woman, a mother. Times when I want to hold my own child in my arms. You have four children now, Fanneh?

FANNEH: No Madam. The youngest died before we left Senehun.

YOKO: Oh, I forgot about that. What about you, Musu?

MUSU: Just two, Madam.

YOKO: Hmm! Go and bring the child now, Musu.

MUSU: Yes Madam. (*Exits*)

YOKO: Fanneh, power transforms people. It breeds fear and that fear makes me dread even shadows at night. I sometimes think.... (*Musu enters with Jeneba*) Ah darling little angel. (*Yoko picks her up and swings her*) Did you eat anything today, my little *suwui*?

JENEBA: Yes, Mama Fanneh gave me pap. Mama Musu gave me roast cassava.

YOKO: Ah, that's good and did you eat all of it? (*Jeneba nods*) Very good. Are you happy here with me, my small queen? (*Jeneba nods again*) Good. How is your mother, Jilo?

JENEBA: *Keke* Ndapi beat her.

YOKO: (*Surprised*) Why? (*Jeneba shrugs her shoulder as guard enters*)

GUARD: Your Highness, there is a man outside. He says he is a messenger sent by the Governor.

YOKO: Musu, go and make the Governor's messenger comfortable. Put him in the best hut; give him the best palmwine and good food. Find him a *Sande* girl versed in bed manners. He comes from the Governor and must be treated with due honors.

MUSU: Yes, Madam. (*Exits*)

YOKO: Fanneh, bring my crown. Guard, summon all the elders: Lavalie, *Ngo* Musa, *Keke* Lamboi, and Ndapi.

GUARD: Yes, your Highness. (*Exits*)

YOKO: Jenneh, go outside and play. I'm having a very important visitor. (*Jenneh exits as Fanneh enters with the crown*) Come, Fanneh. Help me adjust this dress. My royal slippers, go bring them. Wait. Bring my silver bangles too.

FANNEH: Yes, Madam. (*As she exits, noise offstage. Ndapi is pummeling Jilo. He drags her in and throws her at Yoko's feet*)

YOKO: Ndapi, Jilo, what happened?

NDAPI: Let her speak Madam. Let the dog speak for herself.

YOKO: Ndapi, stop beating her. It's enough! Jilo, get up. What happened?

JILO: Nothing, your Highness.

NDAPI: (*Advancing again*) What? What did you say? So I'm a madman? I just beat you without cause? So I'm mad? Go on you liar. Tell the Chief what you did. If you don't want to talk I'll squeeze the words out of your throat with my bare hands.

YOKO: No, Ndapi, be patient. You cannot....

NDAPI: This woman is a liar, Madam. She has deceived me. Tell her Highness whom I caught you flirting with (*Jilo is silent*) You don't want to talk? (*Grabs her and twists her arm behind her back*) Go on, tell the chief the man I caught you flirting with.

JILO: Assiiiieeeeeeuuuuuu! My arm, *Ngo*, you'll break my arm.

NDAPI: Soon, I'll break every bone in this your rotten body if you don't open your wretched mouth and talk.

JILO: Your Highness, he is hurting me. Tell him to stop!

NDAPI: Talk, Jilo. Talk.

JILO: My arm, my arm!

YOKO: Ndapi, stop!

NDAPI: Let her tell you the truth, Madam.

YOKO: I command you to stop! (*Ndapi lets go*) Now tell me what happened?

NDAPI: Madam, a member of your honored and respected household has put fire to the roof of my life.

YOKO: A member of my household? Man or woman?

NDAPI: (*To Jilo*) You answer that!

YOKO: Ndapi, I'm addressing you.

NDAPI: Forgive me, Madam. When such things happen, a hardworking honest man goes mad with anger. A member of your honored and respected household has shattered my life.

YOKO: Who is it, Jilo? (*Pause*) Jilo!

JILO: Lans... Lans... Lansana, Madam.

YOKO: What?

NDAPI: He has been having a secret affair with my wife. The gods led me to the bush today. I found them embracing each other in the undergrowth on the road leading to the river, very near the cotton tree. I had gone to fetch some herbs for my daughter, Jeneba. Madam, he has put fire on the roof of my life. Ah, had I caught Lansana, you would have banished me from the chiefdom forever.

YOKO: May the gods forbid that. Guard!

GUARD: Your Highness.

YOKO: I want Lansana here!

GUARD: He left a short while ago, Madam. He told us he was going to see relatives at Taiama. He will be away for three days.

YOKO: Send two warriors. If they find him on the way they must tie him up and bring him back.

GUARD: Yes, your Highness. (*As the guard exits Lamboi, Musa, and Lavalie enter*)

YOKO: No, you will all have to go back and wait. I cannot receive the Governor's messenger. Not in this state. (*They exit*) Jilo you have shamed me. You mean Lansana whom I saved from the jaws of death when he was brought back as a slave from one of the wars my husband waged? Guard! Take this woman and put her in stocks.

JILO: Madam... your Highness, please... please. (*Jilo is dragged out*)

YOKO: Ndapi, I will deal with this matter myself. By the time they drag Lansana back from Taiama I would have seen the Governor's messenger. Lansana will pay all the damages.

NDAPI: And Madam, Jilo was three months pregnant. Now everything has....

YOKO: ...wasted away. I understand how you feel Ndapi. But you...

GUARD: (*returns*) Your Highness, Jilo wants to....

YOKO: I say put the woman in stocks. Are you mad?(*Lights out, followed by spotlight on Lamboi and Musa returning from the barre*)

LAMBOI: I've never seen the chief so angry.

MUSA: She hates such things. Lansana should never have done that. Ndapi is his friend. What will his wife say when she hears this?

LAMBOI: *Ngo* Musa... I'm thinking of something.

MUSA: What is it? The Governor's messenger? I passed by the guest huts on my way to the *barre*. Musu was leading that beautiful *Sande* girl you wanted to marry to the messenger. They have given him a reception, which will make even the Governor himself jealous. This woman is afraid of that Governor. What I can't understand is....

LAMBOI: No. That is not what I'm thinking of. Look at it this way, *Ngo* Musa. Suppose Jeneba disappears.

MUSA: Jeneba? How?

LAMBOI: Suppose we kidnap her, take her to the bush and you know.... (*He makes the death sign*) Then we tell the warriors and the people that Yoko has sacrificed her to consolidate her position as Chief. We shall tell them that she buried the child alive. That will cause a lot of trouble. Then the people will force her to give up the chiefdom and go into exile. If she refuses, then measures will be taken to depose her. And if that fails, she will definitely be killed.

MUSA: And then you take over?

LAMBOI: Exactly. That way we cannot fail.

MUSA: (*Pause*) But Lamboi, where do we bury the body after killing Jeneba?

LAMBOI: Out there in the bush. That question is irrelevant *Ngo* Musa. How did you dispose of the bodies of Yattah and Mama Kadi's children when you killed them and used their blood for your *bofima* back in Senehun?

MUSA: Lamboi, our plan to kill the Chief the last time failed and...

LAMBOI: This time it will not only be the two of us. Yoko will be facing the wrath, the anger of all the people in the Chiefdom.

MUSA: Do you think she might still be suspecting us of her husband's death?

LAMBOI: *Ngo* Musa, that is history. This new plan must be put into effect immediately. When did you last enrich your *bofima* with the rich and hot blood of a child? Look, your skin does not possess that glow. It's all wrinkled like the buttocks of an old woman. Your farms have not been doing well these past years. Two of your wives died suddenly last planting season all because you have failed in your commitments to the *bofima*.

MUSA: But the chiefdom is not what it used to be in the past. We no longer go to war and hardly get slaves.

LAMBOI: And that is because Yoko is so scared of the Governor. Look at the manner in which the woman is treating an ordinary messenger. You would think the fellow himself, a man of our own color, is the Governor's younger brother—all because she wants him to sing her praises to the Governor. *Ngo* Musa, Yoko is crafty. That little *Sande* girl who used to thrill the entire village has changed overnight. Now she is a vicious woman bent on doing anything to hang on to power. Just five days ago, three chiefs, without any prompting, traveled all the way from Boama to hand over their chiefdoms to her. You were at the *barre*, *Ngo* Musa, and you saw them. When such men have lost the will to fight and defend the land of their ancestors, how then can we go to war? How then do you think you can get the blood of slaves to strengthen your *bofima*?

MUSA: Lamboi, if we have to kill Jeneba we must be very careful. Will the people believe us?

LAMBOI: They have to. Not everybody in the chiefdom is happy about Yoko's growing powers. Most of them would have been wondering what charms she rubs on her body or what herbs she usually drinks before talking to the white man. Those people so love and respect that woman, that it hurts my manhood. We shall tell them that her strength lies in sacrificing little children, burying them alive.

MUSA: Heh! Heh! Heh! Lamboi, you are a crafty man yourself. You are indeed an old monkey. You should be the chief; you have a wise head on you shoulders.

LAMBOI: We must not waste more time then. Everything must...

MUSA: No, Lamboi, wait.

LABOI: What?

MUSA: Everyone loves that child. If she disappears there will be trouble, big trouble, *Keke* Lamboi.

LAMBOI: It will not be your trouble but Yoko's. Come to my hut in the evening. I will have some palmwine and good *jolabete* ready for you. We shall then deliberate further on this plan.

# Scene Three

(*Lights. The barre. Sande music is playing offstage. Madam Yoko is seated with court attendants. Lavalie and Ndapi enter with the Governor's messenger. Ndapi prostrates and introduces the messenger who goes up, shakes and kisses Madam Yoko's hand. As he takes his seat, music intensifies and the "Sande" girls troop in and do a short dance. Applause follows. The girls depart and one returns with a bottle of imported gin, places it at the messenger's feet and exits*)

MESSENGER: May it please your majesty. Let me first of all extend profound greetings from the Governor and deep felt gratitude for this unprecedented reception accorded me since my arrival here in this beautiful chiefdom. (*Applause*) My master, the Governor, servant of her Imperial Majesty the Queen of Great Britain, intimated that you are a shining example not only of African feminine pulchritude but of one who blends grace, magnanimity, bravery, audacity, tranquility, and majesty (*Applause*) to your role as custodian of the greatest Chiefdom here in the primitive heartland of the protectorate. (*Applause*) My sagacious Imperial master, the Governor, extends to you madam, his unbounded felicitations and wishes to your gracious person, the best of positive, physical, mental, surgical, psychological, psychiatric, philosophical and psycho-analytical well being. (*More applause*) For your magnificent execution of the onerous, multifarious, tangential and multi-faceted duties of state, the honored, revered and respected Governor, grand commander of the colony and servant of her Imperial majesty, has kindly and graciously prevailed upon me the honor of your generosity.

(*Music intensifies as everybody rises and lights fade. Lights pick up Jilo getting ready to go to the river. Fanneh is seated with Jeneba in her lap. There is a bucket beside her*)

JILO: Mama Fanneh, will you take Jenneh with you to Madam? I have to go and wash in the river.

FANNEH: Madam has sent me to another village. I only came to greet you and to see my little queen. (*Pause*) Jilo, did Madam tell you when your case is coming up for hearing?

JILO: No, they have not yet brought Lansana from Taiama.

FANNEH: But, Jilo, why did you do it?

JILO: Mama Fanneh, if that question had come from a child I would understand. You know Ndapi. That man has pepper sprinkled all over his temper. There is not a single day, from sunrise to sunset, when Ndapi will not come to this house and beat me up. He is always accusing me of adultery.

FANNEH: But he was not wrong. Did he not catch you and Lansana in the bush?

JILO: That he did. But Mama Fanneh, can you imagine a woman who is constantly abused by a man to whom she gives her body, this sacred gift from the gods, night after night? Can you imagine the frustration of giving your body to a man and not receiving even a kind word in return? For Lansana it was easy. At least I tried to resist him. But as a woman, I need reassurance, Mama Fanneh—reassurance and admiration. That Lansana gave. I would put on the best clothes, cook the most delicious meal and Ndapi would come to this house, eat up all the food and grumble. As for the dress, he would become blind to it for the rest of the evening. But Lansana was different. At least he made me feel proud as a woman.

FANNEH: And so you rewarded him? Did you not think then that it could break up your home? Are your people here strong enough to return Ndapi's dowry? Hmm, I even wonder whether that good-for-nothing Lansana himself will even be able to pay the damages. Jilo, I must be on my way. I've got to return with a reply to Madam by nightfall.

JILO: Mama Fanneh, I'll see you off. Jenneh, you wait here.

FANNEH: Why not bring the child along?

JILO: I want to say something to you in confidence. That child is sharp. She will tell her father all that we have been discussing on his return from the *barre*. (*They exit*)

(*From the other end Lamboi appears with a fruit in his hand. He advances towards Jeneba and gives her the fruit. From the folds of his gown he takes out a bottle, pours some liquid into his hand and runs the liquid on Jeneba's face, hands, and legs. Then he takes the fruit and proceeds to exit, smiling wickedly. Slowly, like a sleepwalker, Jeneba gets up and starts following him. She does not utter a word. They exit. Evening. Lights slowly rise on* "barre." *The elders, Ndapi. Lavalie, Ngo Musa, and Lamboi are seated. They are talking to each other*)

YOKO: (*Enters*) I have got to leave this evening! The Governor has sent me to crown two chiefs in Taiama. On my return we will discuss this business of paying tax for our huts.

LAVALIE: We should discuss that now, your Highness. I don't see any reason why we must pay taxes to the Governor for our huts standing on our own land.

YOKO: It will have to wait, Lavalie. If the Governor says we pay, we pay. I will be in charge of collecting payments for this area and I'll turn over to the Governor any chief who prevents his people from paying. Fanneh, are the bodyguards who should accompany me ready?

FANNEH: Yes, madam.

YOKO: We must be leaving... Lamboi, you will take charge of the chiefdom in my absence.

LAMBOI: Yes, your Highness.

LAVALIE: But, madam, should we not discuss this tax business before you leave?

YOKO: What is there to discuss? I have already.... (*She is interrupted by noise offstage. Two warriors enter with Lansana*) So you have decided to leave your three wives and make love to another man's wife in the bush. Lansana?

LANSANA: Madam, I did not...

YOKO: Shut up! Guards put him in stocks and starve him till I return from Taiama. You want to bring trouble to my household. I will deal with.... (*Another noise and Jilo comes in wailing. She falls to the ground*)

NDAPI: What nonsense is this? What nonsense is this, woman?

JILO: My child, my only child Jenneh, Jenneh, oh Jenneh.

MUSA: What happened to her?

JILO: Oh my child, my child.

NDAPI: Look woman, pull yourself together. What has happened to the child?

JILO: She has disappeared. I have been searching all over the village. I cannot find her.

YOKO: When did this happen?

JILO: I left her this morning to see Mama Fanneh off. On my return she had disappeared from the house. I thought she was with Mama Nancy's children playing, so I went to the river. On my way back, I asked Mama Nancy. She said she had not seen her. I asked her children they told me they had not seen Jenneh. Oh my daughter.

YOKO: We cannot afford to waste time. We must send out a search party. That child must be found at all cost. I must really leave now to carry out the Governor's orders. Lamboi, you act in my absence. *Ngo Musa*, you are second in command. I will be away for a few days. But you must all search for and find that child before my return.(*Exits as Jilo continues weeping*)

LAMBOI: Ndapi, get your wife to keep quiet. You tell the Crier to summon the people to the meeting ground in the center of the village. We cannot waste time. (*Jilo's cries rise. Lights out*)

# ACT THREE

## Scene One

*(At the "barre." Lamboi enters)*

LAMBOI: If the secrets of the heart are known, blood will be spilled, for blood has already been spilled. There is no way through which we can pass to reach the pinnacle of dominion over our fellow men save through a path spread with blood. (*He goes over to the throne and examines it*) I have dreamt of power, of governing here in this chiefdom of Moyamba. It has now come my way but for just a few days. (*Smiles grimly*) How beautiful it is to sit on this throne regarding your subjects, minions, cringing in your presence; passing judgment over them; wielding the power of life or death over all. No wonder Yoko does not want to give it up. I have started walking towards this throne now, towards this seat of supreme power on the road of blood and there is no turning back. First it was Gbanya and now Jeneba. Next it may have to be Yoko herself, for she guards this throne so jealously. (*Lavalie enters*) Any luck?

LAVALIE: No, but the search continues… I'm tired. Let me get some palm wine.

LAMBOI: Why not just send one of the girls?

LAVALIE: They have all joined in the search. You know that Jeneba was the darling of this household. Everybody here loved the child. (*Exits as Ngo Musa enters*)

MUSA: Anyone around?

LAMBOI: Shhh! Lavalie has just gone to get some palm wine. Have you started planting the seed?

MUSA: Lamboi, the seed has already started germinating. You know how women like to gossip. I met a group of them searching for the girl in the bush this morning when I went to collect some herbs. I planted it in their minds right there and soon it would blossom. Rumors have wings, you know, eh Lamboi?

LAMBOI: (*nods*) Do you think we will be able to convince the warriors? A lot depends on them.

MUSA: Lamboi, Ndapi has so much grief for his daughter in his head that he will not be able to think properly. He will believe anything we tell him now. Heh, heh, heh, Lamboi, I must go, I still have more seeds to....

LAVALIE: (*Enters with palmwine*) Any news *Ngo* Musa?

MUSA: Eh.... eh... I journeyed to the shrine yesterday to divine.

LAVALIE: Yes... You mean you went to the *Poro* Bush?

MUSA: Gods! Is this man deaf?

LAVALIE: What did you learn?

MUSA: What the *Gbeni* told me is only for the ears of madam herself.

LAVALIE: Look *Ngo* Musa, the Queen ordered us to find that child and we must.

LAMBOI: The child cannot be found. Madam herself has used her as sacrifice.

LAVALIE: Impossible!

LAMBOI: Go on *Ngo* Musa, tell him the truth.

MUSA: She has used her as sacrifice; buried her alive in a big pot.

LAVALIE: But why?

LAMBOI: Power, my friend. She wants more power. She wants to win the favor of the Governor. (*Enter Ndapi*)

LAVALIE: *Hindo*! Listen to this. The *Gbeni* has divined that your daughter was used as sacrifice by madam, to win the favor of the Governor.

NDAPI: Don't talk such nonsense, *Ngo*! Now can the Queen do that? If she wants human sacrifice, I know parents here in Moyamba who would gladly give up their children to her.

MUSA: Ndapi it is true. That's what the *Gbeni* said and….

NDAPI: Enough! Don't you drag the *Poro* into this, *Ngo* Musa. My daughter must be found and I don't care if I have to turn Moyamba over, tear it with my bare hands. I'll find her.

LAMBOI: But you cannot. Right now she is buried alive. No, she could have died. Right now she is buried somewhere in a big pot.

NDAPI: Then prove it. How do you know?

MUSA: If only you'd control that temper. The *Gbeni* said it.

NDAPI: Leave the *Poro* out of this, I said.

LAMBOI: Do you want to tell me that your grief for your daughter has caused you not to believe in the omnipotent *Gbeni*?

NDAPI: I did not say that.

MUSA: Well?

LAVALIE: *Ngo* Musa, if you are sure the *Gbeni* told you that, then swear.

LAMBOI: What? Are you now doubting the *Poro*? Do you know the dreadful implications of that, Lavalie? Look, Ndapi, don't allow grief to cause you to anger the *Gbeni*. I know you grieve for your daughter. But would you like your nose to rot, would you like leprosy to devour your fingers, cataracts to marry your eyeballs and elephantiasis to cling to your legs like....

GUARD: (*Enters panting*) My Lord! My Lord!

NDAPI: What is it? Have you found her?

GUARD: No my lord, but the women... they are saying Madam used Jeneba as... as sacrifice. They are even swearing to it.

NDAPI: What?

MUSA: Do you now believe me? The word is all over the chiefdom.(*Sande drums sound frantically, briefly, then stop*)

LAVALIE: And what is that?

GUARD: The *Sande* women are summoning a meeting. They want Madam deposed.

LAVALIE: But... but... They can't...

LAMBOI: Yes, they have a right to. The Queen is one of their kind and if she has done this dreadful deed, the *Sande* women want no part of it.

GUARD: Exactly, my lord, that's what they said.

NDAPI: You go and tell them to break up that meeting. We shall deal with this matter ourselves. (*Guard prostrates, exits*) *Keke* Lavalie, what do you think we must do now?

YOKO: (*Enters*) Indeed, when the hen leaves her chicks in the hands of the hawk, she has no one to blame if they disappear. Lamboi, what nonsense is this (*Interrupted by shout as bodyguard tries to contain women offstage, who are showering incentives on madam, labeling her witch, murderer, and devil)?* Is it that I cannot leave the chiefdom for three days under your care and return home to find peace?

LAMBOI: Madam, there is no peace in the minds of those that kill.

YOKO: What?

MUSA: No peace in the mind of a killer.

YOKO: Have you all in this chiefdom gone mad? Can't I pass through my own land without my people shouting murderer, devil, and witch? Is that the way to greet your Queen? Now everybody out, out of the *barre*. Where is the child? Have you found her? (*Pause*) Have you found Jeneba? Guard!

GUARD: Your Highness.

YOKO: Get Fanneh or Musu.

NDAPI: *Hindo*, don't move.

YOKO: What? Who rules this land? Get Fanneh!

NDAPI: Take one step, *Hindo* and my spear will taste the blood in your liver.

YOKO: (*Goes towards the throne*) I must be....

NDAPI: (*Blocks her*) No madam, you don't!

YOKO: What nonsense is this? I command you as your Queen to give way, Ndapi.

NDAPI: (*Sends Yoko sprawling*) You become Queen again only after finding my daughter. (*Sits on the throne*)

YOKO: Ndapi, I forbid you. Don't. (*Heavy thunder*) Yes, I know it. The end is not too far away.

LAMBOI: It cannot be. The end cannot be far away for a murderer.

YOKO: Now, what in the name of the gods are you all talking about?

MUSA: The hawk has not eaten the hen's chicks. It is the hen that has destroyed the hawk's nest.

YOKO: Lavalie, you tell me what has been going on?

LAVALIE: The *Gbeni* said you have sacrificed Jeneba and…

NDAPI: And that is why the Governor has been showering you with gifts, extending your power. Why must I pay to satisfy your craze, your devilish ambition? Look, madam, I want my daughter back. If I don't get her I'll kill you with my bare hands.

YOKO: But…. But…

LAMBOI: The *Gbeni* told us you had buried her alive somewhere in a big pot.

NDAPI: Look, woman, stay right down. You have killed my daughter, but I cannot blame you. You don't know the pain of childbirth, so you don't know the worth of a child. You have never had children of your own, so you don't know what motherly love is. You gave Jilo and the entire chiefdom the impression that you loved the child. All the while, you had been plotting in your mind to offer her to the gods.

YOKO: But I loved the child.

LAMBOI: Yes, you loved her. It was like rearing a sacrificial lamb. You tend it, feed it on the best blades of grass, fatten it, for just one moment, just one purpose.

LAVALIE: This has shocked me.

YOKO: My life is now in your hands, but if I may be allowed to swear by the *Poro* that….

MUSA: Don't utter that word, you witch. You must never utter that word. You are unworthy of it.

YOKO: No, you will have to kill me now, but… (*She reaches for a palm frond*)

NDAPI: (*Rises*) If you do that Yoko, my spear will kill your wicked heart.

YOKO: Then you will have to kill....

NDAPI: (*Attempts to throw*) You.... (*Noise offstage. One of the Sande girls enters. She is hysterical*)

GIRL: We have found her. We have found her. The child. Gods. I couldn't take a second look; it was so awful, so ghastly.

NDAPI: Where? Where did you find her?

GIRL: Behind the *Sande* Bush. We went to dig up some potatoes and we found the body....

LAVALIE: She's dead then.

GIRL: Yes, dead! Killed!(*2nd guard comes in bringing Jeneba's body. The elders indicate putrid scent by holding their nostrils. They crowd around the guard*)

LAVALIE: Gods, the breastbone is broken and the heart pulled out.

MUSA: Her neck was cut with a knife.

LAMBOI: I cannot bear to look on. I cannot bear to look. The girl is without her private parts.

NDAPI: (*Sits down on a bench, his head in his hands*) No. This cannot happen. It cannot happen. Not to my own daughter. Not to Jeneba. Not to my only child.

YOKO: And that is the child I was supposed to have buried alive. That is the child I sacrificed alive to win the favors of the Governor. That is the child that has earned me the scorn of the entire chiefdom; the child that has caused me to be labeled witch, murderer, and devil. That is your child buried alive by me in a big pot.

NDAPI: Madam, you must....

YOKO: Ndapi, hold your peace. That is the child who has caused you to humiliate me, your queen. Leave now, everybody, be gone. I intend to get to the bottom of it. No one will ever live to say that in her time, Yoko did not rule well. Go! Guard! Let them bury the remains at once!

NDAPI: But Madam, you must forgive me. I never....

YOKO: Don't beg for forgiveness from me, Ndapi. Is it not because of my ignorance of the pain of childbirth that I sacrificed your daughter? Is it not because my wicked heart is insensitive and incapable of experiencing motherly love that I reared Jeneba like I would a sacrificial lamb for that one fateful moment? Go away now! Lavalie, prepare the *Poro* Bush. I intend to get to the bottom of this. And if in the process I die, then and only then will my spirit find peace in the land of our ancestors. The maiden *paytaytaying* her water-pot on her way from the river of life has hit her toe against a concealed pebble. There is now no remedy, for the water-pot has crashed to the ground, and the water sipped by the earth. No one should beg for forgiveness. That cannot change the fact that I have been unjustly humiliated. We meet in the *Poro* bush tonight. Now everybody, out! (*They all exit. A dirge rises offstage as Yoko sits. Her head falls and she soon starts sobbing silently. Lights out*)

(*Lightning and thunder rend the air, followed by the sound of rain. Shrill sounds and gun blasts from time to time. Rain fades but thunder continues. Musu and Fanneh enter trembling, one with a basket the other with a bundle of firewood*)

FANNEH: The women have gone to beg for forgiveness from the Queen.

MUSU: Did she give them audience?

FANNEH: No! She spent the whole day in her room.

MUSU: The Queen was unfairly treated.

(*Blasts and shrill sounds again*)

FANNEH: Didn't you hear that Madam will be going to put *Poro* to discover who killed Jeneba?

MUSU: But you didn't tell me that! Yeiyoo! If they find us out here we shall surely….

GUARD: Halt in the Queen's name. Who goes there? (*The women are frightened. They stand close together. Guard emerges with a lamp and examines their faces*) Don't you know you cannot be out on such a night? Evil spirits dare not venture out tonight.

FANNEH: *Ngo*, we are sorry. We were late in collecting firewood and cotton.

GUARD: *Kpako! Kpako!* (*Another guard emerges*) Take these women home and ensure that no harm befalls them. Now hurry! (*They exit and bodyguard returns to shadows. Sounds rise and fade. Messenger comes striding in*) Who goes there?

MESSENGER: What? Who dares address me in that…?

2nd GUARD: (*Emerges and puts messenger in a vicious arm lock*) Struggle and cross life's river of no return.

GUARD: It's the parrot-with-the-big-words, the Governor's messenger. What do you want here?

MESSENGER: Heh! heh! heh! He's throttling me. What… is this the red carpet reception for the servant of his Lordship the Governor, servant of her Imperial Majesty, the Queen of Great Britain?

GUARD: Look parrot, do you want to live long enough to see tomorrow's sunrise? What do you want here? The night is unhealthy.

MESSENGER: I demand an explanation for this vicious welcome. I have missive of the utmost national and international importance. And when I risk my life and limb to bring it here, all I get is a savage attack from you apes. If you thing you can threaten me, then you are in dire need of psychoanalytic....

GUARD: (*Slaps him*) Now, don't you go bursting our eardrums with those big words. If you don't know, tonight is *Poro* night. If you encounter the fearful *Gbeni* as you go around yapping, yapping, and yapping, your nose will rot, leprosy will devour your fingers, cataracts will marry your eyeballs...

MESSENGER: And elephantiasis will cling to my appendages the way mud clings to the pedal extremities of an agriculturist in the swamps?

2nd GUARD: What? You are a member then?

GUARD: *Bu wa?*

MESSENGER: *Bisie.*

GUARD: *Ka hui yena?*

MESSENGER: *Kayei Ngewo ma.*

GUARD: *To-baiti?*

MESSENGER: Baiti-to!

GUARD: To baiti?

MESSENGER: Baiti-to!

2nd GUARD: I don't believe it. The marks then. Show us the Marks. (*Messenger takes off his shirt*)

GUARD: It's true, look at them.

2nd GUARD: Show us your hands. (*Messenger complies*) Yes…now. Tell us about your mission.

MESSENGER: That, I must say openly, my dearest and most amicable colleagues, is strictly confidential. State security, for the queen's tympanums only. But wait… who is putting *poro* at this time of the year? This is not the season.

GUARD: The Queen.

MESSENGER: The Queen? You mean Yoko herself? (*Guards nod*) But why?

2nd GUARD: They claim Madam killed Jeneba, that she had sacrificed the girl to win your master's favor.

MESSENGER: That is pure balderdash.

GUARD: You and your big words again. But the child was discovered. She had been murdered and….

MESSENGER: Sweet Jesus.

GUARD: And her private parts, heart and liver missing.

MESSENGER: Most atrocious! Who is so base as to commit infanticide?

2nd GUARD: Parrot! What does that mean?

MESSENGER: I mean, who killed the child? Who murdered the helpless, little angel?

GUARD: That's what Madam intends to find out in the *Poro* bush tonight.

MESSENGER: Now I get the point. I must proceed. This message from the Governor is urgent.

GUARDS: *Hindo!*

MESSENGER: *Kpako!* (*Attempts to exit*)

GUARD: Wait! I'm sorry for that slap.

MESSENGER: One white cock, two headpan loads of rice, a dozen tobacco, five white and six red kolanuts for hitting a senior *Poro* man. You're lucky. Had this been the actual *poro* season, you know the fine would have been heavier.

GUARD: Collect before you leave.

MESSENGER: No, I collect tonight. My god, *ndake*, that slap was most stinging…

(*Lights fade out and then fade in. The Poro bush. Ndapi is seated in a state of shock*)

NDAPI: What? *Keke* Lamboi and *Ngo* Musa killed my child?

LAVALIE: You heard it yourself. The *Poro* never lies.

NDAPI: (*Moving to exit*) I am going after them.

YOKO: No, Ndapi, you are a *Poro* man. Right now they would be gone. I see them far, far away. They are running, but will not get too far. Their noses will rot, cataracts will marry their eyeballs, leprosy will devour their fingers and elephantiasis will cling to their legs. That is the *Gbeni's* revenge. (*Guard enters*)

GUARD: Your Highness, the Governor's messenger.

LAVALIE: He can't enter the bush. Let him go and wait in the *barre*.

YOKO: No, let the messenger come. He is a *Poro* man, one of us. (*Guard enters and comes back with messenger*) Yes, you bring a message, a message that will cause me great pain. I can feel it. I know it is in that letter. Open it and read….

MESSENGER: From his Highness the Governor. South of Bandajuma, the six villages to the North of the Tabe River now belong to the people of the Chiefdom of Bo. The Tabe River, which was the original boundary mark and which was laid by Major Fairlough, has been declared null and void with effect from...

YOKO: Enough! Say no more. (*There is a long pause*) Lavalie?

LAVALIE: Madam.

YOKO: Come. Go to the brush, south of the Cotton tree, past that small stream where *Sande* girls take their bath in the moonlight. Cross that stream and to the north of the palm tree without branches; you will find the *ndinaba* tree. Now, come. You must do exactly as I tell you. (*She whispers to him*)

LAVALIE: But Madam that is impossible!

YOKO: Lavalie, I command you. I am your Queen. Now go.

LAVALIE: You word is my command Madam but...

YOKO: Lavalie! (*Exits slowly mumbling to himself*)

YOKO: (*To guard*) You follow him. Take whatever he gives you and bring it back here. Let us all go to the *barre*.

(*They all exit. Solitary drumming. Lights out. Drumming continues. Lights return. Madam paces slowly, while the messenger sits down writing*)

MESSENGER: Yes Madam.

YOKO: Tell the Governor that I understand the contents of his letter... Tell him that I thank him.... Tell him that in all my years as ruler of this chiefdom, I have never been disgraced in this manner... Tell him the way he has decided on the boundary marks is a slap in the face for a lady who has been loyal to him all these years... and tell him that....

2nd GUARD: (*Enters*) Madam!

YOKO: Go back, I'm busy. And tell everybody I don't want to be disturbed. (*Guard exits*) Tell the governor that...

GUARD: Madam, Lavalie has sent me to give you this. (*He prostrates and hands over the loot wrapped in a leaf*)

YOKO: Ah, this is good, this is good. Go now, brave guard. Call Musu.

MUSU: (*Entering*) I'm here, Madam.

YOKO: Take this medicine, go prepare it in the usual way. Now, make a thick concoction out of it.

MUSU: (*Examining the root*) But what medicine is this Madam?

YOKO: Musu, do you ask the lightning why it flashes?

MUSU: No, Madam.

YOKO: A little patience then and you will hear the thunder. Go now, good woman.

MUSU: Is it the root of the *Ndinaba* or the *Ndondohai*?

YOKO: There you go again, Musu. There you go again. Come, you have seen the lightning in the way I was humiliated by the entire chiefdom. You have seen the lightning in the treachery of *Ngo Musa*, and Lamboi, my own brother. You have seen the lightning in the way the boundary marks have been laid by the District Commissioner on the Governor's orders. Now go prepare the medicine, woman. (*Musu exits*) Let's continue, young man. Tell the Governor that I have risked my life and throne to carry out his commands. And it is only now that I have come to realize—now that I am getting old—that I have been a fool. I have been used. Tell him it is a great insult to my integrity and honor as Queen. Tell him I will be very thankful to his Excellency the Governor if he will be kind enough to send someone to examine the way the boundary marks have been laid. Tell him I sent my representatives but the DC and the other chiefs refused to wait for them to arrive. But young man… why am I telling you all this? Why should I?

GUARD: Madam, Ndapi and his wife Jilo are outside. They request an audience.

YOKO: (*Pause*) Call them in.

GUARD: Yes, your Highness. (*Exits*)

YOKO: And now, the thunder is set with all its anger to shake the land with the speed of its birth.

NDAPI: (*Enters*) Madam, you may not want to hear this, but we won't sleep soundly ever again if you don't forgive us. Indeed your Highness. You must forgive us. *Ngo* Musa and Lamboi misled us.

YOKO: Ndapi, Jilo, forgiveness, like all good things in this world, like evil itself—for there are times when it is good to do evil—should come from the heart. But who can blame you, Ndapi, for humiliating me? Who can blame you too, Jilo, for inciting the other *Sande* women? You loved your child and naturally you should vent your anger and seek to avenge her death. It is too late to beg for forgiveness. The chiefdom has seen the lightning and it now waits, with mounting expectation, for the thunder.

JILO: But Madam, you must understand…

YOKO: Indeed I understand. Why shouldn't I? I who have never known the pain of childbirth. I who professed to love your little daughter, Jeneba, only to sacrifice her for power.

NDAPI: But your Highness…

YOKO: Enough. Say no more.

JILO: But our daughter is dead. She cannot be brought back to life. They fooled us all, Madam.

NDAPI: It was a hidden trap, your Highness, and we all walked right into it.

YOKO: Enough I say! If you could see my heart—this heart that has known happiness, this heart that has known love and power. It has also known humiliation and treachery this day. My late husband, Gbanya, warned me. Behind every set of white teeth there lurks an evil plotting mind. But I am ready. Go now. Go mourn for the death of your fine daughter, Jeneba, and leave me to suffer in my distress alone.

(*They exit as Musu and Fanneh enter*)

FANNEH: Madam, I have served in this household long before you became Queen. I even served the mother of your late husband. But I cannot understand, Madam... Madam...

YOKO: Musu, is the medicine ready?

MUSU: (*Steps forward*) It is here, Madam.

FANNEH: But Madam, what sickness is this?

YOKO: That which cannot be cured—the sickness of the mind. My husband suffered from it and now it's my turn.

FANNEH: But Madam, this is no more cure for a sick mind.

YOKO: Has there been any cure for a sick mind? The only cure is peace, woman, that peace which is only found in the eyes of a sacrificial lamb after the sharp knife of the *totogbemui* has done its ghastly work.

MUSU: Madam!

YOKO: Here, Musu, take the medicine again. This is too much. Pour it on the ground. Don't put it into any calabash that you might want to use in the future.

MUSU: Yes, Madam. (*Exits*)

YOKO: (*To messenger*) You may leave us now. Give my regards to the Governor.

MESSENGER: But your Highness, as a friend it is my duty to ask...

MUSU: (*Enters*) I did it Madam, I poured it on the ground.

YOKO: That is good. (*Faces messenger. He exits. Wind starts offstage*) And now, my journey is ended. Let me begin another cycle; the cycle of peace.

FANNEH: (*Restraining her*) No, Madam. If you are to drink that, let me drink it first.

YOKO: Fanneh, you know I have always loved you. You know I have shared the secrets of this heart, though it is now heavy with untold grief, with you. No. You cannot. I don't want two graves to be prepared. I have savored the fruits of power alone; I have known and enjoyed the grandeur of high office alone; if I'm to die, then let me die alone. (*She drinks as wind intensifies. Yoko puts the calabash down and grips her stomach*) And now I will know peace. Now I will never be used again. Gbanya, make way, Yoko is coming. Make way, my husband. Make way, you noble ancestors, Yoko is coming in search of peace. (*She slumps to the ground*)

FANNEH: Quick, Musu, get some palm oil. Yeiyoo! (*Musu dashes out as Fanneh tends to Madam*)

MUSU: Here it is, Mama Fanneh.

FANNEH: Madam, quick. Drink this.

YOKO: (*Raising her head*) No, Fanneh, I... I... I... did not bring a child into this world, so let no one mourn my death. Tell the entire.... entire.... entire chiefdom... none.... should mourn... my death.

(*Wind gives way to slow drumming as dirge rises*)

# LIGHTS OUT

# THE PATRIOT

A HISTORICAL DRAMA BASED ON THE LIFE OF BAI BUREH OF KASE

BY
JULIUS S. SPENCER

*Julius S. Spencer*

# CHARACTERS

◇◆◇

| | |
|---|---|
| KPANKA | Bai Bureh of Kase |
| KPATEH RONKO | His Father |
| ISATU | His Senior Wife |
| FATMATA | His Junior Wife |
| NARRATOR | Also plays Gbamellah and Bai Bangura |
| | |
| BUTEH | Kpanka's Brother |
| PA SANTIGI | |
| PA KUMRABAI | |
| BRIMA SANDA | Elders of Kase |
| BAI SUBA | |
| | |
| BAI FORKI | |
| BAI FARIMA | Temne Chiefs |
| BOCKARI BAMP | |
| SORIE BUNKI | One of the elders in Port Loko |
| GOV. FREDERICK CARDEW | Governor of Sierra Leone |
| CAPTAIN SHARPE | District Commissioner of Karene District |
| MAJOR TARBET | In charge of Frontier Police |
| SERGEANT | |
| MESSENGER | |

Townspeople, Policemen, Warboys

# ACT ONE

◊◆◊

## Scene One

*(Lights come up on a bare stage and after a few seconds are extinguished as if they had been put on by mistake. An old man shouts from the audience)*

NARRATOR: Come on, stop wasting time. (*He proceeds to the stage*) Let the play begin. (*He addresses the audience*) This play is about Bai Bureh, the great Bai Bureh. Anyway, you all know Bai Bureh. The one we sang about as children. Many of you young people still sing about him. I suggest we sing it whilst waiting for them to start their play. Maybe that will speed them up. (*He starts singing and encourages the audience to join in, cajoling and bullying them until they are all singing*)

> Bai Bureh was a warrior
> He fought against the British
> The British made him surrender
> *I ala koto maimu*
> *Ah koto bekithong*
> *I ala koto maimu*

Stop! Stop! Stop I say. (*He waits for the singing to stop*) Actually that's a song we should be ashamed of because we denigrate those who gave their lives for our freedom. See how lustily we sang, a song intended to make fun of one of the greatest Africans who ever lived, who fought for the freedom of his people. (*Pause*) But why do I chastise? It is not our fault. It is the fault of those who have thought it fit to keep us in blissful ignorance, while elevating themselves to demigods, trampling on the tombs and bones of those who fought to make our nation great. But I, Gbamellah, with the aid of this group of players will enlighten you. (*Music rises in the background, and a group of players dance on to the stage singing. The Narrator continues speaking with the music and singing in the background*) So, come with us on a journey into the past. To a time when men were men, and valor and prowess in war were the surest means of achieving fame. Come with us to Kase Chiefdom in the latter part of the 19$^{th}$ Century when the name of one Kpanka, nicknamed Kablai, was on everyone's lips. His prowess in war had earned him the nickname, and his name had begun to instill fear in the hearts of enemy warriors.

(*The music rises to full volume and the dancing and singing increase in intensity. An elderly man, Kpateh Ronko, enters and is hailed by his men. Another song is raised and the dancing continues. Gbamellah moves to join Kpateh Ronko on stage and they engage in silent conversation, obviously enjoying the dancing. After some time, three warriors, including Kpanka's brother, Buteh, emerge from the auditorium. It is obvious from their demeanor that they are bearers of evil tidings. The two old men immediately notice this. As the warriors approach them, the dancers seem to sense that some bad news is about to be broken, and they progressively fall silent until there is absolute silence broken only by the measured footsteps of the warriors. As they approach, Kpateh Ronko rises. He has sensed the nature of the news*)

KPATEH RONKO: Kpanka? (*Buteh nods*) What happened?

BUTEH: He is dead.

(*There is shocked silence for a few seconds, then one of the women begins to sing a dirge and the wailing of the women starts. Kpanka's wives, Isatu and Fatmata, throw themselves on the ground and have to be restrained by the other women*)

# The Patriot

GBAMELLAH: Dead did you say? Are you sure?

BUTEH: Yes.

KPATEH RONKO: (*Making an effort to sound calm*) How did he die? What happened?

BUTEH: He was knocked into the river.

GBAMELLAH: Kpanka? Knocked into the river?

BUTEH: Yes. We were attacked by a large group of Limba war boys. There were only ten of us, so we ... (*shrugs*)

1st WARBOY: We thought he had escaped too.

BUTEH: We went back when we noticed he was not with us.

2nd WARBOY: You should have seen him. Wham! With his machete, Zwap! With his whip. They were falling all around him.

BUTEH: We found him surrounded by about fifty Limbas. He was standing with his back to the river, on top of a large rock.

KPATEH RONKO: You did not try to help him?

1st WARBOY: Ah! ... There were only ten of us.

GBAMELLAH: So? Ten of you could not stand up to fifty Limbas? Ah, in my day ...

BUTEH: We did not even have the chance. Before we could decide what to do, one of them threw a stone with his sling and Kpanka fell backwards into the river.

KPATEH RONKO: The stone hit him?

1st WARBOY: We did not see...

2nd WARBOY: We were not sure.

KPATEH RONKO: (*Suddenly alert*) You did not see the stone hit him?

BUTEH: No, but we saw him fall.

KPATEH RONKO: Did you actually see him fall into the river?

BUTEH: Into the water?

KPATEH RONKO: Yes…

BUTEH: No, but….

KPATEH RONKO: (*Becoming excited*) So you did not see him fall into the water?

BUTEH: No, but he fell off the rock and he did not come up, so he must have drowned.

KPATEH RONKO: But you did not actually see him hit the water?

GBAMELLAH: (*Puzzled*) They have said he fell into the river. What…

KPATEH RONKO: Wait. (*To Buteh*) Where exactly did this happen?

BUTEH: Where?

KPATEH RONKO: Yes. (*Turns to the women*) Hey, you women, stop that noise! (*They take no notice of him*)

BUTEH: You know the area near the road to Mafonda, where a large rock juts out over the riverbank?

KPATEH RONKO: Yes.

BUTEH: It was there.

KPATEH RONKO: You mean the place where there is a lot of grass growing?

BUTEH: Yes, that's the place.

(*Kpateh Ronko bursts out laughing. Everyone is taken aback. The women stop their wailing momentarily, and then continue with renewed fervor. They have concluded that Kpateh Ronko has gone mad at the news of his son's death. Buteh moves towards him)*

BUTEH: Father....

GBAMELLAH: (*Restraining him*) Careful! The news must have.... (*makes a sign to indicate madness*)

KPATEH RONKO: (*Struggling to control his laughter*) Cave... Cave...

GBAMELLAH: What? (*To Buteh*) What is he saying?

BUTEH: I don't know. (*To Kpateh Ronko*) What is it? What's wrong?

KPATEH RONKO: Cave... ha, ha, ha.... fooled all of you... ha, ha, ... there's a cave... ha, ha, ha

GBAMELLAH: A cave?

(*At this point, Kpanka appears at the back of the auditorium. He is a powerfully built man and has a long whip in one hand and a machete in the other. The 1st warrior is the first to see him*)

1st WARBOY: (*Pointing*) Look!

(*There is pandemonium when they realize it is Kpanka who is supposed to be dead. The women scream. Kpateh Ronko is the only one unaffected, and he laughs even louder. Kpanka surveys the scene, realizes what has happened, and his laughter rings out. He moves down to the stage amid shouts of "O krifi ko e! krifi ko e!" Kpateh Ronko moves up to him while everyone else falls back. They are both still laughing*)

KPATEH RONKO: The cave? (*Kpanka nods*) Bring food! The man is hungry. (*The women scurry off and Kpateh Ronko leads Kpanka off. The men follow slowly, still puzzled. Gbamellah watches them go, then turns to face the audience, resuming the role of narrator*)

NARRATOR: It was simple really. There was a well-concealed cave below the rock he was supposed to have fallen from. And so his fame grew. He was rumored to be invincible, to have supernatural powers that enabled him to appear and disappear at will. (*Laughs*) It was even said that he could live under water for several hours. And he reveled in it. He even went out of his way to fan the rumors. He became much sought after as a war leader. The mere mention of the name Kablai--for so he came to be called--was enough to turn an enemy warrior's liver to water. But there was one man who wielded immense influence over him. That man was Alimami Rassin, the peacemaker king, ruler of Gbinti; a man who hated war and did all in his power to ensure that all men lived at peace. Rassin was a devout Moslem, a peacemaker for whom the very thought of war or killing was distasteful. Kpanka became a changed man. No longer Kablai—he whose basket is never full--but something else.

ISATU: (*Off stage*) Fatmata! Fatmata ey…!

NARRATOR: Ah! Kpanka's wives. (*He hurries off*)

ISATU: (*Isatu enters struggling with a mortar and pestle. She places them centre stage and goes off again to re-enter shortly with a bowl of rice*)

ISATU: Fatmata! Ah Ah! Where is this woman? Fatmata!

FATMATA: (*Off stage*) Na! I am coming oh.

ISATU: (*In an undertone*) Probably dressing to go out.

(*She proceeds to pound the rice. After a short while, Fatmata enters. She is obviously on her way out. She is the younger of the two women*)

FATMATA: Yes, you called?

ISATU: I said it, dressed to go out. Where are you going to so early in the afternoon?

FATMATA: Is that what you called me for?

## ✠ The Patriot ✠

ISATU: No, that is not what I called you for. But where are you going?

FATMATA: I am going to my friend Kadiatu. She promised to plait my hair for me.

ISATU: So early in the day? Have you finished cooking?

FATMATA: I will cook when I come back.

ISATU: When will that be? Have you given your children food?

FATMATA: Not yet. (*Sweetly*) I was thinking of asking you to give them some food for me.

ISATU: What do you mean? Oh! My soup! (*Rushing off*) Hold this for me.

(*Fatmata catches the pestle, which is on the verge of falling and taking the mortar with it*)

FATMATA: Is it burning?

ISATU: (*Off stage*) Yes. Can't you smell it?

FATMATA: (*Sniffing*) Oh yes. Is it okra?

ISATU: Yes. (*Entering*) I have taken it off the fire. Ah Fatmata! You could not even help me beat the rice?

FATMATA: *Bo*, you only asked me to hold it for you.

ISATU: So? Give me the thing. (*Taking the pestle from her and resuming her pounding*)

FATMATA: What were you calling me for?

ISATU: I wanted you to help me beat the rice while I finished cooking the soup. But you are already dressed to go out. Just make sure you don't take too long. I won't be able to answer questions.

FATMATA: I won't stay long. (*Starts exiting and stops halfway*) Will you give Sorie and Ami food for me?

ISATU: I will, but it will be the last time. You seem to be making it a habit. Don't forget I have my own children to feed.

FATMATA: (*Already going*) Thank you. I'll be back soon.

(*Isatu watches her exit and shakes her head. She continues pounding, singing a work song. After a short while, Kpanka enters. He is carrying a hoe, machete and a bundle of cassava*)

ISATU: Welcome.

KPANKA: Thank you. (*He divides the cassava into two portions, giving Isatu the larger of the two. He calls*) Fatmata!

ISATU: She is not in.

KPANKA: Not in? Where has she gone to at this time of the day?

ISATU: She has gone to plait her hair.

KPANKA: At this time?

ISATU: Em …the woman who is going to do the plaiting is only free at this time.

KPANKA: I see. (*He proceeds to perform ablutions preparatory for prayers*) What about her children, has she fed them?

ISATU: They are going to eat with me.

(*Kpanka looks at her but says nothing and proceeds with his prayers. Isatu continues pounding. After sometime she notices one of the children performing some mischief off stage*)

ISATU: (*Shouting*) Hey! You Manso, stop that! What is wrong with you?

(*Kpanka is visibly startled by the shout but recovers and continues praying. Isatu finishes pounding and exits with the rice. Buteh enters, sees Kpanka praying and sits down watching him. Isatu enters to take the mortar and pestle. She sees Buteh*)

## The Patriot

ISATU: Ah, *koto*! You are here? (*Buteh signals to her to be quiet, pointing at Kpanka who by this time is counting his beads. She lowers her voice*) How are you? It's a long time since we saw you.

BUTEH: (*Almost in a whisper*) I can't complain, except that enemy warriors are keeping me very busy.

ISATU: (*Looks at Kpanka and sighs*) Well I have to go back to the kitchen.

KPANKA: (*Without looking up and in a voice expressive almost of physical pain*) Why do you always disturb my prayers? (*Buteh and Isatu looked at each other puzzled*) Isatu, it is you I am talking to. "*Te nan ansol me dis mu-e.*"

ISATU: I am not biting any fingers. What have I done?

KPANKA: You know. You are always doing something to distract me when I am praying.

ISATU: I am sorry o. I have not yet got used to my new husband.

KPANKA: What new husband?

ISATU: The one who is always praying. You know I am used to my warrior husband. Forgive me, it will take some time. (*Isatu exits*)

KPANKA: She does it on purpose.

BUTEH: I don't think so. She is a good woman. She probably has not yet got over the change in you.

KPANKA: Isatu? You don't know her as well as I do.

BUTEH: I know. But you must admit that the change in you has been rather drastic and sudden. You leave home a warrior and come back an *alpha*.

KPANKA: Are you going to start again? By the way, if you have come to try and persuade me to fight, don't waste your time. The answer is no.

BUTEH: Ah, Kpanka. Don't say that.

KPANKA: Why shouldn't I say that? I mean it. I am serious when I say I have finished fighting.

BUTEH: But why? Are you not going to protect your people anymore?

KPANKA: Not by fighting and killing. I am finished with that.

BUTEH: But how else are you going to protect your people when they are being attacked, captured and killed by enemy warriors?

KPANKA: (*Reflective*) I don't know. All I know is I am not going to fight. I am trying to make peace with Allah. Anyway, let's not waste time arguing about that. What did you come to see me for?

BUTEH: Well … I … need some advice. The Limbas are again attacking our people when they go to the river. Several men and women have been captured in the last four days. I have posted guards, but the river is big and the Limbas always seem to know where we are.

KPANKA: Have you tried setting traps?

BUTEH: Traps? What kind of traps?

KPANKA: I mean baits. Bait them with some women, or warriors posing as fishermen and let them lead you to their camp.

BUTEH: Hm … I hadn't thought of that. (*Pause*) Kpanka, you know you should be leading the men. Things are not the same without you. The men are not even as courageous as they used to be.

## The Patriot

KPANKA: Look, how many times do you want me to say the same thing? I have finished with fighting. I am now a farmer.

BUTEH: You are taking the coward's way out.

(*Kpanka's reaction is sudden and violent, and for a moment, as he seems on the verge of attacking Buteh, we see the old Kpanka. He visibly struggles to bring his anger under control. He finally succeeds. Buteh is shaken. He knows he has had a narrow escape*)

KPANKA: (*Calm*) You know I am not a coward. I have stopped fighting not because I am afraid, but because I now believe that it is wrong. I was growing to love killing, and that is *haram*. What has resulted from all the fighting and killing? Nothing but more and more fighting and killing. I have made up my mind and nothing you or anyone else says will change that.

BUTEH: I did not mean it that way.

KPANKA: Which way did you mean it? (*Laughs*) Me, coward? It is not bad. If you have finished, I have work to do.

(*Kpanka rises and sets about cleaning and sharpening his farming implements*)

BUTEH: (*Rising*) I am sorry. (*Pause*) Em ... by the way, father asked me to tell you that he wants to see you.

KPANKA: Okay, I hear.

(*Isatu enters*)

ISATU: Ah, *Koto*, are you going? Will you not stay to eat with us? Food is almost ready.

BUTEH: We ...e...l...l...em ...I have to see some other people.

ISATU: But you will at least eat.

BUTEH: (*Glancing at Kpanka who shows no interest in the discussion*) Em...I don't think so.

ISATU: Why? (*To Kpanka*) Won't you ask him to stay?

(*Kpanka makes no reply. Isatu looks from one to the other and seems to sense that they have quarreled*)

BUTEH: Well, I am going. (*Kpanka does not respond*)

ISATU: Okay. Do come and see us more often.

(*Buteh exits, stopping at the doorway to look back at Kpanka*)

KPANKA: (*Laughing cynically*) Coward. Me.

ISATU: What?

KPANKA: Hm?... Oh, nothing.

(*Isatu looks at him, shakes her head and exits. The Narrator enters, this time from the back of the auditorium. His opening utterance should be delivered so that the audience is startled, and their attention shifts from Kpanka on stage, but ends up somewhere in the middle of the auditorium*)

NARRATOR: Do you still feel like singing, or do you begin to understand? Our people say *Muno Won akoftha-e, muno tara are me thoymu-e*. It is the person who wears the shoe that knows the place where it is burning him. (*Pointing at Kpanka*) There is a man in whom conscience and societal pressure are at war. Coward! Coward, his brother called him. Is it cowardice for a man to follow the dictates of his conscience against the dictates of his society? Who is the coward? He who crumbles under pressure and engages in acts he has no belief in, or he who even though he stands alone refuses to bow or break before the wind which carries the mass along? (*Pause*) The years roll by. The pressure mounts, then recedes as the resilience of this spirit shines through. (*Isatu and Fatmata come on stage, and together with Kpanka, mime farming activities during the rest of the narrator's speech*)

### The Patriot

The affluence of the warrior gives way to the serenity of the farmer. Roles change from destruction to creation. Times are hard, as the once famous is relegated to near obscurity. But there is growing peace and tranquility where there was excitement and anxiety. The women too have gradually come to an understanding and acceptance of their new husband. Are there regrets? Well, who knows? (*The sound of a solitary voice wailing floats in. It is echoed by various voices*) The chief is dead. The search for a successor is on.

(*Isatu and Fatmata exit. Kpanka sits on the ground and is soon deep in thought. After some time, one of the chiefdom elders, Pa Santigi, enters. He is an old man in his seventies*)

PA SANTIGI: (*Greeting Kpanka*) Impiari!

KPANKA: (*Jolted out of his reverie*) Ah! *Seke*, Pa. You are welcome. (*He rises hastily and helps the old man to sit*)

PA SANTIGI: How are you my son?

KPANKA: Allah be praised, I have no cause for complaint.

PA SANTIGI: Good. Good. (*Pause*)

KPANKA: Let me get you some kola nuts.

PA SANTIGI: Ah! That will be good; something to make tired legs strong.

(*Kpanka exits and returns almost immediately with some kolanuts that he gives to Pa Santigi. Pa Santigi splits one and gives half to Kpanka. They chew in silence for a while*)

PA SANTIGI: I am sure you must be wondering what has brought me here. Well, I have a message for you from Pa Kumrabai. (*Pause*) He has asked me to tell you that we will be *hanging heads* tonight and we would like you to be there. I will come to your house as soon as it is dark to take you to the meeting place.

KPANKA: What Pa Kumrabai wills must be done. (*Pause*) May I ask why this sudden call?

PA SANTIGI: Don't worry. When you get to the meeting you will know. (*Seems to sense the cause of Kpanka's apprehension*) We are not going to ask you to fight if that is what you are worried about.

KPANKA: (*Relieved, but hiding it*) No. I'm not worried about that. It's just that the call is rather unexpected and I am curious. I will be waiting for you. More kola? (*Offering it to him*)

PA SANTIGI: No. I have to get back to town, and these legs are not as strong as they used to be. (*He rises*) Well, I'd better start going back. I will see you tonight.

KPANKA: If it is the will of Allah. (*Pa Santigie exits. Kpanka stands staring after him thoughtfully for some time, then starts collecting his farming implements. He looks up and calls*) Isatu! Fatmata!

(*The two women enter*)

KPANKA: I am going home.

FATMATA: Why? Are you not feeling well?

KPANKA: I am alright.

ISATU: Then why are you going home so suddenly?

KPANKA: Pa Santigi was here.

FATMATA: Pa Santigi? What did he come for?

KPANKA: He brought me a message from Pa Kumrabai. There is a meeting tonight and they want me to be there.

ISATU: A meeting? What sort of meeting? I hope it is not another war.

KPANKA: No. I don't think so. It probably has to do with the chieftaincy. Maybe they want to ask me to find and bring the successor back.

FATMATA: Oh, like you did with Bai Lamina?

KPANKA: Yes.

ISATU: Will you do it?

KPANKA: I don't know. Allah will guide me. (*He picks up his things*). I am going home.

ISATU: We are coming. (*Kpanka exits*) We had better hurry up so we get home before dark.

(*The two women exit. Almost immediately, the sound of drumming and singing starts and seems to move closer and closer until a group of old men, including the narrator, and led by Pa Kumrabai, enter. They sit in a large half circle with Pa Kumrabai roughly in the center. The drumming continues. After some time, Kpanka and Pa Santigie enter. Kpanka is directed to sit D.S.C. with his back to the audience. The singing and drumming continue in the background throughout this scene. Pa Kumrabai rises*)

PA KUMRABAI: Is it your wish that I speak as we had discussed?

ELDERS: Speak.

PA KUMRABAI: It is the sun that sees the people traveling a long distance. Kpanka, before we called you here like this, we have thought long and hard over the matter we are about to place before you. You know that since our chief, Bai Lamina, died, we have not been able to name a successor. I have been Regent Chief now for three full moons. Do you know why this is so? (*Contemptuously*) Because the men who hold claim to the chieftaincy are afraid. Yes, afraid of a curse dead these past ten years. A curse you were instrumental in removing. They have run away … from a curse that no longer exists. Should we go and beg them to come back, or should we go and drag them back? No. We will not do that. If one plants bean seeds, is it not beans one should expect to grow? These men have all shown that they are cowards. We have decided that we do not want a coward to rule us. We are not going to ask you to find these men and drag them back. No. (*Pause*) Kpanka, the child that washes his hands does not make a selection of old people. You have washed your hands, and although you have no claims to the chieftaincy, we have decided that we want you to be the next chief of Kase.

KPANKA: (*Jumping up in surprise*) What? Me? … b…but I can't em … I…

PA KUMRABAI: (*Gently*) Sit down, my son. Allow yourself to think about it … (*Kpanka slowly subsides*) Don't think this proposal has been made lightly. We have weighed all the odds. Think about it, we are in no hurry. (*The music in the background rises in volume. The rhythm is suggestive of the turmoil in Kpanka's mind and the mood of breathless expectancy of the people and the elders who watch Kpanka closely. For the space of about thirty seconds, they are all motionless; then Kpanka rises*)

KPANKA: I will not fight.

PA SANTIGI: We are not asking you to fight.

KPANKA: A chief is expected to be a warrior capable of leading his people in battle. I am no longer a warrior and do not intend to become one again. You know I have taken a vow never to fight again.

PA KUMRABAI: We know of your vow and, as Pa Santigi says, we are not asking you to fight. We are not at war.

KPANKA: Yes, but what will happen if and when we are at war?

PA KUMRABAI: Don't worry about that now. We will cross the river when we get there. We are asking you to be chief because we believe ... all of us ... we believe you are the best choice at this time.

PA SANTIGI: You have proved yourself a man of valor, and although some may question your decision not to fight, all respect your courage in sticking to it. Was it not yesterday we received a message from Alimami Rassin?

PA KUMRABAI: Yes. Urging us to select a man of peace as chief.

KPANKA: Alimami Rassin?

PA KUMRABAI: Yes. You know he has been waging a relentless campaign to get non-warriors accepted as suitable chiefs. Through his influence, the people of Sanda Loko, Romedi and Sanda Tendaran have made non-warriors chiefs. He is now urging us to do the same. So, in asking you who have sworn never to fight again to be our chief, we are not isolating ourselves.

(*The music stops abruptly and there is complete silence and immobility for about fifteen seconds*)

KPANKA: (*Slowly*) If it is understood and accepted that my vow never to fight again will not be broken, then I accept the honor of being made chief of Kase.

(*There is a thunderous shout of joy from off stage. A song is raised and the townspeople come dancing in. Kpanka is carried shoulder high and they all dance off. He has been taken to "Kantha," the place where he will be prepared for the mantle of leadership. There is silence for some seconds, and then the voice of Pa Kumrabai can be heard calling from off stage*)

PA KUMRABAI:

| *Koi no! Koi no!* | I greet you! I greet you! |
| *Sa yema thono wura obai* | We want to bring out the |
| *Kere so yema e koftha yong* | Chief today but we want his |
| *dei ang ronko ngong* | shoes and his *ronko* (gown). |

(*Buteh runs across the stage carrying the two items. Almost immediately after he exits, a song is raised. Kpanka, now Bai Bureh, enters from the back of the auditorium, flanked by his wives and preceded by his sub chiefs. They move in a procession to the stage. This is followed by homage paying and the presentation of gifts by people living in his domain——Mendes, Limbas and Temnes. They all dance off leaving the narrator alone on stage*)

NARRATOR: For several years, peace reigns in Kase Chiefdom under the wise rule of Kpanka, now Bai Bureh. But the mouth can only hold what it can hold and so things begin to change. The influence of the white man has begun to be felt. The pounding boots of his civilization are marching inland, crushing underfoot the foliage that has sustained life for centuries. (*A group of chiefs and their attendants, carrying mats, enter and sit. They are about to have a meeting. Bai Bureh is one of them*) Change, that most potent destroyer and creator is on the move and the responses are varied. (*The chiefs start their discussion in undertones such that we cannot make out what they are saying. The narrator speaks above their voices*) From some quarters, quiet acquiescence, from others skeptical acceptance, and from still others, vehement resistance. (*From this point, the narrator assumes the role of Bai Bangura. He joins the other chiefs*)

BAI SUBA: (*Vehemently*) I say no! I will go to war when I feel there is a need. Who are they to tell me what to do?

BAI BUREH: Although I do not agree with Bai Suba about going to war, I join him in saying no. We do not need the white man's protection. We have lived on these lands…. Our fathers and grandfathers lived on these lands without the white man's protection. As soon as we start asking for protection, we will lose our sovereignty.

BAI FORKI: I do not agree. All we are being asked to do is to put our marks on a piece of paper which says we shall allow the white strangers in Rokamp to mediate in our quarrels with the neighboring tribes and that we will not go to war without first consulting them.

BAI SUBA: Why should we consult them? Are we no longer chiefs over our own people? We have signed treaties of friendship with the white men, but that does not make us answerable to them.

BAI BANGURA: My brothers, let us not quarrel over this. The way I see it is this. The White men are traders from a land far across the sea. They have come to live among us to trade, and in order to do this successfully, they need peace in the area. That is why they want us to assure them that we shall not go to war, or at least inform them before we do so.

BRIMA SANDA: Exactly! What Bai Bangura has said is the truth. That is exactly why the white men want us to sign the treaty.

BAI SUBA: Are you one of the white men that you now speak for them and seem to know their minds? Or are they your masters?

BRIMA SANDA: *(Rising in anger)* I will not take that from you. Have I not got the right to speak my mind? After all, I am a chief, same as you are.

BAI SUBA: *(Laughing derisively)* You, a chief like me? Puppet!

*(The two men confront each other, but are separated by the other chiefs)*

BOKARIE BAMP: My brothers, let us control our tempers. This is a meeting of chiefs. Let us behave in a manner befitting our positions. Brima Sanda is one of us and is entitled to express his views. So, let us listen to him. *(He signals to Brima Sanda to speak)*

BRIMA SANDA: I have said what I wanted to say.

BOKARIE BAMP: Then, I will speak. What we need to ask ourselves is whether signing the treaty is in our interest and that of our people, or whether it is not in our interest to sign. How can we determine this? We need to examine the treaty. What is it we are being asked to do and what do we get in return? From what I understand, the white men want us to sign a treaty agreeing not to go to war without at least first consulting them. In return for that promise, they will promise to give us protection from the aggression of neighboring tribes and those who may seek to invade our lands. The way I see it, we do not stand to lose anything. We are not giving up our rights as a sovereign people. The white men are not coming from Rokamp to rule us. We will still maintain all our rights, except the right to go to war as and when we feel the need. For that, we can call on the white man's soldiers with their guns for help whenever we are threatened. To me, it seems we have nothing to lose and a lot to gain. I say we sign.

BAI BUREH: I do not agree. It is not as simple as Bockarie Bamp has put it. There are other things we should think of. The white men are very crafty and are not to be trusted. They always ask for less than they want, but take more than you want to give. Today they say we want a room in your house, we give them. Tomorrow they will say it was not only a room you gave us, you gave us the whole house. I, more than most of you, should be happy that the white men are offering us the opportunity of laying down our arms permanently. But I have doubts, grave doubts.

BAI FORKI: Bai Bureh has spoken well. But his fears are largely unfounded. The white men have not given us any reason not to trust them. Up to now, they have always kept their word.

BAI BUREH: Up to now, we have not given them the right to tell us when and how we should do anything. In fact, up to now, they have been asking us for protection. If we sign the treaty, our roles will be reversed.

BAI FARIMA: I want to agree with Bai Forki and Bockarie Bamp that we should sign the treaty. As far as I can see, we have a lot to gain and nothing to lose. Bai Bureh's fears are not likely to be realized. They are based largely on his own prejudices, with no facts to back them up. We have nothing to fear from the white men. They come as friends and are only interested in trade. I say we should sign the treaty.

BOKARIE BAMP: It seems therefore that only Bai Bureh and Bai Suba are against signing the treaty.

BAI FORKI: *Koni*, let us speak with one voice. I think we should ask Bai Bureh and Bai Suba whether they will agree to sign the treaty if we all decide we should sign.

BAI SUBA: I will not object to signing the treaty, as long as it is made very clear to the white men that they will not dictate to us what we should do.

BAI BUREH: I still feel we should not sign. My fears are very real, and I am afraid that signing the treaty will be an action, which we will regret. However, if it is the wish of all of you that we should sign the treaty, then I will not stand against your wishes. I will sign, but like Bai Suba has just said, I want it to be impressed on the white men that we are not giving up our rights of sovereignty.

BAI FORKI: So, are we all now agreed that we should sign the treaty?

ALL: Yes.

*(They all rise and as they are exiting, two policemen enter from opposite directions carrying a table and two chairs which they place on stage to represent Governor Cardew's office. Governor Cardew, a middle aged Englishman, enters with Captain Sharpe,*

*who is also an Englishman, but several years younger, and whose bearing indicates someone with military training)*

SHARPE: All the chiefs in the north also signed the treaty?

CARDEW: Yes. *(Moving to sit)*

SHARPE: Then we shouldn't have any problems. They owe allegiance to us.

CARDEW: Tell that to the French.

SHARPE: You mean they are going to ignore the treaties?

CARDEW: They are not going to ignore them. They are going to claim that they are ineffectual. The French have a penchant for seizing the bull by the horns, and since we don't really have administrative jurisdiction over these areas …*(shrugs)*

SHARPE: They are going to claim them as being in their sphere of influence.

CARDEW: Precisely!

SHARPE: Just like the French to grab such an opportunity. *(Pause)* I hear there have also been complaints by traders of harassment.

CARDEW: Unfortunately, yes. Both British and Creole traders have reported several incidents of attacks and the theft of their goods by local tribesmen.

SHARPE: Anything done yet to arrest the situation?

CARDEW: Well, Major Tarbet … You know him?

SHARPE: We have met. I can't say it was a pleasant experience.

CARDEW: He's not such a bad chap when you get to know him. Anyway, he's in charge of the Frontier Police in the north, and he claims he doesn't have enough men to police the area.

## The Patriot

SHARPE: From what I hear, his men spend their time doing other things.

CARDEW: I've heard the rumors myself. One begins to wonder whether the whole business of the Frontier Force wasn't a mistake.

SHARPE: Well, it's no use crying over spilt milk. *(Pause)* What are you planning to do?

CARDEW: It's all in the hands of the British government now. I have submitted a proposal to the Colonial Secretary for the setting up of a protectorate over all the areas now within our sphere of influence.

SHARPE: A protectorate? Are you sure the people will take kindly to that?

CARDEW: They may not, but it is in the interest of the British Empire.

SHARPE: Wouldn't a protectorate involve the setting up of viable institutions of British administration throughout the hinterland?

CARDEW: Yes. I've already made some suggestions. The details will be worked out if it receives government approval.

SHARPE: Hm… Well… I'd better go and see my men. I'll drop in again later.

CARDEW: Right, see you later. *(Sharpe exits)* Ah, Captain Sharpe! *(Sharpe enters)* I forgot, Margaret would like you over for lunch today, say half past one. Can you make it?

SHARPE: With pleasure.

CARDEW: Right. See you later.

*(Sharpe exits. After a short while Cardew also exits followed by the policemen who carry the furniture off. On the other side of the*

*stage, Bai Bureh and his sub chiefs enter, followed by a government messenger)*

BAI BUREH: Let us hear the message you have for us.

MESSSENGER: The District Commissioner for Karene District …

BAI BUREH: District Commissioner? What is District Commissioner?

MESSSENGER: Captain Sharpe, the white man who is like governor in this area.

BAI BUREH: So the governor is no longer staying in Rokamp?

MESSSENGER: The governor is in Freetown. Captain Sharpe is the District Commissioner.

BAI BUREH: I see. *(Looks at his chiefs and shrugs)* What does this… em… what do you call him?

MESSSENGER: District Commissioner.

BAI BUREH: Yes. What does he want from me?

MESSENGER: He says I should tell you that now that you have been made paramount chief of this chiefdom in the protectorate, you have to go to Port Loko to be given your staff-of-office.

BAI BUREH: Paramount Chief? Protectorate? What is that? And staff-of-office? I do not understand.

MESSENGER: That is the message I was asked to bring to you.

BAI BUREH: Hm…well, I have heard the message but I do not understand it. Go back to whoever sent you and tell him that I do not understand why I should go to Port Loko. If anybody wants to give me a present, he should bring it here.

MESSENGER: The District Commissioner will not be pleased with that answer. He...

BAI BUREH: Look, I do not know who this your District Commissioner is, and I do not care if he is pleased or not. I do not understand his message, and I am not going anywhere. Tell him that.

MESSENGER: But …

BAI BUREH: *(Vehemently)* Go! *(The messenger is startled and quickly exits)* Foolish man!

PA SANTIGI: Maybe he is the dis…ditikt komsona. *(They all laugh)*

BAI BUREH: I wonder what he meant by "protectorate" and "paramount chief"?

PA SANTIGI: I am sure he has misunderstood the message he was asked to bring. That man is obviously a fool.

BAI BUREH: I don't think so. There … *(Brima Sanda comes hurrying in)* Ah! What is chasing you?

BRIMA SANDA: *(Greatly agitated)* Bai Forki has been arrested.

BAI BUREH: Arrested? What do you mean arrested?

BRIMA SANDA: Arrested. His hands tied, taken to Port Loko and locked in the police barracks. *(There are expressions of shock and disbelief from all present)*

BAI BUREH: Bai Forki, tied and locked up? Who … which mad man has done that?

BRIMA SANDA: Those …em …frontier police. About six of them went to his compound, tied his hands and took him away.

BAI BUREH: But why? Why should they do that?

BRIMA SANDA: They say he has refused to go to Port Loko to receive his staff.

BAI BUREH: What staff?

BRIMA SANDA: Oh, you have not yet heard? The white men say they are now ruling us.

BAI BUREH: Ruling us? What do you mean?

BRIMA SANDA: They have declared a…em…a protectorate. They say they are now our rulers.

BAI BUREH: *(Laughing)* These white men are not serious. How can they say they are now ruling us? Did we tell them that we are no longer able to rule ourselves?

BRIMA SANDA: They are serious o.

PA SANTIGI: So, the messenger was not mad.

BRIMA SANDA: Messenger? What messenger?

BAI BUREH: Oh, one foolish man who came to tell me that somebody called district commissioner wanted me to go to Port Loko to be given some present … em … I think he called it … staff-of-office.

BRIMA SANDA: It is true. I received the same message. I have just come from Port Loko two days ago. I was given a walking stick with a golden head. There is a white man there called Captain Sharpe who says he is the District Commissioner. He says they are now protecting us, so they are now our rulers.

BAI BUREH: *Kurumasaba*! It has happened. I said it. I said it. I knew something like this would happen.

BRIMA SANDA: Bockarie Bamp is asking us to meet to decide what to do. We meet tomorrow.

(*As they rise and begin to exit, all the other Temne chiefs enter to meet Bai Bureh and Brima Sanda who remain on stage whilst*

## The Patriot

*Bai Bureh's sub-chiefs exit. At the same time, on the other side of the stage, Governor Cardew, Captain Sharpe and Major Tarbet enter, accompanied by two policemen carrying the furniture for Governor Cardew's office. The chiefs spread mats or place stools, sit down and freeze. Focus is on Governor Cardew's office)*

SHARPE: The bloody cowards all ran away.

TARBET: They were taken by surprise.

SHARPE: Surprise? A bunch of thirty so-called policemen routed by a bunch of savages?

TARBET: They were armed.

SHARPE: And so?

CARDEW: Major Tarbet, you seem to be making excuses for what can only be described as the disgraceful behavior of your men.

TARBET: I am not …

CARDEW: Why did you arrest the man anyway? Don't you know that Bai Forki is one of the most important Temne chiefs?

TARBET: I did not arrest him.

SHARPE: Oh you took him to a party then.

TARBET: There's no need to be sarcastic.

SHARPE: The man was handcuffed and locked up, and you say you did not arrest him.

TARBET: That was a result of the men misunderstanding my instructions. I told them to make sure they returned to Port Loko with him.

CARDEW: And they took that to mean he was to be arrested.

TARBET: Exactly.

SHARPE: The whole thing has placed us in a very bad light.

CARDEW: Yes. Particularly the forcible release of Bai Forki by his people. Makes us look foolish. We must make sure this sort of thing doesn't recur. Particularly now that we are soon going to start collecting the hut tax.

*(They freeze. Focus shifts to the chiefs)*

BAI SUBA: Hut tax? What is hut tax?

BOCKARI BAMP: We are being asked to pay a tax of five shillings for every house in our country to the white district commissioner.

BAI FARIMA: Five shillings? For what?

BOCKARI BAMP: For our houses.

BAI SUBA: They must be mad. You mean they want us to pay a tax on our own house?

BOCKARI BAMP: Yes. *(Everyone starts speaking at once)* My brothers! My brothers! That is not all. The British say they have declared a protectorate over our countries and we are no longer the rulers of our people. They say we are now paramount chiefs and have to obey the District Commissioner who is the Governor's representative. Bai Forki here was arrested, tied and led to Port Loko where he was locked up. A chief, tied and locked up.

BAI FORKI: Yes. Because I refused to go to Port Loko to be given a walking stick which they call staff-of-office.

BRIMA SANDA: You should have gone. See my own staff that I was given. *(He proudly displays his staff. The other chiefs are shocked, and stare at him with a mixture of embarrassment and disgust. He realizes they are unimpressed and sheepishly puts it away)*

BAI BANGURA: Staff! Is that what you are proud of?

BOCKARI BAMP: (Breaking the embarrassed silence) Em … if it had not been for the timely action of Bai Salamansa in rescuing Bai Forki, who knows what would have happened by now.

BAI SUBA: But why are they doing these things?

BOCKARI BAMP: There is still more which they plan to do. They say under their protectorate, we are no longer allowed to judge land cases, witchcraft, murder and all other serious cases. The District Commissioner will judge those cases.

BAI FARIMA: We have to pay tax for our houses; we, as chiefs, can no longer judge serious cases. What is left then? We are no longer chiefs.

BAI BANGURA: And we no longer own our land and houses.

BAI BUREH: *(He has been strangely silent, sitting slightly apart from the others)* Several years ago, I warned you about the white men, but you all chose to ignore my warning. Do you remember what I said then? …I warned that they were not to be trusted, but you all said we should sign the treaty with them. Now I have been proved right. We gave them a room and they are now claiming ownership of the house. They will soon drive us out of the house.

BOCKARI BAMP: We know you warned us. And you were right. But the mistake has been made. What are we going to do now?

BAI FORKI: I think we should send our complaint to the governor, explaining that we cannot accept what they are asking us to do.

BAI FARIMA: Yes. We should tell him that they have no right to ask us to pay a tax on our own houses.

BOCKARI BAMP: Are we all agreed that we should send a letter to the governor in Rokamp?

ALL: Yes.

BAI BUREH: Well, you can send your case, but it will not make any difference.

(*All the chiefs freeze as the focus shifts to Cardew, Tarbet and Sharpe on the other side of the stage*)

TARBET: Listen to this. (*Reads*) "We ask that the ancient rights and privileges enjoyed by chiefs be returned to us. We assure His Excellency the Governor that we shall maintain peace within our chiefdoms and shall not engage in wars with neighboring tribes, as we now know the benefits of peace"…em…tar ra ra ra… "It seems that the British people want to take our country from us …We cannot agree to pay the tax, as paying tax for our houses means we no longer own them. We therefore ask that you reconsider the tax issue" …Who do these people think they are? I hope you've given them a suitable reply sir?

CARDEW: Certainly. That is, in fact, the second petition we have received from the Temne Chiefs. There have, in addition, been several protesting the actions of your men, Tarbet.

SHARPE: And I believe their claims are valid.

TARBET: What claims?

CARDEW: Claims of harassment, incessant arrests, floggings …you name it, your men have been accused of it.

SHARPE: A little power seems to have gone to their heads. They have become tyrants and take pleasure in showing utter disregard for the chiefs.

TARBET: We …e…l…l… I have received complaints myself, but some of these claims are difficult to prove.

SHARPE: I think the whole force should be disbanded and completely restructured.

CARDEW: That is going to be difficult. We don't have the resources right now.

## The Patriot

TARBET: I agree with Captain Sharpe to some extent sir. The force needs restructuring. Some of the men should be thrown out. I believe you've seen the proposal I submitted to the Secretary for Native Affairs, sir.

CARDEW: Yes. But I doubt whether we can afford all of what you suggest. We are looking into it anyway.

SHARPE: What are you going to do about the petitions related to the hut tax?

CARDEW: Well, like I said, I've sent a reply to them. Maybe I should read sections of it to you. *(Looks in a file and pulls out a sheet of paper. He skims through, running his finger down the page)* Right, here is the section dealing with the Frontier Police. *(Reads)* "I would like to assure you that your complaints about the actions of members of the Frontier Police Force are being looked into, and if found to be authentic, disciplinary action will be taken against erring members of the force. However, the government cannot, as you request, leave your country to itself. If it were to do so – say withdraw the police and District Commissioners – slave raiding and inter-tribal wars would commence again. In a short time, there would be such anarchy and confusion, and our neighbors would so suffer from the disturbances that they would step in and occupy and control your country themselves. Be rest assured that if England does not rule you, another European power, notably France, will do so." I then point out the advantages of British rule over French rule, then go on to the need for the hut tax. *(Scans through the page)* Ehen! Here it is. *(Reads)* "I regret to inform you that the government is in no position to rescind its decision with regards to payment of a hut tax of five shillings per house. The money collected will be used to finance British Administration in the protectorate and provide some services such as roads. I would therefore urge you to comply with government directives in this regard and pay your taxes promptly.

*(They freeze and focus shifts to the chiefs)*

BAI FORKI: That is the reply from the Governor, which we have all heard. What do we do now?

BRIMA SANDA: What can we do? We have to pay.

BAI SUBA: Just like that. *(Mimicking him)* "We have to pay." What are we? Children? If we pay, we lose all our rights of ownership.

BOCKARI BAMP: I agree with Bai Suba. I do not see how we can pay. But then, what will we do when they start arresting us?

BRIMA SANDA: Ehen! What will we do? I do not want to be locked up. We should just pay and forget about the whole thing.

*(Bai Bureh who has been sitting with head bowed, suddenly erupts, startling the other chiefs)*

BAI BUREH: No! I say no! I will not stand by and watch our lands, the lands of our ancestors, usurped by people who have left their own country far away. Why do we sit here arguing like women? Some say pay, others say don't pay. I say I will not pay and nobody else will pay. *(Becoming more and more worked up)* Two years ago, I broke my vow and became a warrior once more. Through your insistence, all of you looking at me, I broke my vow to fight beside the white men against the Sofas. I led you in battle. And what for? Was it not to defend our lands and our people from domination by strangers? Hm? Tell me, were we not fighting so our children and grandchildren could continue living on the lands where their ancestors lived and died? Or were we fighting so that others could take the land and make it their own? The white men say they need money to finance British administration. Did we tell them we want their British administration? *(Pause. When he speaks again it is with a calm resulting from a hardened resolve)* I prefer to die than watch what belongs to me, what belongs to all of us—-our children and grandchildren, stolen. I will not allow my people to become enslaved. As chief, I intend to maintain the dignity and status bestowed on me by tradition and I will fight for it if I have to. So, I say again, I will not pay any hut tax or any other tax imposed by those who seek to dominate us.

*(There is silence for a few seconds)*

BOCKARI BAMP: You have heard Bai Bureh speak. He has spoken well, but I want to ask him one question. *(To Bai Bureh)* Will you lead us in battle if we have to fight?

BAI BUREH: *(Without hesitation)* Yes. But it will be a defensive war. I will defend our lands against domination by the usurpers.

BAI FORKI: That is all we need. Now that we have heard Bai Bureh, shall we pay the hut tax and accept domination, or shall we say "no," even if it means giving our lives in battle?

ALL: We say no! *(Brima Sanda is noticeably silent)*

BAI BUREH: Give me your hands on that. Let us seal our resolve. *(They all rise and clasp hands, Brima Sanda rather reluctantly. They freeze and focus shifts to Cardew, Sharpe and Tarbet)*

SHARPE: When should I start collecting the taxes?

CARDEW: As soon as you get back to your station. I suggest you start in Port Loko. Being a trading centre, you're likely to collect appreciable sums there. I suspect there will be some resistance from the chiefs, but it shouldn't be anything serious.

SHARPE: I intend to do effective collection. Anyone who refuses to pay will be arrested.

CARDEW: That's the spirit. Major Tarbet, I suggest you hold your men in readiness in the unlikely event of a revolt.

TARBET: That's highly unlikely. These people are all bluster. Once they realize we mean business, they'll quiet down and tow the line.

CARDEW: Well, good luck gentlemen. (*Shakes hands with both men*) Keep me posted.

(*Sharpe and Tarbet exit. On the other side of the stage all the chiefs, except Bai Bureh, also exit. Bai Bureh stands apparently deep in thought. Cardew assumes a similar posture. For a few seconds, both are immobile, and then at the same instant, they turn and stride purposefully off stage in opposite directions. Bockari Bamp enters where Bai Bureh exits and Captain Sharpe enters where Cardew exits. Captain Sharpe is quite angry*)

SHARPE: Bockari Bamp, you have been threatening reprisals against those who are willing to pay the hut tax.

BOCKARI BAMP: (*Taken aback*) Captain Sharpe!

SHARPE: Don't Captain Sharpe me. Why have you been threatening people?

BOCKARI BAMP: Who says I have threatened him?

SHARPE: All the traders say they are afraid to pay tax.

BOCKARI BAMP: Ah, Captain Sharpe. If they are afraid, is that my fault?

SHARPE: Don't try to be clever with me. They are afraid because of what you've threatened to do to them.

BOCKARI BAMP: Captain Sharpe…

SHARPE: I want to know why you have been threatening people.

BOCKARI BAMP: I have not been threatening anybody.

# The Patriot

SHARPE: The traders say they are afraid you'll destroy their goods and even kill them if they pay the tax.

BOCKARI BAMP: Did they say I told them that?

SHARPE: Don't ask questions. Answer.

BOCKARI BAMP: I have already answered your question Captain Sharpe. I have told you that I have not threatened anybody.

SHARPE: Then the traders are lying?

BOCKARI BAMP: If they say I have threatened them, they are lying.

SHARPE: (*Suspicious*) Are you sure you are telling me the truth?

BOCKARI BAMP: Will I lie to you?

SHARPE: Yes, you would. Anyway, if I find that you have indeed threatened the traders, there will be trouble. Goodbye! (*Glares at Bockari Bamp and exits*)

BOCKARI BAMP: (*Smiling to himself*) Goodbye Captain Sharpe. So the District Commissioner has started collecting the tax and the people are refusing to pay. (*Laughs out loud*) I must send a message to Bai Bureh and Bai Forki. (*Exits*)

*Almost immediately, an orderly or policeman comes in carrying a desk and chair. We are now in Captain Sharpe's office. Sharpe enters and sits. (To Policeman)*

SHARPE: You! Get me Major Tarbet.

(*The policeman exits and Sharpe paces restlessly to and fro. After a short while, policeman and Tarbet enter*)

TARBET: You sent for me?

SHARPE: I have just ordered the imprisonment of a group of traders for refusing to pay their taxes.

TARBET: Good. Set a few examples and the rest will fall in line.

SHARPE: That's the general idea. However, I believe the people are genuinely scared of reprisals from the Chief.

TARBET: Bockari Bamp?

SHARPE: Yes. That's the impression they gave me yesterday, although they have now decided to be clever and are pretending not to understand anything I say.

TARBET: A few days in jail will teach them some sense.

SHARPE: Anyway, I want the Chief brought here.

TARBET: No problem. Sergeant!

SERGEANT: (*Off stage*) Yes sir! (*He runs in*)

TARBET: Get a detachment together and bring the Chief here.

SERGEANT: Yes sir (*He begins to exit*)

TARBET: I haven't sent you to arrest him. Invite him here. Tell him the District Commissioner wants to see him.

SERGEANT: Suppose he says he is not coming sir?

TARBET: Then arrest him and bring him here. But don't handcuff him.

SERGEANT: Yes sir. (*Exits*)

TARBET: They will soon be here.

SHARPE: Good. (*Pause*) The way things are going, I may have to take some rather harsh measures in order to induce compliance among the people. I'll need your full support.

TARBET: No problem. I now have a force of about a hundred stationed here. We can easily handle any problems the people here may pose.

SHARPE: Good. I suggest you have a detachment of your men on standby in case they are needed to provide escort to Freetown. I am going to see if I can persuade Bockari Bamp to give an assurance of safety to those who want to pay the tax, failing which I want him arrested and taken to Freetown immediately for trial.

TARBET: Couldn't you try him here?

SHARPE: I could, but I'd hate to have a repeat of the Bai Forki incident.

TARBET: You're right. I'd forgotten about that. Anyway, I always have a company on standby.

SHARPE: Good.

TARBET: Ah, here they come.

*(Bockari Bamp and his sub-chiefs are escorted in by a group of policemen. They are followed by a large group of townspeople)*

BOCKARI BAMP: Good afternoon Captain Sharpe. You sent for me?

SHARPE: Yes. It's good you have come with your sub-chiefs. I am going to ask you some straightforward questions. But before I ask them, let me warn you that my patience has been tried to its limit and I'm not going to tolerate any more delaying tactics. I want a simple "yes" or "no" answer to both questions. Do I make myself clear?

BOCKARI BAMP: Quite clear.

SHARPE: Good. Now, will you permit the traders to pay the tax without any reprisals from yourself, your chiefs or people?

BOCKARI BAMP: I …

SHARPE: Yes or no?

BOCKARI BAMP: *(After a slight hesitation)* No.

SHARPE: Fine. Will you set about immediately assisting in the collection of the tax in the Port Loko area?

BOCKARI BAMP: No.

SHARPE: Right. Arrest him and all his sub-chiefs. (*The policemen hesitate to carry out the order*)

TARBET: You heard the man. What are you waiting for? Arrest them! (*The policemen jump to obey. There is uproar from the townspeople*) And clear these people out of here.

(*Townspeople are herded out, protesting*)

TARBET: Take the chiefs to the barracks. We will take them to Freetown tonight.

BOCKARI BAMP: (*As he is being led out*) What do you hope to achieve by this, Captain Sharpe?

SHARPE: I intend to make an example of you, so the other chiefs will realize we are serious. You will be taken to Freetown where you will be tried.

BOCKARI BAMP: And you think that will make the people pay? (*Laughs*) You do not understand our people.

SHARPE: Take them away. (*The chiefs are led away unresisting, except for one of them, Sorie Bunki, who is struggling. Tarbet whispers something to Sharpe, points at the struggling man*) Bring that one over here. (*Bunki is led to Sharpe*)

SHARPE: What is your name?

SORIE BUNKI: Sorie Bunki, sir.

SHARPE: Do you know what will happen to you when you get to Freetown? You will be tried and sent to jail.

## ✹ The Patriot ✹

SORIE BUNKI: Ahhh! B...b...but I...I... have not done anything. I told them we should pay the tax, but they refused.

SHARPE: Okay. I have a proposition to put to you. Supposing I were to install you as Acting Chief, will you help in the collection of taxes?

SORIE BUNKI: *(Eagerly)* Yes sir, I will. Everyone will pay the tax.

SHARPE: Are you sure?

SORIE BUNKI: Yes sir.

SHARPE: Good. You are now the Acting Chief of Port Loko.

SORIE BUNKI: Thank you, sir. God will bless you, sir.

SHARPE: Yes, yes, go. I will inform the people in the morning that you are the new chief.

SORIE BUNKI: Yes, sir. *(He exits)*

TARBET: That one will serve us well.

SHARPE: What makes you so sure?

TARBET: The man is a coward. As long as he remains frightened about what we can do to him, he'll tow the line.

*(There are angry noises from the townspeople who have gathered outside)*

SHARPE: We'd better go and see that the prisoners are dispatched to Freetown before their people work up enough courage to try freeing them. *(They both hurry off)*

*(There is silence for a short while, then the sound of drumming and singing fill the air and a group of warriors enter at a rush. They do a war dance. Several other groups of warriors arrive at intervals and join in the dance. This continues until the stage is crowded with wildly dancing warboys. Bai Bureh enters with Buteh)*

WARBOYS: Kablai! Kablai! Kablai!

BUTEH: Quiet! Quiet! Kablai wants to speak.

(*The warboys quiet down slowly. Bai Bureh surveys the assembled warriors*)

BAI BUREH: Welcome. I welcome you all. May you return home as you left.

ALL: *Amin-a.*

BAI BUREH: My brothers you all know why we are here. We are here because strangers want to take our country from us. They say we are no longer the owners of our country and we have to pay tax for our houses. That is what we are saying no to. (*Pause*) As I look around me, I see men eager for battle. I see faces that are familiar. Faces that have fought with me in the past. Faces of strong and brave men willing to die for the protection of our people and our lands. I welcome you all. (*Pause*) This war is a different war. It is going to be a difficult war, because we are fighting an enemy who has plenty of weapons, which can destroy a whole army like that. (*Snaps his fingers*)

1st WARBOY: We are not afraid.

2nd WARBOY: We shall fight.

1st WARBOY: We shall fight the usurpers.

2nd WARBOY: Drive them off our lands. (*Warboys nod in agreement*)

BAI BUREH: Yes my brothers, we shall fight. Be we shall fight in a different way.

BUTEH: What about guns? Do we need guns?

BAI BUREH: We already have some guns.

BUTEH: I don't mean *chakabula*. Guns like those that the strangers have.

BAI BUREH: We do not have that kind now, but Bai Suba and Bai Farima have promised to try and get some.

(*The sound of singing floats in from a distance. Everybody listens. A warboy who had been on guard rushes in*)

3rd WARBOY: There is a group of warboys approaching.

BUTEH: Who is leading them?

3rd WARBOY: I don't know. They are still far away.

BUTEH: Fool! Go and find out.

(*The warrior rushes out and comes back almost immediately*)

3rd WARBOY: It is Bai Bangura and Bai Suba

(*There is a shout of joy from the assembled warriors and they start singing and dancing wildly. Bai Bangura and Bai Suba join in the dance. Buteh leads the warriors off*)

BAI BUREH: Welcome. How many *warboys* have you come with?

BAI BANGURA: Two thousand.

BAI BUREH: Good. What about Bai Farima? He promised to get some guns.

BAI BANGURA: I don't know. I have not seen him for a long time.

BAI BUREH: There is one thing I want us all to agree on. We shall not harm anyone not directly involved in the fight. Missionaries and traders should not be harmed.

BAI BANGURA: Even if they are white men?

BAI BUREH: Yes.

BAI SUBA: But they may be spies.

BAI BUREH: As long as they are not carrying weapons, they are not to be harmed.

BAI SUBA: But …

BAI BUREH: I am leading this fight for one reason only, and that is because I feel I have a duty to defend the rights of my people. I am not fighting missionaries and traders, or women. So, none of them should be harmed. I want you to make sure your men understand this. I will not be called a murderer.

BAI BANGURA: Okay, we will tell them.

BAI SUBA: We should attack them in Port Loko now and drive them away from our country.

BAI BUREH: No. We cannot win that type of war now. We have allowed them to plant their roots too firmly for that.

BAI BANGURA: But how many men do they have in Port Loko?

BAI BUREH: They do not have many men there now. But if we start attacking them, they will send for more men and guns from Rokamp.

BAI SUBA: So, we should just sit here and wait for them to attack us?

BAI BUREH: We are not going to sit down. We are going to organize the defenses of our towns.

BAI SUBA: How are…

BAI BUREH: Stockades! We will build stockades along all the roads leading to each town. In places where the enemy will not expect them. If they break one down, we build another. We will always be moving so they will not know exactly where we are.

BAI BANGURA: We have agreed that you lead this war, so we will fight the way you want.

BAI BUREH: Good. *(Looks at Bai Suba, expecting him to say something)*

BAI SUBA: *(Shrugging his shoulders)* Well … you are in charge.

BAI BUREH: Good. Let us go and organize the men, so we can start building the stockades.

*(They all exit. Tarbet and Sharpe enter from the opposite direction. They are deep in conversation)*

SHARPE: We have to arrest him immediately.

TARBET: I know. But how? We don't even know where he is.

SHARPE: His name is on everyone's lips. "Kablai", that's all one hears. "Kablai will attack us if we pay the taxes." I tell you, the fellow is behind all the resistance to the taxes.

TARBET: That's true. The acting chief here, Sorie Bunki, is absolutely terrified of him.

SHARPE: We have to arrest him, or we'll never succeed in collecting the tax.

*(A policeman enters in a hurry)*

POLICEMAN: Excuse me sir.

SHARPE: *(A bit annoyed)* Yes, what is it?

POLICEMAN: There is a man who says he wants to see you, sir. He says he is called Brima Sanda, sir.

TARBET: Brima Sanda? What's he doing here?

SHARPE: *(Shrugs)* Let him come.

POLICEMAN: Yes sir. *(He exits)*

TARBET: I wonder what he wants?

SHARPE: Probably wants some favor. He's always asking for favors.

TARBET: A rather shifty character.

(*Policeman enters, followed by Brima Sanda*)

POLICEMAN: This is the man, sir.

SHARPE: Thank you constable. You may go.

POLICEMAN: Yes sir. (*He exits*)

BRIMA SANDA: Good afternoon, Captain Sharpe and …

SHARPE: Yes, what is it you want? We're rather busy, so speak up.

BRIMA SANDA: Em… I have some information for you.

SHARPE: Information? What sort of information?

BRIMA SANDA: (*Fawning*) Ah! Very important information, which I know you will be glad about. (*Pause*)

TARBET: Come on what is it about? We haven't got all day, you know.

BRIMA SANDA: But there is the small… em… a reward?

SHARPE: A reward for what?

BRIMA SANDA: Ah, Captain Sharpe. For Bai Bureh.

SHARPE: Oh, that reward.

TARBET: Do you have information about Bai Bureh?

BRIMA SANDA: Yes. (*Pause*)

SHARPE: Well?

TARBET: Let's hear it, man!

BRIMA SANDA: Will I get the reward?

SHARPE: That depends on what sort of information you have.

BRIMA SANDA: It is about Bai Bureh.

SHARPE: That may be so, but it has to be information leading to his capture for you to get the reward.

TARBET: Do you know where he is?

BRIMA SANDA: Yes.

SHARPE: You do? Where?

BRIMA SANDA: He is at Mahera.

TARBET: Mahera? Are you sure?

BRIMA SANDA: Yes. I am supposed to meet him there today.

SHARPE: *(To Tarbet)* You know the place?

TARBET: Sure. It's only a few miles from Romeni.

SHARPE: Good. Let's get some men together and go get him.

TARBET: Right. *(They both exit)*

BRIMA SANDA: *(Shouting after them)* What about my reward?

SHARPE: *(Off stage)* If and when we capture him. *(Brima Sanda is left alone on stage. He looks around rather furtively, then exits quickly. Almost immediately, we hear the sound of marching, and a group of policemen enter with Tarbet and Sharpe bringing up the rear, Tarbet shouting orders. They march across the stage and exit. After some time, they emerge from the opposite direction. Suddenly there are shouts and gunshots. There is chaos. The men are confused)*

TARBET: Take cover. Enemy attack.

*(The policemen begin to flee, some dropping their guns)*

SHARPE: Come back. Come back.

TARBET: Stand and fight. Cowards! Stand and fight!

(*The men pay no heed. Realizing they are going to be left alone, Tarbet and Sharpe also beat a retreat. One of the policemen seems to be injured and is limping off when a group of warriors enter at a rush. The policeman is captured. The men do a quick victory dance around him, then dissolve in laughter. Bai Bureh, Bai Suba and Bai Bangura enter*)

1st WARBOY: Did you see the white men?

2nd WARBOY: Like *Fritambo*. (*Mimicking them*)

BAI BANGURA: But look at this one. (*Pointing at policeman*) Black. (*Slaps him*) Black, like all of us.

BAI BUREH: Bring him here.

(*Policeman is dragged to him and forced to sit on the ground*)

POLICEMAN: (*Crying out in pain*) Aahh ...my foot o!

2nd WARBOY: (*Slapping him*) Shut up!

BAI BUREH: No! Leave him. (*The policeman is left whimpering on the ground*) Now my friend, tell, why are you fighting me?

(*The policeman continues whimpering. Bai Bangura kicks him*)

BAI BANGURA: Answer!

POLICEMAN: I... I... I ... am not f... f... fighting you.

BAI BUREH: You are not fighting me? You are fighting for my enemy and you say you are not fighting me?

POLICEMAN: Em... I mean... I am a policeman.

BAI BANGURA: You are a policeman, so?

POLICEMAN: I have to obey orders.

## The Patriot

BAI BUREH: You have to obey orders. So if your masters order you to kill your mother, you will kill her?

POLICEMAN: Ah, that is different.

BAI BUREH: I see. What about your brother? Will you kill your brother if your masters order you to do so? *(Policeman shakes his head)* Then why do you want to kill me? Why do you want to kill these men? *(Indicating warriors)*

POLICEMAN: B...B...But...

BAI BUREH: Where are you from? Are you not a Loko man?

POLICEMAN: I am Loko.

BAI BUREH: Puppet! Slave! I am a Loko too. Some of these men are Loko, some are Temne, and we are all fighting to save our country from being taken over by strangers. And you, a Loko man like me, you are fighting for these strangers who want to take away the lands of your forefathers.

POLICEMAN: I...

BAI BANGURA: Shut up! What do you want to say? Dog!

BAI BUREH: We are going to treat you the way we treat slaves. Then we will send you back to your friends, the other slaves fighting against their own people, so that you will tell them what happened to you. Any one of you we catch again ... *(Makes a sign to indicate slitting of throats)* Lie down. *(The policeman is reluctant to obey. The warriors grab him and stretch him out on the ground. Bai Bureh throws a whip to one of them who proceeds to whip the screaming policeman)*

BAI BUREH: Enough! Let him go.

*(The policeman is released and chased off)*

BAI BANGURA: That will teach him a lesson.

BAI BUREH: Let's go.

(*They all exit, but Bai Bangura stops at the entrance, removes his cap, symbolizing his resumption of the narrator's role. He moves back centre stage and addresses the audience*)

NARRATOR: For four months Bai Bureh held the initiative against the enemy forces. Forces better equipped and as they arrogantly believed, better trained. What they had failed to realize was that they were fighting in the bush and Bai Bureh was a master of bush fighting. Not only did they fail to arrest him as they had planned, but he constantly kept them under pressure. He controlled the countryside and prevented them from moving out of Karene, the district headquarter town. They could not collect their tax. But might usually overcomes right, and soon, things began to change.

(*He dons his cap and exits as Bai Bangura. Almost immediately, a policeman enters in a hurry*)

POLICEMAN: Major Tarbet! Major Tarbet! Major Tarbet! Come quick.

TARBET: (*Rushing in*) What is wrong with you? Are you mad? What do you mean, shouting my name like that?

POLICEMAN: Sorry sir. Sir…

TARBET: Attention!

POLICEMAN: Yes sir. (*Clicking awkwardly to attention*) Sir …

TARBET: Quiet!

POLICEMAN: Yes sir.

TARBET: (*After a suitable pause during which it is obvious the policeman is anxious to say something*) Now, what is it?

POLICEMAN: Sir, the patrol that went out this morning, enemy have attacked it. I saw them coming back … just now. Only four, four men.

## The Patriot

TARBET: What? Four? Are you sure?

POLICEMAN: Yes, sir.

TARBET: Out of thirty, only four … is Lieutenant Woods with them?

POLICEMAN: No sir, I did not see him. Maybe he is dead sir.

*(A group of four policemen stagger on. Two of them, including a sergeant are injured and are being helped by the others)*

TARBET: What happened to you? Where is the rest of the patrol?

SERGEANT: Dead sir. All dead.

TARBET: What about Lieutenant Woods? Is he …

SERGEANT: Dead sir. He was the first to be killed.

TARBET: Damn! That's the fourth officer in less than a month. But what happened? There were thirty of you.

SERGEANT: It was Bai Bureh sir. We were ambushed. We had no chance.

TARBET: But thirty of you?

SERGEANT: We ran into a stockade and whilst we were trying to overrun it we were attacked from behind by a group of warriors led by Bai Bureh himself.

TARBET: You saw him?

SERGEANT: Yes sir.

POLICEMAN: He was appearing and disappearing.

TARBET: What? What do you mean?

POLICEMAN: He would appear here, then over there, then there.

SERGEANT: We tried to escape sir, but whichever way we turned Bai Bureh was there, blocking the path. It was terrible sir. The men panicked.

(*Tarbet stands staring into space, deep in thought. The other wounded policeman begins to moan*)

TARBET: Take him away and see that he gets treated. (*The wounded man is carried away*) At this rate, we will all be wiped out if reinforcements don't arrive soon.

SERGEANT: Sir?

TARBET: Hm... Oh, nothing. You go and get yourself treated.

SERGEANT: Yes sir. (*He starts going*)

TARBET: Hopefully, reinforcements will arrive soon. Captain Sharpe has gone to Freetown to see the Governor.

SERGEANT: Very good sir.

(*They all exit. Cardew and Sharpe enter from the opposite entrance. They are carrying chairs which they place centre stage and sit*)

CARDEW: It's cooler out here. (*Pause*) Are you sure you are not exaggerating the gravity of the situation?

SHARPE: Far from it sir. If anything, I've understated it.

CARDEW: Come on.

SHARPE: I'm serious sir. The Frontier Police Force is not up to the task. Bai Bureh's forces have swamped them.

CARDEW: But there are over three hundred of them and several British officers have been posted to your district.

SHARPE: There's only Lieutenant Woods left sir.

CARDEW: How come?

### The Patriot

SHARPE: We've lost three officers in as many weeks.

CARDEW: What?

SHARPE: It's as serious as that sir. The men cannot operate effectively by themselves, and I don't know how long Woods will last. He doesn't have much experience.

CARDEW: He's been well trained. And you are only fighting a bunch of Temnes, not real soldiers.

SHARPE: *(Laughs bitterly)* Have you read Major Tarbet's report sir?

CARDEW: Yes, load of balderdash. How can he claim the Temne forces are superior to his?

SHARPE: It's a different kind of war sir. The men are not trained to fight in the bush. Most of the time they can't even see the enemy. We need real soldiers, experienced ones too. *(Pause)*

CARDEW: Hm… I'm reluctant to commit the West India Regiment.

SHARPE: But why sir?

CARDEW: I don't think it's really necessary. I don't believe you people have made enough effort. *(Sharpe is dumbfounded)* Yes Captain Sharpe, I believe involving the West India Regiment will be committing the government to unnecessary expense.

SHARPE: I don't think you are being fair sir. We have been fighting Bai Bureh's forces in the country where they are at home. After four months, we are still as far away from achieving our original objective as at the beginning and it's not from want of trying. Bai Bureh is in control of a very disciplined fighting force, which outnumbers our forces by about ten to one.

CARDEW: But you are better armed.

SHARPE: Even that is not really true any more. The Temnes seem to have been able to get hold of good quality guns, which I suspect have come from the French.

CARDEW: Hm!

SHARPE: We need those reinforcements sir and we need them now. In a few more weeks we are likely to be overrun.

CARDEW: *(After a lengthy pause)* Well, I will instruct … very reluctantly of course … I will instruct that B company of the West India Regiment be transferred to Karene district to prosecute the war against the Temne rebels.

SHARPE: That will be good sir. But can't we have two companies?

CARDEW: Two companies? No sir! You don't need two companies of soldiers to capture one rebel.

SHARPE: You don't seem to understand the situation sir. It's …

CARDEW: *(Beginning to get annoyed)* What do you mean I don't understand the situation? I understand it perfectly and I am not going to commit two companies of the West India Regiment at the same time. And that's that. (Pause) Now, I am also going to send Colonel Marshall to assume command of operations in your district. He is a well-experienced officer and I'm sure he will be able to bring things under control.

SHARPE: What about Major Tarbet?

CARDEW: Major Tarbet will still be in charge of the Frontier Police, but he will be answerable to Marshall.

SHARPE: When should we expect the soldiers?

CARDEW: I will give the instructions in the morning so they should get to you in about a week.

### The Patriot

SHARPE: Thank you sir.

CARDEW: Just make sure this Bai Bureh fellow is captured quickly so you can get on with collecting taxes.

SHARPE: We will try sir. *(Rising)* Shall I return the chair sir?

CARDEW: Yes please. I'm going in too. *(Rises)* Ah, I almost forgot. Don't you think we should raise the reward?

SHARPE: For Bai Bureh?

CARDEW: Yes. Maybe if we raise it to… say… one hundred pounds, we'll have people volunteering information about him.

SHARPE: Well… I guess it's worth trying.

CARDEW: Good. I'll issue a notice to that effect.

*(They both exit. Shortly after there is the sound of gunshots and shouting, women and children screaming. People dash across the stage. Shouts of "fire, fire" can be heard. Bai Bureh emerges from the wings, having been disturbed by the noise. He grabs a warrior who is dashing across the stage)*

BAI BUREH: What is happening?

WARBOY: Fire! They are burning the bush.

BAI BUREH: Who?

WARBOY: The British.

BAI BUREH: The British burning the bush?

WARBOY: Yes. They are setting fire to the bush. They are also burning houses. *(Bai Bureh releases him and he dashes out shouting)* Yebu! Yebu!

BAI BUREH: Isatu! Fatmata! …Fatmata!

*(The two women run in)*

ISATU: What is happening?

BAI BUREH: Get the children and go immediately to Rogbalan. Stay there till I either send for you or come myself.

FATMATA: Why? What is happening?

BAI BUREH: Do as you are told woman. Go!

ISATU: Are we being attacked?

BAI BUREH: Will you stop asking foolish questions and take the children away? Come on. Go!

(*The women exit. Almost immediately, Bai Bangura and Bai Suba rush in from opposite directions, with some of the warriors. Both begin talking at the same time*)

BAI BANGURA: They are burning the bush.

BAI SUBA: They are attacking.

BAI BUREH: (*Calmly*) I know. Get all the men together and let us move out quietly.

BAI SUBA: Move out? Are we going to give up the town without even fighting?

BAI BUREH: Yes. There is no point in fighting here.

BAI BANGURA: But we can't just leave the town for them.

BAI BUREH: We cannot fight here. They are burning the bush. If we do not move quickly, we are either going to get trapped in the fire or by the soldiers.

BAI SUBA: This is the third time they are doing this.

BAI BUREH: (*Reflectively*) Yes. There is a new man in charge. Marshall I think they call him. Maybe this is his way to fight.

BAI BANGURA: Burning farms and our towns?

## ✶ The Patriot ✶

BAI BUREH: They are determined to win at all costs.

BAI BANGURA: But why are they burning the bush and our farms?

BAI BUREH: When the bush is destroyed they will be able to see us easily.

BAI SUBA: But our farms, our houses...

BAI BUREH: When we are hungry we can't fight. *(Silence)*

BAI BANGURA: Some of the men no longer have their hearts in the fight.

BAI BUREH: It has started.

BAI SUBA: What?

*(Bai Bureh shrugs but doesn't reply. Silence. Suddenly there is a scream from off stage; it ends abruptly)*

BAI BUREH: What was that?

BAI SUBA: I am going to check. Hey, you! You and you! Come with me!

*(They exit. Expecting an attack, Bai Bureh signals to his men to take cover. After a short while a group of four warriors posted on guard duty come stumbling in, followed by Bai Suba)*

BAI BANGURA: What was it?

BAI SUBA: They have killed a white man.

BAI BUREH: A white man? Was he alone?

BAI SUBA: *(To* warriors) Answer!

1st WARBOY: Yes.

BAI BUREH: A soldier?

1st WARBOY: No.

BAI BUREH: Who was he?

2nd WARBOY: He said his name was Humpis.

BAI BANGURA: Humpis? Hum… Hum… Humphreys?

1st WARBOY: Yes, yes that was the name.

BAI BANGURA: *Ogbo!*

BAI BUREH: *(To Bai Bangura)* Do you know him?

BAI BANGURA: Mr. Humphreys? Yes, the man is a missionary.

BAI BUREH: What? A missionary? Are you sure?

BAI BANGURA: If it is Mr. Humphreys…

BAI BUREH: *(To a group of warriors)* Go and bring the body. *(They exit)* If it is the missionary, then you are finished. *(The culprits fall at his feet pleading)* Don't beg. I warned you.

1st WARBOY: We did not want to kill him.

2nd WARBOY: He forced us.

BAI BUREH: He forced you? He forced you to kill him?

2nd WARBOY: He refused to use another road.

BAI BUREH: He refused to use another road, so you killed him?

1st WARBOY: He wanted to come this way. We warned him. We told him not to use this road, to turn back. But he refused. He said he was not going to turn back. When we tried to stop him from coming here, he started to fight us.

BAI BUREH: And so you had to kill him? Why did you not bring him to me?

*(No response)*

BAI SUBA: Answer! Why did you not bring him here?

## The Patriot

2nd WARBOY: We...we... thought...

BAI BANGURA: You thought what? Had you not been warned?

*(The body of Mr. Humphrey is brought in and the Bais go over to look at it)*

BAI BANGURA: It's him.

BAI BUREH: The missionary?

BAI BANGURA: Yes.

BAI SUBA: *(He has been examining the body)* They cut his throat. *(Bai Bureh and Bai Bangura rush over to see)*

BAI BUREH: *(Boiling with anger)* You shall be treated the same way. *(The culprits begin pleading and wailing)* Take them away. *(They are dragged away. Bai Bureh moves over to the corpse and stands looking at it. There is an uneasy silence. He signals to some warriors)* Take him to Captain Sharpe in Port Loko. Tell him that Mr. Humphreys was killed without my permission and I have punished the men who killed him. Tell him I am sorry about Mr. Humphreys. Go! *(Warriors lift the body and exit)* Let us find another place to sleep. We cannot stay here anymore. Let us move on.

*(The men rise silently, pick up their things and exit. Bai Bangura remains behind. He watches them leave, then removes his cap, resuming the narrator role)*

NARRATOR: They burnt our farms, they burnt our towns. Even the forests were not spared. Then the rains came, and hunger stared us in the face. Attitudes began to change as men's bellies began to feel the rumblings of hunger and their hearts felt the fear of losing wives or children in their absence. Bai Bureh who had been surrounded by people willing to die for the freedom of their country began to find he was standing more and more alone. (*He hears the sounds of approaching people and quickly dons his cap. It is a group of three warriors who greet him on entering*)

WARBOY: *Obai impiari.*

BAI BANGURA: *Seke.* (*Pause*) Are you not going to join the others?

WARBOY: We are coming.

(*Bai Bangura and warriors exit. There is silence for a short while, and then a war song is raised in the background. It builds up to a crescendo, and then suddenly gunshots are heard. The song stops abruptly and is replaced by shouts and screams, then silence. Bai Bangura, Bai Suba and Bai Farima enter*)

BAI FARIMA: So, I think we should try and convince him to negotiate peace with the District Commissioner and the Governor.

BAI SUBA: You say you have stopped fighting. Have you negotiated peace with them?

BAI FARIMA: Well… they say it is Bai Bureh himself that has to talk to them.

BAI BANGURA: Then why have you stopped fighting?

BAI FARIMA: Can't you see that it is useless? Our men are dying from the soldiers' bullets, our women and children are starving, our houses, our farms, all destroyed.

BAI SUBA: So, you have surrendered?

BAI FARIMA: (*Evading the question*) They say we should all stop fighting and give ourselves up … including Bai Bureh … then they will talk with us.

(*Bai Bureh enters quietly and stands listening*)

BAI BANGURA: He will never agree to that.

BAI FARIMA: Talk to him. They are planning to send many more soldiers here. They are determined to defeat us. They will completely destroy our country if we continue fighting.

BAI SUBA: Whom will they rule? Are you saying we should give up our country to strangers?

BAI FARIMA: I am not saying that.

BAI BUREH: *(Quietly)* Then what are you saying? *(The chiefs are startled)* You are not saying we should give up our country to strangers, yet you say we should stop fighting. So, what are you saying we should do?

BAI FARIMA: *(Defiantly)* If we continue fighting, we will soon have no country. They will destroy it completely. Our women and children will die of hunger. Then, what would all the fighting and dying have been for?

*(Bai Bureh is struck by the truth of Bai Farima's words, which echo thoughts that have been plaguing him for some time. He seems to sag)*

BAI SUBA: *(To Bai Farima)* Coward!

BAI FARIMA: I am not a coward, and you know it.

BAI SUBA: Then why are you afraid to fight?

BAI FARIMA: I...

BAI BUREH: You say they are sending more troops here?

BAI FARIMA: Yes, two companies.

*(Bai Bangura has withdrawn from the action and now stands D.S.R. away from the group. He removes his cap, thus resuming the role of narrator, and stands watching)*

BAI BUREH: It is finished. *(He moves to sit, dejected and dispirited. Pause)* Alimami Rassin was right. It is wrong to fight.

BAI SUBA: So, we should have folded our arms and watched them take our country from us?

BAI BUREH: Fighting has not stopped them.

BAI SUBA: At least we fought like men to protect what is ours.

BAI BUREH: *(Lifelessly)* Yes, like men.

*(Silence. Bai Suba and Bai Farima look at each other, surprised at the change in Bai Bureh)*

BAI FARIMA: I… *(Silence)*

BAI BUREH: *(Sighs)* It is true, what Bai Farima has said. It is time to stop fighting.

BAI SUBA: But we can't just give up like that.

BAI BUREH: It is no use. The men's hearts are no longer in the fight. You know that. Everyday their numbers get smaller. They are going away quietly in the night. Who can blame them? Hunger and death are coming closer every day. No matter what we do now, we always seem to be trying to escape from the soldiers. *(Pause)* It is me they want. It is me they have wanted from the beginning. *(Pause)* Go home.

BAI SUBA: What?

BAI BUREH: Take your men and go back quietly to your homes. Use the bush paths and avoid the soldiers.

BAI FARIMA: What are you going to do?

BAI BUREH: I am going to give myself up to Captain Sharpe.

BAI SUBA: You can't go alone. We will all …

BAI BUREH: No! I go alone.

BAI SUBA: But you did not fight alone.

## The Patriot

BAI BUREH: I did not fight alone, but there is no reason for all of us to suffer when I can carry it alone.

BAI SUBA: The load belongs to all of us, so must all carry it. Anyway, how do you know they will not hang you?

BAI BUREH: An old man cannot run, but he knows how to hide. I know these people. You go home.

BAI FARIMA: *(Relieved)* Bai Bureh is right. He is the one they want. They are not worried about us. So, let us do what he wants and go home.

BAI BUREH: Yes, go home. You have fought well with me, but it is all over. Finished!

*(Bai Farima and Bai Suba exit reluctantly. Bai Bureh remains. He is motionless for sometime, lost in thought. He comes to a decision, rises and exits briskly. The sound of a dirge floats in from off stage. It seems to be rising and falling in volume. Against this background, the narrator speaks)*

NARRATOR: And so it all ended. The rest you know. This great man, exiled, pardoned, returned and died. Died a broken man. He had fought and lost, and in losing, we lost our freedom––a thing we are still struggling to regain. *(The whole cast begins to assemble on stage singing the dirge)* Do you now understand, or begin to understand the story of Bai Bureh, Kablai, the man who fought that we may be free from oppression? So, shall we sing a dirge for the death of freedom? *(The dirge rises to full volume. After a short while, the narrator signals for the singing to stop)* Or would you rather we ended the way we began?

*(The cast bursts into the opening song, "Bai Bureh was a Warrior," and scatters among the audience)*

# ☽ ☾
# THE POOL
# ☽ ☾

### BY
### TONIE FRENCH

# CHARACTERS

◆

| | |
|---|---|
| KHADAY KAMARA | Student at Typing institute |
| MABEL JONES | Student at Typing institute |
| AINA COLE | Student at Typing institute |
| MARION MACAULEY | Student at Typing institute |
| JAMES MACAULEY | Marion's father |
| ALICE MACAULEY | Marion's mother |
| MISS COKER | Owner of Typing institute |
| MR. BUCKLE | Teacher at Typing institute |
| IYA ALIMAMY | Khaday's mother |
| MR. JUSU | James' friend |

❰ The Pool ❱

# ACT ONE

◇◆◇

## Scene One

*(Curtain opens to reveal a stage set that is partitioned into three parts. The first part, stage right, doubles as the home of the Macauleys and a bar. The second part, center stage, features a teacher's desk. Adjacent to this desk is a door with an "office" sign on it. The typing institute staff use this entrance into the classroom. Students use this door only when they have some office business. This section also doubles as Khaday's house when the "office" sign is taken down. The typing pool classroom occupies the third section, downstage left and slightly center. There are desks, chairs, and typewriters dating back to the seventies in this section. There is also a door——stage left——that students use to enter the classroom. In this scene, Miss Coker is typing at teacher's desk in the typing pool. Mabel enters and crosses over to Miss Coker)*

MABEL: Miss Coker, yesterday, after you interviewed me, I went and told my friend and she says she wants to come too. So I brought her with me today. May I bring her in? *(Exits and enters with Khaday)*. Miss Coker, this is Khaday.

KHADAY: *(From a distance)* Good morning, Ma.

MISS COKER: Come here, child *(Khaday does not respond)*. Don't you understand English?

KHADAY: Of course I understand English. I got a grade one, and a one in language.

MISS COKER: What language?

KHADAY: English, of course.

MISS COKER: But you got a nine in good manners.

KHADAY: Mabel, you brought me here for such insult?

MISS COKER: Mabel, did you say this is your friend?

KHADAY: Are you ashamed to say that you are my friend?

MABEL: (Aside) Khaday, keep your voice down, I did not say that. She is older than you.

KHADAY: But I am paying for the lesson. *Lai lai* she has no right to talk to me like that.

MABEL: But she is old enough to be your mother.

KHADAY: So what? Even my mother watches what she says to me. I am not going to tolerate any nonsense from anyone. Let's get out of here. I have to meet a client in half an hour. You know how difficult it is to find transportation these days.

MABEL: Khaday, you must stop seeing him. He is too old for you.

KHADAY: Who cares how old he is if he pays the bills. I'm off.

(*Turns to exit*)

MISS COKER: Excuse me, Miss lady,

KHADAY: (*To Mabel*) She's talking to you.

MISS COKER: No, I was talking to you.

KHADAY: Who? Me?

MISS COKER: Yes.

KHADAY: Yes?

MISS COKER: Why do you want to attend this institute?

## The Pool

KHADAY: Because Mabel asked me and I have nothing better to do.

MISS COKER: Is that the only reason?

KHADAY: I haven't even thought about it.

MISS COKER: What do you do all day? Don't you have a job?

KHADAY: Job? Since I left school I have been looking for work. And the only one I got is at night. I find it pays well. I enjoy myself very much. I go to the best places. I wear expensive clothes.

MISS COKER: How long are you going to be doing this… this job?

KHADAY: For as long as it pays well.

MISS COKER: If you are so well paid, then, you do not need to attend my classes.

MABEL: Khaday…

KHADAY: *Bo*, go ahead and tell her I don't take any nonsense. Otherwise I will leave.

MABEL: Miss Coker, I had no idea Khaday would behave like this.

MISS COKER: Never mind my dear. Obviously, she doesn't know what to do with the good friend that she has. I only hope she doesn't find out too late.

KHADAY: (*To Mabel*) What does she mean?

MISS COKER: Here. (*Hands application form to Khaday*) Take this home. Read it carefully and fill it out. Bring it back here if you're still interested in this class.

KHADAY: (*Walks up to Miss Coker, snatches form and exits. Lights Out*)

《 *Tonie French* 》

# Scene Two

(*Classroom in the typing pool. Marion is in her seat. Aina is at Mr. Buckle's desk*)

MR. BUCKLE: How in heaven's name do you hope to take the Pitman exam and pass it, if you do a slipshod job like this?

AINA: Mr. Buckle, you know my problem.

MR. BUCKLE: What's your problem?

AINA: I'm a widow with four children all under ten years of age. I'm only doing this so I can get a better paying job. My husband died and left me nothing. All the children's responsibilities are on my shoulders.

MR. BUCKLE: Aina?

AINA: Sir?

MR. BUCKLE: Aina?

AINA: Yes sir?

MR. BUCKLE: I know all that, but this is a simple composition. An essay on the last book you read.

AINA: Mr. Buckle, when I leave here and I get home, I have to start preparing the meal and by the time I am finished, I am so tired that all I am fit for is my bed.

MR. BUCKLE: So why do you bother to come to the class if you cannot do your homework properly?

AINA: Mr. Buckle, I'm sorry.

MR. BUCKLE: Oh, you're always sorry.

AINA: Ehhh, Mr. Buckle, what else do you want me to say? I don't remember the last time I read a book in my life. So

## ❰ The Pool ❱

it is difficult to write an essay about the last book I read. I'm sorry.

MR. BUCKLE: Don't you read your children's books? Surely you can write an essay on that.

AINA: Mr. Buckle, my eldest is ten years old. He got books from his cousin. Most of the pages are missing and the others are badly scratched. I don't have the patience to read those books.

MR. BUCKLE: So what do you read? *Woman's Own?*

AINA: What's that?

MR. BUCKLE: You mean you haven't heard of *Woman's Own?*

AINA: No, Mr. Buckle.

MR. BUCKLE: I see. It's a female magazine which shows women how to apply makeup and look slim.

AINA: Mr. Buckle, where would I get money from to buy makeup?

MR. BUCKLE: How would I know?

AINA: Mr. Buckle, why are you always picking on me?

MR. BUCKLE: Oh, am I? I...I didn't realize that.

AINA: You're always picking on me. If it is not one thing, it is another. Why are you always picking on me?

MR. BUCKLE: Because all the other girls are making an effort and you are the only one who always gets low marks. I won't tolerate this any more. You either shape up or I hand you over to Miss Coker. And about your attitude in English class...

AINA: Don't tell Miss Coker. If she forces me out of here, I have no future (*a knock on the door*).

MR. BUCKLE: Who is it?

MISS COKER: (*Sticks head through office door but does not enter*) Mr. Buckle?

MR. BUCKLE: Yes madam? (*He moves from desk to door. Goes back to desk to pick up folder*)

MR. BUCKLE: Excuse me, ladies. (*Exits*)

MARION: Miss Aina, why is Mr. Buckle always picking on you?

AINA: Marion, Mr. Buckle isn't picking on me. He is right. I cannot cope with the work here. Perhaps I should leave. (*Begins sobbing with her head down. Mabel enters*)

MABEL: What are you doing now Marion? Why are you making Miss Aina cry like this?

MARION: Who? Me?

MABEL: Yes, you, Marion Macauley.

MARION: You and your friend are the same. You come in here and don't know what is happening and you start shouting at me.

AINA: Girls, girls, please don't quarrel on my account. Marion, Mr. Buckle isn't picking on me. You girls are lucky your brains are still young. For me it is different.

MARION: But Miss Aina, once you get book learning in school it stays with you for the rest of your life. You're always going on about the school you went to.

AINA: But do you know what happened to me after I left school?

MARION: Miss Aina, what happened to you?

MABEL: Ah, Marion, you're too inquisitive. Leave the woman's private business alone. She may not want to talk about it.

## ❰ The Pool ❱

MARION: Miss Aina, please tell me. (*Aina starts crying again*)

MABEL: Now look what you've done. Miss Aina, wipe your face. Mr. Buckle will be here soon.

MARION: Mabel, it's not good to keep a problem to yourself. It causes hypertension.

MABEL: Hey, Dr. Marion.

MARION: It's true! It's better to tell someone. What's the saying? "A problem shared is a problem halved."

MABEL: Suppose Miss Aina told you her problem. What would you do? You're still living with your parents. You're not earning any money on your own. In fact, your parents pay for your fees here. So how can you help Miss Aina?

MARION: Mabel, it's not every problem that is solved with money.

MABEL: Oh yeah? Show me one problem that you don't solve with money. (*Mr. Buckle enters*)

MR. BUCKLE: Aina, Miss Coker would like to have a word with you before you go home today… Did you hear me?

AINA: Mr. Buckle, I'm not feeling well. I think I will go home. I will see Miss Coker tomorrow. (*Picks up bag and leaves*)

MR. BUCKLE: What's the matter with her? (*Notices Mabel*) I say Miss Lady, when did you come in here? You were not here when I took the attendance. Anyway, look for your paper in this pile and give the rest to me.

MABEL: Aina Cole.

MR. BUCKLE: Give that to me.

MABEL: Mabel Jones. (*Keeps her own paper*) Khaday Kamara.

MR. BUCKLE: Give that to me as well.

《 *Tonie French* 》

MABEL: Mr. Buckle can I pick it for her? She's my friend.

MR. BUCKLE: She should see her marks first. Why is she not here anyway?

MARION: She was on duty last night.

MR. BUCKLE: Ah, praise God. She works during the night and studies during the day. Quite sensible. That girl will go far. She writes very good essays and she's very good in English.

MARION: And all other things.

MR. BUCKLE: What did you say, Marion? (*Marion giggles*) Come on. Let's share the joke.

MABEL: It's not a joke, Mr. Buckle.

MARION: Who asked you? Is your name Marion?

MABEL: Why are you shouting at me?

MARION: I'm not shouting!

MABEL: Mind your own business. (*She throws Marion's paper at her*)

MARION: Birds of a feather.

MABEL: I don't go out at night, o. I stay at home and….

MR. BUCKLE: Ladies. (*School bell rings*) Hmmm. Look through your vocabulary. We will discuss the corrections tomorrow. (*Exits*)

MARION: How do you spell receiving?

MABEL: "E before I after C."

MARION: What?

MABEL: "E before I after C."

MARION: What's that?

☾ **The Pool** ☽

MABEL: That's how we were taught to remember spellings. R-e-c-e-i-v-i-n-g. So what did you get?

MARION: I just made it. I got 50. And you?

MABEL: I got 55 and Khaday got 70.

MARION: (*Not too happy at the news*) I'm hungry. It's lunchtime. Let's go and have something to eat. What do you have?

MABEL: You just go ahead.

MARION: I have bread and omelet. Are you coming? (*No answer. Starts to leave. Khaday enters. They eye each other*)

KHADAY: (*To Marion*) What are you looking at? (*Marion exits*)

MABEL: Khaday, you promised me you would be regular this week. You made me come late to class today. I stayed there waiting for you so that we could walk together.

KHADAY: I'm tired. (*She sits*)

MABEL: Of course you're tired. (*Look of disgust and pity. Khaday takes wallet out of her bag and hands money to Mabel*)

KHADAY: Count this for me.

MABEL: What's here? (*Takes money*) With you dressed the way you are, any fool walking in would know what you have been up to. Haven't you been home yet?

KHADAY: You know I don't like going home before I count my money. If my mother offers to count it, half of it disappears.

MABEL: Hey, you have dollars.

KHADAY: Give me that. These are special. I'm saving for my ticket.

MABEL: And who will give you a visa?

KHADAY: Honestly Mabel, you talk as though what I do is written all over my face. If I'm out of these working clothes, I look quite respectable.

MABEL: I know, and I wish you would stay out of those working clothes permanently. (*Hands money back*) By the way, you had very good marks for the essay.

KHADAY: Where is the paper?

MABEL: Mr. Buckle wouldn't give it to me. You know how stiff he is. He says that you should be the first to see your marks. He does not know what you do at night. He thinks you have a job where you are permanently on night duty and study during the day.

KHADAY: Well.

MABEL: He thinks very highly of you.

KHADAY: Well, what do you know?

MABEL: Except for that loud mouth Marion.

KHADAY: What did she have to say? Tell me.

MABEL: Easy Khaday. I handled it quickly.

KHADAY: Mabel, thank you for being a friend.

MABEL: But Khaday, you must try to… to…

KHADAY: Are you going to start preaching at me again?

MABEL: No.

KHADAY: Good. What do you have to eat? I'm hungry.

MABEL: You know I never bring any lunch. I had my leftover rice for breakfast and that's it until I get home and have my evening meal.

☾ **The Pool** ☽

KHADAY: I'm going to treat you today. Let's go to Lamar and eat chicken, chips, and salad.

MABEL: How can you eat chips and salad?

KHADAY: Just come and see.

MABEL: We should be back in half an hour.

KHADAY: Mabel, just for today, relax and enjoy the good life.

MABEL: And where will the good life lead me?

KHADAY: Mabel, try to understand. I'm not trying to lure you to my kind of life. We've been friends ever since we were little. You have a mind of your own. Nothing I do now will influence you to the extent that you want to follow my footsteps. There are many girls who want to be friends with me, Mabel, but you are the only one I trust. The only one. (*She hugs Mabel*)

MABEL: Khaday, you're crying.

KHADAY: I am tired, that's all.

*Lights Out.*

## Scene Three

(*At a restaurant*)

JAMES: I don't think Khaday is coming. It's late. I have to get back to the office. We will leave a message with the waiter. I say, waiter! Oh, these boys. They're not business-minded at all. They serve us one drink and they disappear.

JUSU: Well, Mark, I'm tired of talking to them. Each time I come here, I tell the proprietor about the way things are abroad. I mean the waiters greet and follow you around to make sure you get served. And it follows of course, the more you order, the more tips they get. But here they are not business-minded at all. (*Mabel and Khaday appear at the door*). Hello, who are these?

JAMES: Ah, that's her.

JUSU: And who is that with her?

JAMES: I don't know, maybe her friend.

JUSU: (*Adjusts tie*) Do you think she will like me?

JAMES: (*Adjusts Jusu's tie for him*) Well, let's hope so.

JUSU: I hope she is as good as you say your Khaday is.

JAMES: Maybe.

JUSU: Tell me, how did you meet Khaday?

JAMES: Well, you know my problem at home.

JUSU: Yes, I do indeed. It has been such a long time since I saw the missus. She still refuses to go anywhere with you?

JAMES: Unfortunately, yes.

JUSU: Well, okay. Tell me about your Khaday.

JAMES: Well you know how it is in our position.

JUSU: She applied for a job?

JAMES: Yes, but this one was innocent.

JUSU: Wait for me man. You mean she was intact when you first…uh…the very first time? Wow! You should be proud man! You should be proud! You don't get them like that anymore. They are all too fast for anyone's comfort.

JAMES: Damn it man, she is the same age as my daughter, if not younger.

## ☾ The Pool ☽

JUSU: Come on, pull yourself together man. The other one with her doesn't look that worldly wise either (*laughs*). Maybe I will be lucky like you.

JAMES: Khaday is a good girl, really. (*Khaday enters followed by a reluctant Mabel*) Hello, I thought you had changed your mind. (*Hugs Khaday*) This is Mr. Jusu.

KHADAY: Delighted to meet you, Mr. Jusu. (*They shake hands*) This is my friend Mabel. (*Roughly pulls Mabel closer to Jusu*)

MABEL: How are you sir?

KHADAY: Sorry James, I was held up.

JAMES: So do you want a drink or shall we go? You know I have to get back to the office.

MABEL: Khaday, what about me? Are you going to leave me here?

JUSU: Oh, my dear Mabel, don't you trust me?

MABEL: (*Scared*) No sir, I mean, yes sir.

KHADAY: Oh, relax Mabel, he won't eat you. (*Jusu laughs hysterically. This scares Mabel even more*)

MABEL: Khaday, I'm coming with you.

KHADAY: Where will we go?

MABEL: To the Institute.

JAMES: Which Institute?

JUSU: Mark, I say Mark, (*Pulls James aside*) I don't seem to have much luck. Talk about being green, this one takes the cake (*Both laugh and he walks over to Mabel*). What do you think I'll do to you in this public place? I'm not that hungry, I can wait until we get to the hotel.

MABEL: (*Alarmed*) To where?

JUSU: The hotel is upstairs.

KHADAY: James and I are going upstairs. We'll be right back.

MABEL: Ehh???

KHADAY: Should I meet you here?

JAMES: Come on, Khaday, we don't have all day.

KHADAY: (*Angry*) For goodness sake James, if you are in such a hurry let's fix another appointment. Mabel is my friend. I brought her here. If she is upset, I won't leave her.

JUSU: (*Tries to hug Mabel*) Oh Mabel darling. (*Mabel pushes him off*)

MABEL: What are you doing? (*Sends Jusu sprawling on the floor. He gets up angrily and puts some money on the table for Mabel*)

JUSU: Take this. Mark, I'm off. This girl is not serious. Perhaps next time I'll be lucky. (*Exits*)

MABEL: What does he mean by this? (*Points to money*)

KHADAY: Take the money and let's go.

JAMES: And what about me?

KHADAY: Can't you see my friend is upset?

JAMES: Your friend? After all that I've done for you?

KHADAY: James, please try and understand.

JAMES: I'm trying, but I am not pleased. (*Khaday comforts Mabel, goes to whisper something in James' ear. James exits. Khaday and Mabel laugh out loud in victory*)

*Lights Out*

## Scene Four

*(Same Day at the typing pool)*

MISS COKER: So that was what happened. Now tell me honestly, how are you getting on with Mr. Buckle? *(Silence)* Aina?

AINA: Yes, Miss C?

MISS COKER: Did you hear what I said?

AINA: Yes, Miss C.

MISS COKER: Then I would like an answer. The last time Mr. Buckle spoke to me about you, you had not completed an assignment he had given you. You had not completed it satisfactorily. Is that correct?

AINA: Yes, Miss C.

MISS COKER: But why is that Aina?

AINA: Well, Miss C, Mr. Buckle asked us to write an essay about the last book we read and I don't remember the last time I read a book in my life. As for newspapers, that is out of the question. I just can't afford to buy them.

MISS COKER: Then what did you write about?

AINA: I don't remember. I haven't seen Mr. Buckle since to collect my paper from him.

MISS COKER: Don't you want to continue your classes here?

AINA: I want to continue. You yourself said that the typewriting is improving but it is the English and the shorthand that are very difficult to handle.

MISS COKER: So what do you want to do?

AINA: Well, I was thinking that if you would let me continue with the typing and give up the shorthand and the English...

MISS COKER: I am tempted to say yes but, on the other hand, looking back a couple of years from now, you would wish you had persevered and taken all three subjects here.

AINA: But I am taking them seriously, Miss C.

MISS COKER: This is a misconception young people have about being a good secretary. They do not want to concentrate on English but they want to become excellent typists. How do you know that the draft you are typing is correct if your English is not good? Bosses will not admit it, but they do appreciate an intelligent and smart secretary who will tactfully correct their mistakes. You can only do that if your English is good. As for the shorthand, well, you definitely need good English and a good ear. If you persevere with English, you will find shorthand a little easier. (*Buckle enters*)

MR. BUCKLE: Excuse me. I hope I'm not interrupting anything. Aina, I have not seen you since that day.

AINA: Mr. Buckle, I'm sorry, I have not been to collect my paper.

MISS COKER: Please sit down, Mr. Buckle.

MR. BUCKLE: Yes, of course. (*Sits*) Forget about collecting your paper, you haven't been in class since.

AINA: I'm sorry.

MISS COKER: Is this true Aina? That you haven't been in class since you did the last exercise?

AINA: Yes, Miss Coker.

MISS COKER: But why is this Aina?

## ☾ The Pool ☽

AINA: Miss Coker, I am forty years old. All the other girls in the class are in their teens. If I had been fast, they would have been my children. It is very difficult to be criticized in front of them all the time.

MR. BUCKLE: (*Excited*) I'm forty years old too. I have never been married. I don't have children. I never thought you were that old. You can pass for a twenty-five year old. You see, it is very difficult to understand young girls. But you are always chatting with them. You seem so close to them. When they have a joke, they share it with you. You are their friend. I am just the outsider.

MISS COKER: Just a minute, Mr. Buckle. Do I hear you two right? Are you telling me that Aina's relationship with the other girls in the class is affecting the way you teach them?

MR. BUCKLE: No madam. What I am saying…

MISS COKER: If you find out that teaching the whole class together is difficult because of the difference in age, would you consider giving private lessons to someone like Aina?

AINA: Miss Coker, where would I get the money from to pay for private lessons? I can barely pay for my fees here.

MISS COKER: (*To Buckle*) You insist on your fee, or your reputation as an excellent teacher?

AINA: Out of the question. The neighbors with whom I leave my children would like me to pick them up at two after four.

MISS COKER: Aina, don't you think you should give Mr. Buckle a chance to speak for himself.

MR. BUCKLE: I would like to give Aina lessons. You see, I don't have much to do at home except mark homework.

And that takes no time at all. As a matter of fact, we could have the private lesson out here.

MISS COKER: Mr. Buckle, come to see me about it then. Aina (*Takes Aina aside*)

AINA: Miss C. thank you very much for the time spent with me. I really appreciate it. May God bless you.

MISS COKER: You're most welcome, my dear (*Aina exits. To Mr. Buckle*) You seem suddenly happy. I wonder why.

MR. BUCKLE: Oh, I do?

MISS COKER: You came to see me about something.

MR. BUCKLE: Did I?

MISS COKER: What is it?

MR. BUCKLE: I have forgotten. The next period is here already. I'll see you later. (*School bell rings. Buckle exits*)

(*Marion, Mabel, and Khaday enter class and take their seats*)

MISS COKER: Please turn to page 132. I'm going to time you. It's now 1:30. I will be back at 2 to check your work. Comport yourselves. (*Students begin typing as she exits*)

KHADAY: Shit.

MABEL: Khaday!

KHADAY: What?

MABEL: Mind your language.

KHADAY: I made a mistake.

MABEL: No foul language.

MARION: Shut up you two for goodness sake. The rest of us are trying to concentrate.

KHADAY: And so the story E-N-D-E-D. Full stop. Finish.

## ❨ The Pool ❩

AINA: Khaday, you are impossible.

KHADAY: Why?

AINA: The rest of us are still struggling and you're finished already?

KHADAY: No I'm not.

MABEL: Yes, you are.

KHADAY: No I'm not.

AINA: Stop being modest, the last time we did an essay, you had the best mark. And you're hardly ever in class.

KHADAY: I read a lot.

MABEL: Okay, you read a lot. We accept that. But how do you explain finishing typing in record time?

KHADAY: Finishing in record time isn't the thing. Making as few mistakes as possible is what's important.

AINA: Let me see your sheet.

KHADAY: My what? When I said it just now, Mabel screamed as if I had killed her mother. But when Miss Aina says it, it's alright.

MARION: Well, she's older than us so she can…

KHADAY: I know you will put your big mouth in it.

MARION: Who has a big mouth?

KHADAY: That's not all; you are stupid as well.

MARION: Are you telling me I'm stupid?

KHADAY: My dear lady, if you weren't stupid you'd know the difference between shit and sheet.

AINA: Oh, oh, now I understand what Miss Coker meant. If you have good English, your shorthand and typing would be better. Perhaps I should take up that offer of private lessons with Mr. Buckle after all. (*Marion giggles*)

KHADAY: You see? Stupid.

MARION: Who is stupid?

KHADAY: That's the second time you're asking the same question.

AINA: Let me see your paper. (*Picks up Khaday's paper*) "And they all lived happily in the house and that is how the story ended."

MABEL: How many errors?

AINA: Guess.

MABEL: Four?

AINA: How did you guess? You two know each other too well.

KHADAY: Is everyone else finished? I'm hungry.

MARION: But we have just had some lunch.

KHADAY: I didn't have any lunch. I wish I could go back to Lamar. Mabel, do you remember when we went there the other time? (*Laughs*)

MABEL: I don't want to talk about it.

KHADAY: You remember that man who wanted to take you out?

MABEL: Khaday!

KHADAY: I thought he was very funny.

MARION: Don't you ever talk about anything else? Boys, boys, boys, all the time!

KHADAY: Not boys my dear. Men. Go ahead and vomit.

## ☾ The Pool ☽

MARION: Why should I vomit, just because you insist on talking about men all the time? My mommy says I should not encourage any boy until after my studies. As for my father, he just about bursts with anger if any man, beside him, is around our house. That's why our houseboy is a very old man. He has been with us since before I was born.

AINA: You see Khaday, she's daddy's favorite child.

KHADAY: Miss Aina, what do you think I am? I'm also a favorite child. Her father thinks she's the only child in this world. If he doesn't have time for it during the week, he takes out on Sunday. Imagine that. Every Sunday!

MARION: Let me tell you, I am the only child of my parents. Sometimes it is nice, other times it isn't. We have everything at home but I still wish I had someone to share with.

KHADAY: I am the oldest in my family. My mother made all the sacrifices and spent every cent she could spare on my schooling. I plan to go to university, but she cannot understand why I want to learn anything more. She thinks I can work anywhere. How do I explain to her that jobs are hard to come by these days——even for university graduates, let alone us? It is even worse for girls than it is for boys. Girls have to (*sways hips*) or else no way. These big men, they live double lives. They tie chastity belts on their daughters yet they want to know the color of panties everybody else's daughter is wearing.

MARION: All that I know is that my own father is not like that. (*Exits*)

KHADAY: Sleeping beauty. One day she will wake up and find not Prince Charming but the devil himself in the shape of a father.

MABEL: But, why are you always picking on Marion? What have you got against her?

KHADAY: You remember when we went to Lamar?

AINA: Yes, that's what we were talking about when all the mix up began.

KHADAY: Miss Aina, this my friend let me down. He couldn't have done anything there. The only thing the man wanted was a little (*rubs fingers together*) "play-play."

MABEL: I don't know. You never know where "play-play" will lead to; the next thing, I would be pregnant. My father would kill me.

KHADAY: You could have walked out of that place with fifty thousand Leones, easy.

MABEL: You have that kind of money?

KHADAY: Where will I get it from?

MABEL: Khaday, you mean you did not have any money that day?

KHADAY: Of course I did, I had enough money to buy myself a drink and I had my transport fare home.

MABEL: So who would have paid for the lunch?

KHADAY: Marion's father.

MABEL: So you know him? Where did you meet him? Have you been to their house?

KHADAY: That was him there at Lamar who wanted to take my clothes off like he does almost every lunchtime. That day I was tired so I decided to take you with me. When it is about two or three of us, he's usually a little restrained.

MABEL: (*Shocked*) So that's the famous James Macauley? (*Marion enters*)

KHADAY: Miss Aina, I hear you're with Mr. B?

## The Pool

MARION: Who told you that?

AINA: Who is Mr. B?

MARION: Khaday, where did you get that information from? We stay here with Miss Aina day in and day out. We don't see or hear anything. You walk in here one day and you start throwing hints.

KHADAY: I use my eyes. In my game, you have to be able to use your eyes.

AINA: What are you two girls going on about? Who is Mr. B?

KHADAY: (*Whispers to Aina*) Mr. Buckle.

AINA: Ahhhhh, I didn't even get it.

MARION: Khaday, what does it feel like? You know, what you do?

KHADAY: Why don't you join me one night, baby? Then you can find out first hand. You'll be surprised whom you will meet.

*Lights Out*

## ACT TWO

### Scene One

*(The living room in Khaday's house. Sparsely furnished)*

IYA: Khaday, Khaday.

KHADAY: What is it?

IYA: He is here. Do you not hear him blowing his horn? You're not even dressed yet. Where is he taking you today?

KHADAY: Iya, I am tired today. I'm not going anywhere with anyone. Leave me alone.

IYA: I like it when you pretend to be annoyed. It suits you well.

KHADAY: Who says I'm annoyed?

IYA: Well I thought you were annoyed. Khaday, who was that teacher? The one who walks like this? (*Imitates Miss Coker's gait*)

KHADAY: Oh. Miss Coker. That one, she is like a mother to us in that school. If you don't go for one day, she is so worried.

IYA: But tell me something, Khaday, why are you still going to school? Haven't you learned enough book? What is it you had the other day at your school when they gave you all those *boku boku* books? I was so proud. The woman who was sitting near me kept saying: "Ahh this *pekin*, she's so clever."

## ☾ The Pool ☽

Khaday: That was our prize-giving ceremony.

IYA: It was? (*Car horn is heard*)

IYA: You see… the man is still waiting. Let's go!

KHADAY: I'm not going anywhere today.

IYA: Look, if you were up country, you would have been married and had three children by now.

KHADAY: But the man doesn't want to marry me. Neither does he want me to have any children for him.

IYA: Then why do you go out with him?

KHADAY: Iya Alimamy, are you asking me that question?

IYA: Don't disrespect me. The man is blowing his horn and you are not going? Wait. Let me bring your clothes. (*Exits and returns with clothes*) Which of these two do you want to wear? Here, wear this.

KHADAY: I feel so ashamed each time I go to classes with those girls.

IYA: Why should you be ashamed? Are you not more beautiful than all of them? Don't you dress well? I don't know what's wrong with you today. If you know how proud I am of you…

KHADAY: I wish I could say that about myself. I feel so dirty each time I go with these men.

IYA: But they give you *boku boku* money. Khaday, you're a very good daughter to me. Look at this *lappa*. Do you remember when you got it for me? The people in this compound were so jealous. They can never afford to buy this type of *lappa*.

KHADAY: Iya Alimamy. You sound as if I owe you something and I have to pay it back.

IYA: Owe me something? Wait Khaday. All those years I was walking down to King Jimmy Market barefooted, under rain and under sun, your father did not care. I starved myself to get school fees for you. Your father always told me "if you see me bring a bag of rice into this house, you should be grateful. If you want your children to go to school, it is not my business" and now you're asking me if you owe me something? Of course you owe me something. Let me tell you something else. I'm not getting young. Your father is marrying a wife every blessed day. But I am determined to make something good out of you.

KHADAY: But Mama, how are you going to make something good out of me if I go on like this? Everyday a new man, *bo*? Except for the three regular customers I have?

IYA: Have you not heard the saying, "*Wan man nor de full box?*" A single man can't satisfy.

KHADAY: Well, all my years in this house I have never seen you look at any other man except my father and your box is not full.

IYA: Do you want your father to kill me? He is entitled to marry as many wives as he wants but I should not do anything to draw attention to myself.

KHADAY: Then how do you explain your wanting me to go out with so many different men? Just because you expect me to pay the fees of my younger brothers and sisters and buy you expensive *lappas*? (*Horn blares*)

IYA: You see? The man is waiting. Come on, let's go. (*Pushes a reluctant Khaday to the room to get dressed*)

*Lights Out*

☾ The Pool ☽

# Scene Two

(*The Home of the Macauleys. They are having breakfast*)

JAMES: That was a very nice breakfast, Marion. You're fast becoming an expert in the kitchen.

ALICE: Marion did not cook breakfast, I did.

JAMES: Oh.

MARION: Daddy, is that all you're going to say? "Oh?"

ALICE: Marion, hurry up, your father will be leaving soon. You know you will be late if you go by public transport.

JAMES: Let the driver take her and come back for me.

MARION: Oh yes, please mommy.

ALICE: Well, in that case, I will go with Marion to pick up a few things from the supermarket for lunch this afternoon. Let me get my purse.

JAMES: Well, we might as well all go together.

ALICE: Oh well, in that case, I'll go in my own car later on.

MARION: Mommy, why are you being such a spoiled sport?

ALICE: What makes me a spoiled sport, Marion?

JAMES: Ladies, ladies where are we now? Are we all going together or is Marion going alone?

ALICE: I'm staying at home. You go with Marion.

JAMES: Why don't the two of us, uh, you and I talk for a few moments until the driver comes back from dropping Marion at Miss Coker's Institute.

MARION: Excuse me, I'll be back. (*Runs out*)

ALICE: Marion, Marion, wait for your father. He will be late for work. (*The car is heard leaving*)

JAMES: (*Quite pleased*) They are gone.

ALICE: Yes, I heard.

JAMES: Thank you for a lovely breakfast. (*Hugs Alice*)

ALICE: (*Shrugs him off*) I have to clear the table.

JAMES: Since when did you start doing dishes in this house? What does the boy do when you wash the dishes?

ALICE: I have to clear the table.

JAMES: Alright. Why are you always running away from me?

ALICE: Who says I'm running away?

JAMES: Even Marion has noticed. That's why she wanted to get out of the house fast so that we could be alone together.

ALICE: We sleep in the same bed, how much more alone can we be?

JAMES: Sleeping in the same bed is not always the same as being alone. Most nights when I come home, you're fast asleep.

ALICE: You always come back late and at the end of the day, I'm tired and I want to sleep.

JAMES: But I'm usually home by eight, the latest. And that's when I've been to the club after work.

ALICE: Look, what is it you want to talk to me about? You're going to bring your friends home to lunch, aren't you?

JAMES: Yes I am. But this is very important. If you cannot make it, I'll take them out for lunch.

## ☾ The Pool ☽

ALICE: If you stop all this nonsense and let me go to the supermarket, I'll be back in time to finish up. I already started the sauce yesterday.

JAMES: Never mind. (*Takes wife from breakfast table to living area. They sit on sofa and he tries to be romantic*)

ALICE: (*Shrugs him off*) What is all this about? A grown man of a twenty-one year old daughter behaving like a little boy?

JAMES: Let's just say, I'm in love all over again.

ALICE: What?

JAMES: I never stopped loving you since the first day I set my eyes on you. You still look good, babe. (*Tries to hug her*)

ALICE: Are you mad?

JAMES: Don't you believe me?

ALICE: Being in love is for young people.

JAMES: You see, you drive me crazy. Each time I make an attempt to come near you, you shove me off. What do you want me to do? Become a priest?

ALICE: That's a sacrilege.

JAMES: Not at all. Not at all. You do not expect a healthy man like me with a wife at home to be treated like this.

ALICE: How are you being treated in this house? Food is on the table and on time. Your clothes are washed and ironed. The house is well kept. Your friends are well treated when you bring them home. I think I do my best so you have no right to complain.

JAMES: I'm not complaining. I will say, lets go out on Sunday and you refuse to go. You prefer to be cooped up in this house like an old woman. For goodness sake, Alice, wake up and live. Life is too short.

ALICE: Have I ever stopped you from doing what you wanted to do? Have I ever interfered in your life?

JAMES: Never, but I goddamn wish you would. You're my wife, not a housekeeper. Everybody knows about us. We never go anywhere together. Your friend spent three weeks with us in this house. Her husband has invited us for holidays in Banjul. Would you get out of this house and go? Never. Whenever I travel abroad, I bring you something. All the thanks I get is, "Oh, you're too extravagant… but this is too expensive." Alice, let's try to be happy again, we've still got time. (*Sound of car arriving*)

ALICE: Your car is here.

JAMES: Oh, never mind the car. This is very important.

ALICE: You're late enough as it is. (*Marion enters*)

MARION: Hello, you two. I forgot my homework behind. Dad, will you drop me off at the institute? Or perhaps you are taking the day off for a change? Hey mommy?

ALICE: What?

MARION: I think daddy should spend the day at home?

ALICE: What will he be doing at home all day?

JAMES: Helping you around the house, of course.

ALICE: No such thing. (*Gets up and exits to bedroom; returns with James's briefcase and coat. He takes them and exits with Marion*) Foolish man.

*Lights Out*

## ☾ The Pool ☽

# Scene Three

(*Morning class at the Typing Pool*)

AINA: At least when I'm here, I can rest from their shouting and their fighting.

MARION: Miss Aina, how old is Junior? He's the oldest isn't he?

AINA: Yes, he is.

MARION: I won't like to be called Junior. I think it is silly calling someone Junior.

AINA: Well, what can you do? He is the first-born. He is a boy; he's the first grandchild; so he has all the qualifications for being called Junior. He is ten and he is the spitting image of his father.

MARION: Talking about fathers, Miss Aina, why is it that Khaday's always going on about my father? I don't like it. I wish she would stop doing that.

AINA: I understand how you feel. When I was young, I did not appreciate anybody saying bad things about my father. But the older I got, the more I understood why my mother was so unhappy.

MARION: What was your father doing to your mother?

AINA: He got beastly drunk sometimes and would beat her.

MARION: That's terrible. I have never seen my father raise his hand to my mother. One thing I notice though is that they hardly ever talk to each other. Otherwise, he comes home fairly early. And he doesn't go out again except to the club. Sometimes he takes a trip up to the country.

AINA: Those are the sly ones––like cats. They do whatever they want to do quietly and by the time you miss them, they are back again licking themselves clean. But my poor husband was not like that. It is true when they say the good die young.

MARION: You say Junior looks just like his father. How does it feel to have him around you looking just like his father?

AINA: Good and bad. Good because I have a living picture of my husband and bad because the pain is too much sometimes. We were quite happily married and then he was gone. (*Sobs. Mabel enters*)

MABEL: Hey, what are you doing now, Marion? Why do you make Miss Aina cry like this?

MARION: Now, don't you start. Leave me in peace, okay? Khaday is not here today. (*Khaday enters*)

KHADAY: Oh yes she is. And she would like to hear what you have been saying about her.

MARION: Who wants to waste time talking about you?

KHADAY: I know one person.

AINA: We were talking about my son Junior being the spitting image of his father.

KHADAY: Which is as it should be. Boys should look like their fathers and girls like their mothers. Carry on.

MARION: Miss Aina wasn't talking to you.

KHADAY: You're darn right. You were digging to see what you could find to spread about her.

MARION: That's not fair. I don't snoop around and I never repeat other people's secrets.

KHADAY: I am not complaining. I have nothing to hide. It's you who have something to be ashamed of.

## ☾ The Pool ☽

MABEL: Miss Aina, please tell us about Junior. These two will never stop fighting.

MARION: We are not fighting.

MABEL: Well stop shouting then.

KHADAY: Don't look at me, tell her.

MARION: Tell your friend to stop picking on me. The place is nice and quiet until she walks in, then bang.

MABEL: Miss Aina, please tell us about Junior.

KHADAY: Miss Aina, be careful. Pick the places that are not too… you know…

AINA: (*Smiling*) Junior is only a child. The neighbors with whom I leave them told me Junior offered to split some wood. They were reluctant to let him handle the axe. But he persuaded them and they let him split one piece of wood. He felt so proud of himself, he went into my pile, took another piece and exchanged it. And he put the wood he had split in the middle of the parlor. I almost fell over it. "Who put wood in my parlor?" I asked. I was raving mad because I thought their games had gone too far. Well, Junior put his hand in his pocket. "Mommy, I did. I split the wood. Now you don't have to pay anyone to split wood for you anymore."

MARION: Good boy.

MABEL: Now you have a man in the house.

KHADAY: I'm proud of him.

AINA: Wait for it. This morning when we were leaving the house, I asked him to split some wood for me when he comes home from school. Do you know what he said? "Have you finished the one I split for you yesterday already?" (*Everyone laughs as Miss Coker enters*)

MISS COKER: What's all the merriment about? Have you all finished? (*Students turn in assignment to Miss Coker*) This is very good Khaday, only two mistakes.

KHADAY: Shit.

MISS COKER: What was that?

MARION: That's what Khaday says when she makes a mistake.

KHADAY: Who asked you?

MISS COKER: Ladies, let's not behave like stray dogs. Now tell me what you were so happy about.

MARION: Miss Aina was telling us about Junior splitting wood for her.

MISS COKER: At that tender age? He's so young. You must be proud of him.

AINA: Yes, Miss C, I'm very proud of him.

MISS COKER: He's the one who looks like his father, isn't he? (*Silence*) Why are you all so quiet all of a sudden? Have I said something wrong?

AINA: Well, Miss C, they are afraid I am going to break down and cry again.

MARION: Miss Aina always cries when she talks about her late husband.

AINA: Well, I haven't quite got over my husband's death. But, it's all right, Miss C. Perhaps it is better if I talk about it. And these girls have been so good.

KHADAY: Except Marion, busybody.

MISS COKER: Khaday, do not call others names.

MARION: You wait until we finish.

KHADAY: Really?

## ☾ The Pool ☽

MISS COKER: I hope you girls don't fight in class.

KHADAY: Oh never, Miss C.

MARION: God forbid.

KHADAY: I like it here, I know you will expel me if I fight.

MARION: Miss Aina, you were about to tell us about your husband.

MISS COKER: Marion. Now I know why Khaday calls you a busybody. Some things are difficult to talk about because they're private and they hurt. You must learn to respect each other's privacy.

AINA: It's all right, Miss C. Perhaps it is providential that I should face reality with the help of these young girls here. You see, Jacob, my late husband, was quite strong till the day he died. He never wanted me to work really. He wanted me to be at home to look after our children.

KHADAY: (*Sarcastic*) And be his housemaid?

MISS COKER: Young lady, you have to mind your own business. (*Bell rings*) Anyway, we will talk another time.

*Lights Out*

# ACT THREE

## Scene One

*(Mabel, Khaday and Marion are in their seats at the typing pool)*

MABEL: Keep your voice down.

KHADAY: No, I'm not going to keep my voice down after all the trouble that woman has gone through. Doesn't she deserve someone to do something for her? Today, I'm going to tell this bitch that she's not better than anyone in this class or this Institute for that matter.

MARION: Who are you calling a bitch?

KHADAY: Please, there are only three of us in this room and I never call Mabel a bitch. She's my friend.

MARION: You're beating around the bush, you're afraid.

KHADAY: Of whom? You? *(Hisses)*

MARION: Are you hissing at me?

KHADAY: Since you asked, yes, bitch!

MARION: This is it. I'm going to report you to Miss Coker. *(Heads for office)*

KHADAY: Aha, after all your "mouth-mouth," all you do is report?

MARION: *(Turns back)* I am well brought up. I come from a decent home, so I will not fight with you.

KHADAY: Who comes from a decent home? Why don't you go and ask your father where he was between 12:30 and 2:00 yesterday. Then come back and tell me about your decent home. Decent home my foot.

MABEL: Khaday, Khaday.

MARION: No, let her finish what she was going to say. I want to know what business she has with my father. Between 12:30 and 2:00 my father was fast asleep and so was the rest of us in our house.

KHADAY: Between 12:30 and 2:00 pm, in the afternoon, stupid.

MARION: My father was at work. He works through the lunch period so that we can have family meals together in the evening. In any case, you don't know him.

MABEL: Stop it, both of you. Just stop it!

KHADAY: (*To Mabel*) Whose side are you on?

MARION: You tell me where you know my father. What business do you have with him?

KHADAY: Why don't you go and ask him what business he has with me?

MARION: You started it.

KHADAY: I'll give you a hint. Those bastards who keep their daughters locked up and fool around with other people's children.

MARION: Liar. My father would never look at a slut like you.

KHADAY: Want to bet?

MARION: I don't even know why they accepted you at this school in the first place. You are wild and rude.

KHADAY: And tall… and clever… (*Miss Coker enters*)

MISS COKER: What in God's name is going on here?

MARION: Miss C, this girl called my father a bastard.

MISS COKER: And what is this girl's name?

KHADAY: And what did you call me? Tell the whole story. In fact Mabel, tell Miss C. (*Mabel is silent*)

KHADAY: Whose side are you on Mabel? (*Mabel is still silent*) Is that how you help a friend?

MARION: You see? You need someone to lean on… someone to fight for you.

KHADAY: Who me? You wait till we leave this place.

MISS COKER: Then what will you do, Khaday?

KHADAY: Ah Miss C, you don't know.

MISS COKER: And what were you talking about?

KHADAY: The way men take advantage of women.

MISS COKER: Is this what you're talking about? Boy-friends?

MARION: I don't have a boyfriend. Me? Not until I finish my studies. Me? Talk to a boy?

KHADAY: But they don't even see you.

MARION: You, they don't look at twice because you show them everything.

MISS COKER: Ladies.

KHADAY: This Marion is too low-down dirty. She's going around telling everyone about Miss Aina. If she is frustrated because no boy will talk to her, she doesn't have to get her kicks out of other people's affairs.

MISS COKER: What's going on with Miss Aina?

## ☾ The Pool ☽

KHADAY: Well Marion, go on, go on. You were telling us about Mr. Buckle with his shirt off.

MISS COKER: (*Alarmed*) Where? At my Institute?

MARION: No, Miss C. No, Miss C.

MISS COKER: Where then? (*Marion mumbles something*) Speak up child.

MARION: I'm sorry.

KHADAY: So you are sorry…

MISS COKER: Hold your tongue, Khaday.

MARION: You have no respect for authority.

MISS COKER: Marion, if you do not mind, I do the disciplining in this Institute. Now, Khaday, what happened?

KHADAY: You see, we all know Miss Aina's story. She does not have a husband. She is barely trying to make ends meet. Mr. Buckle is helping her with private lessons. But sometimes, because she has to get her children by 4:00, Mr. Buckle goes to her house to give her the lessons. Miss lady here saw Mr. Buckle splitting wood for Miss Aina one day. Mr. Buckle had his shirt off and lo and behold Marion is going around telling everyone that Mr. Buckle was without his shirt in Miss Aina's house. She doesn't have the decency to tell the whole story. And poor Miss Aina, she is having a bad reputation because of that.

MISS COKER: Marion, is that correct?

MARION: (*Fawning*) Well, Miss C, uh, I'm sorry. (*Bell rings. Mr. Buckle enters. Marion giggles and sits down quickly, suppressing a laugh*)

MR. BUCKLE: Excuse me, is Aina not here yet? (*Marion laughs hysterically. This annoys Khaday. She descends on Marion, slapping her. They begin to fight, with Miss Coker and Mabel trying to separate them. They exit through the office door. Aina enters stage left)*

MR. BUCKLE: Wonders never cease. Well I'm sure those girls won't make it to class today. Will you mind us going through your private lessons, Aina? No one else is here.

AINA: Yes, why not? Although I feel bad doing this during official time.

MR. BUCKLE: Would you rather we go to your house where we would be more comfortable?

AINA: Ah, Mr. Buckle, please stop. Anybody will think you and I are lovers. I wish you wouldn't talk to me like that. Don't think you can take liberties with me just because you are giving me private lessons.

MR. BUCKLE: Now, there is nothing to worry about. Please sit (*pulls a chair close to his desk*).

AINA: Mr. Buckle, you're very kind.

MR. BUCKLE: Oh, call me Joseph.

AINA: Why?

MR. BUCKLE: Because, I want you to. (*He adjusts glasses, opens books and touches her slightly on the shoulder*)

AINA: (*Jumps up at the touch*) Don't take liberties with me. I have my self-respect. Besides, what will people say?

MR. BUCKLE: Uh, you mean you haven't heard?

AINA: Heard what?

MR. BUCKLE: Talk of the town.

AINA: (*Surprised*) About us?

MR. BUCKLE: Who else?

AINA: Oh my God, what will my in-laws say?

## ( The Pool )

MR. BUCKLE: How long have you been a widow now?

AINA: Three years.

MR. BUCKLE: How old is your youngest?

AINA: Two and a half. Why, what is this? The inquisition?

MR. BUCKLE: Don't you think you have mourned long enough?

AINA: My husband was a good man.

MR. BUCKLE: Yeah, and I'm not good enough for you.

AINA: Mr. Buckle! Anyway, why did you never marry?

MR. BUCKLE: Please call me Joseph.

AINA: You have not answered my question.

MR. BUCKLE: Why… I… never… married?

AINA: Yes, why, Joseph (*looks into his eyes*)?

MR. BUCKLE: (*Looks deeply into her eyes*) Because I never found the right woman.

AINA: (*Recovers quickly*) Here is the work you gave me to do. (*He checks it*) So, what do you think?

MR. BUCKLE: I think you can enter for the Pitman Stage One English now.

AINA: Are you sure?

MR. BUCKLE: Yes, Aina.

AINA: Then I don't need any more private lessons. I can look for a job.

MR. BUCKLE: Well, yes and no. You do not need to come to this Institute full time after this academic year, but I can still come to your house and give you private lessons.

AINA: (*Quickly*) That won't be necessary. The neighbors would like me to be at home to look after my children. It's holiday time.

MR. BUCKLE: But what happens when you get a job? Who will look after them when you are off at work? (*Silence*) Aina?

AINA: Yes, Mr. Buckle?

MR. BUCKLE: Ah, this mister, mister business again. Look Aina, your husband died because God willed it so. But it is not fair for you to be miserable the rest of your life just because he is not here anymore.

AINA: And he spoiled me so.

MR. BUCKLE: (*Mumbles something*)

AINA: What did you say?

MR. BUCKLE: Can I come over to split some more wood this weekend? Junior is just a little boy.

AINA: That is what you think. He is very clever and he is beginning to notice things.

MR. BUCKLE: There is nothing to notice. At least not yet.

AINA: What do you mean by not yet?

MR. BUCKLE: Look Aina, I'm not young anymore. If I marry someone much younger, she will want to have children. I don't think it will be fair for me to leave her the responsibility of bringing children up alone.

AINA: I can tell you it is not easy.

MR. BUCKLE: I have been observing you since you have been at this Institute. I have never seen you in the company of any man. You may have little, but you are respectable and dedicated to your children. No man can ask for anything more.

## The Pool

AINA: My children are all I've got and memories. If only Jacob had not let me live such a sheltered life, I would have been better able to cope with life without him. If only he had let me take on a job, I would have been better able to handle things. If... only... (*begins to cry*)

MR. BUCKLE: (*Comforts Aina*) Aina?

AINA: Yes? (*Looks up from crying*)

MR. BUCKLE: Will you marry me? (*Aina sobs even louder. Miss Coker enters*)

MISS COKER: (*Alarmed*) What is happening here? Mr. Buckle, what are you doing? Aina, what has come over you? Do you realize the gossip that has been spreading around my Institute?

AINA: Miss C, Mr. Buckle has asked me to marry him.

MISS COKER: Well, that's nothing to cry about. What do you say?

AINA: What can I say? (*Buckle runs to her. They both embrace and exit*)

(*Marion and Khaday enter through office door. They are still chasing each other*)

MISS COKER: Are you two still at it?

KHADAY: I'm going to teach her a lesson.

MISS COKER: Stop it, Khaday. Do you realize what time it is? (*Mabel enters*)

MARION: Miss C, she called my father a bastard.

MISS COKER: Is that true Khaday? Answer me.

MABEL: Miss C, since you left us, these two have not stopped arguing. They are still accusing each other and they are saying the must awful things.

KHADAY: Why is it that when someone has a problem, the whole world seems to be against her?

MARION: Who says I'm against…

KHADAY: I'm not talking to you. Shut up, busybody.

MISS COKER: Well, well, Khaday, this is most disappointing. At least you should have respect for my presence.

KHADAY: I respect your presence.

MISS COKER: Then why are you behaving like this?

MARION: Because she has no manners.

MABEL: You see, Miss C, I would like to go, but I can't leave them like this. And Khaday won't come with me.

KHADAY: You go ahead, Mabel. I go on duty after this.

MARION: Liar.

KHADAY: Who are you calling a liar?

MARION: You are a liar. Which duty are you going on?

KHADAY: The duty that gives me money to pay my fees and take care of my family.

MISS COKER: I don't understand, Khaday. What exactly do you mean?

KHADAY: *(To Marion)* It's all right for you. Your father gives you everything. Your mother sits at home like a puppet and has a servant do every piece of work.

MABEL: Khaday, please. Miss C, I must go. I have to go to the market and cook the sauce for the evening meal. My mother will be worried about me.

KHADAY: You hear that? You hear that? Some of us work. We have to earn our living. All you do is watch videos and waste your father's money at this Institute. Not that he deserves any better.

## ☾ The Pool ☽

MARION: Miss C, you hear her? She is abusing my father again. Why are you abusing my father?

KHADAY: Did I abuse your father? I said he deserves nothing better, that's all.

MABEL: Khaday, I have to go. Miss C, I can't stay any longer. (*Exits*)

MISS COKER: Now, come here you two.

MARION: Now your defender is gone.

KHADAY: You think I need her? She is my friend, yes, but I can defend myself.

MISS COKER: Stop this at once both of you. At this Institute, I expect you to become ladies but you have both let me down. Now, one at a time, what is it?

(*Khaday and Marion speak at the same time*)

KHADAY: Miss C, Marion...

MARION: Miss C, Khaday...

MISS COKER: Stop, both of you!

(*James enters stage left*)

JAMES: I didn't realize that my daughter studies this late at the Institute. (*Marion runs to her father*)

MISS COKER: You must be Marion's father.

JAMES: As a matter of fact, I am.

MISS COKER: Thank goodness you are here. These two girls have done nothing all afternoon but quarrel.

JAMES: These two girls?

MARION: Daddy, this girl has been calling you names.

MISS COKER: Speak the truth, Marion. You both have been calling each other names. (*James turns, recognizes Khaday but recovers quickly from the shock*)

JAMES: (*Hurriedly*) Never mind, never mind. Let's be going darling. Your mother has been worried that you haven't returned so she insisted that I check on you before going to the club. Come along.

KHADAY: (*Laughs sarcastically*) Hey, hey, hey, what club?

MISS COKER: Khaday, behave yourself.

MARION: Will you behave like that in front of your own father?

KHADAY: Certainly not. My father may be a poor laborer, my mother a poor trader, but they took time to give me good home training. They sacrificed everything to send me to school. But thanks to people like your father, there are no jobs for us when we leave school. We're not going to go to a university either because our parents are too poor to bribe for scholarships. So how do we support our younger brothers and sisters?

JAMES: Marion, darling, don't you think we ought to be going? (*Pulls Marion gently towards the door*)

KHADAY: (*Gently pulls Marion towards her*) We sell our bodies in cars and hotel rooms and secret flats. Not so darling? (*Walks over to James and kisses him and then slaps him. James is too shocked to respond. Marion watches scene in shock. Khaday begins to pack her bag. Aina walks in at that moment*)

AINA: I forgot my handbag. (*Picks it up and begins to leave*)

KHADAY: Wait for me, Miss Aina, I was just leaving. (*Exits with Aina*)

MARION: Daddy, is it true?

JAMES: Well, you wouldn't understand.

MARION: How could you?

JAMES: It's been a long day, Marion. (*Touches her gently*) You must be tired.

MARION: (*Screams*) Take your filthy hands off me. (*Runs out*)

MISS COKER: Marion, Marion! (*In confused silence, James exits after Marion*)

MISS COKER: (*In shock*) Whatever is the world coming to?

*Lights Out*

# Scene Two

(*Next day at the typing pool*)

AINA: What are you doing here so early in the morning?

MARION: Oh Miss Aina, I'm so tired. I just want to sleep.

AINA: You look terrible. Didn't you sleep last night?

MARION: How could I after that terrible scene between Khaday and my father. I could not bear to sleep under the same roof with him.

AINA: You mean you didn't sleep at home? What is the meaning of this?

MARION: Just that. I have moved out of the house.

AINA: Yesterday evening when I came back to collect my handbag, I noticed that everybody was sort of tense. But I didn't realize it was as bad as this. Was your father annoyed because you were quarrelling with Khaday?

MARION: I wish it were as simple as that. (*Begins to cry and is comforted by Aina. James enters*)

JAMES: Good morning…

AINA: Good morning, Mr. Macauley. How are you today?

JAMES: Very well thank you. Marion, shall we go? I would like to talk to you privately.

MARION: Say whatever you want to say in front of Miss Aina. I'm not going anywhere with you.

JAMES: Please Marion.

MARION: No.

JAMES: Don't be naughty now, Marion. Be a good girl.

MARION: Father, please don't talk to me like that ever again.

JAMES: Since when did you call me father? It's always been "daddy."

MARION: Well, you don't deserve to be called that anymore.

JAMES: That may be so, but please let's find somewhere quiet where we can talk like two grownups. You're behaving like a child, Marion.

MARION: No, I'm not going anywhere with you. As a matter of fact, I don't even want to be seen with you. Please go quickly before the others come.

JAMES: (*Speaks with fatherly authority*) Where the hell did you spend the night? I looked into your room. You were not in bed. Your mother was worried. She insisted that I come back to see if you would turn up before I go to the office today. (*Marion ignores him. He changes his tone and pleads softly*) Where did you sleep, huh, Marion?

AINA: Marion, do as your father says. Go home and sleep. I will explain to Miss Coker you are not feeling well. She will excuse you for today.

☾ **The Pool** ☽

MARION: Miss Aina, did you hear what he said? He only came here because my mother insisted that he stop by here before going to the office. Last night he came because my mother insisted that he stop by here on his way to the club.

JAMES: Look, Marion, don't be unfair. I would have come.

MARION: You would have come? After what…

AINA: Marion that is no way to talk to your father.

MARION: Miss Aina, this man is not my father. From now on, I will see him on the streets and I will not greet him.

AINA: Why would you do a thing like that? What has he done that is so terrible?

JAMES: Please let's leave this place. Marion?

MARION: No, stop calling my name. Leave me alone. Forget you have a daughter. I am dead to you.

JAMES: So what do I say to your mother?

MARION: What have you been telling her all these years? Go and invent one more lie.

JAMES: No, I can't do that. I can't tell her a lie.

MARION: You mean you won't lie to her this time? Ah, but you have always lied to her. "I can't come home for lunch, I have a meeting at the club." "I'll be back after the weekend." Now I know why my mother is so unhappy.

JAMES: That's enough!

MARION: Don't you raise your voice to me.

AINA: Marion, listen to me. (*Pulls her aside. Mabel enters*)

MABEL: Good morning, everyone. Mr. Macauley.

JAMES: Hello, young lady. Where have I seen you before?

MARION: Are you one of my father's playthings too?

MABEL: Don't mix me up in this. Khaday took me out to lunch.

JAMES: I think I better leave. I'll see you this evening. (*Bumps into Buckle who has just entered*) Excuse me, sir, I was just leaving. I am James Macauley, Marion's father. (*Khaday enters*)

MARION: He is not my father.

MR. BUCKLE: I am Mr. Buckle, the English teacher. How may I help you?

JAMES: I was here to see Marion but I...

MARION: He is here to see his girlfriend, Khaday.

MR. BUCKLE: What?

KHADAY: Don't you call my name.

MABEL: Not again.

MR. BUCKLE: (*Confused*) Your daughter? Your girlfriend?

(*Khaday and Marion speak at the same time*)

KHADAY: Mr. Buckle this...

MARION: Mr. Buckle this...

MR. BUCKLE: One at a time! (*Silence*)

AINA: Mr. Buckle, are you the only one who does not know what is going on around here?

MARION: Mr. Buckle, Khaday is sleeping with my father.

MR. BUCKLE: But what has that got to do with you?

AINA: Joseph Buckle! How can you talk like that?

MARION: Men are all the same. Now I understand my mother.

MR. BUCKLE: (*Baffled*) Okay, the class is cancelled, everybody out! (*Students exit*)

MR. BUCKLE: (*To James*) What's the meaning of this?

JAMES: It's a long story.

MR. BUCKLE: The affair with Khaday, is that true?

JAMES: Unfortunately, yes.

MR. BUCKLE: Can I ask a personal question?

JAMES: What question?

MR. BUCKLE: Is Khaday the only one, or are there others?

JAMES: Mind your business.

MR. BUCKLE: I take back the question.

JAMES: I'll answer the question. (*Miss Coker enters*)

MR. BUCKLE: No, you don't need to.

MISS COKER: What's going on here?

MR. BUCKLE: Miss Coker, Marion's father and I are just trying to solve the problem at hand.

MISS COKER: Mr. Macauley, Mr. Buckle here isn't married yet, so he probably doesn't understand a thing you've been saying.

JAMES: (*Dismayed*) I say Mr. Buckle you are not married?

MR. BUCKLE: No.

JAMES: Then for goodness sake don't ever get married. Stay as you are——a jolly old bachelor.

MISS COKER: Don't you think your advice is a little too late?

JAMES: Well, then, he will learn by his mistakes. Where is my daughter?

MISS COKER: Oh, Marion's mother came to pick her up. They both left together. I think you should be planning your defense. I suppose Marion is going to tell her mother her side of the story.

JAMES: Oh... my... God!

## LIGHTS OUT

# NOT YOU TOO

**BY**

**MOHAMED SHERIFF**

*Mohamed Sheriff*

# CHARACTERS

◆

| | |
|---|---|
| GULAMA | Head of the House |
| MARY | Gulama's Wife |
| GINA | Gulama's Daughter |
| GRANNY | Mary's Mother |
| BORBOR | Gina's Lover |
| CHRISTIE | Mary's Friend |
| KULA | Mary's Sister |
| KATE | Mary and Kula's cousin |
| CHIEF JAIA | Town Chief |

Background: Drummers, Singers, Chiefdom Policemen

☾ Not You Too ☽

# ACT ONE

◊◆◊

*(Indistinct background singing, ululation and drumming with the tempo rising now and again in sympathy with the ebb and flow of the emotions expressed by the characters and with the rising tension created as a result. It is midnight. A kerosene lamp held by Gulama, who emerges through a door, left, dragging a reluctant, thrashing, and wailing Gina behind him, lights up the stage. Granny Neneh and Mary, both holding out their hands and wearing a hesitant pleading expression on their faces, follow them from the same room. The light of the lamp reveals a sitting room that does not seem right: A naked unlit bulb hangs from the ceiling; the walls and floor of the room is of mud plastered with concrete; there are several cracks, and the plasters have fallen off here and there, revealing dark ugly patches; the room is furnished with comfortable old leather arm chairs. Settees, a few dinning chairs, a center table, and some stools. The luxurious state of the furniture is in sharp contrast with the poor physical state of the room, giving the impression of the former being handed to the family by a richer relative from the city. There are two doors in the center wall facing the audience, the one on the left leads to Gulama's room while the one on the right to the back of the house. The walls extreme left and right of the stage perpendicular to the center wall have a door each. The one on the right leads to Mary's room, and the one on the left to Granny's room, which also serves as the guest room and from which Gulama, Gina, and the two women have just come)*

GINA: *(Struggling to free her hand from the firm grip of her father)* Papa, please don't throw me at those bloodthirsty *Bundo* Society women. I am convalescing and still anaemic. I can't afford to lose blood now and you know my wounds don't heal easily. I'll die, Papa. I know it.

GULAMA: (*Sets the lamp on a stool*) Shut your mouth, girl. You don't believe your Mama and Papa will do anything to endanger your health, do you? Woman, talk to her. Tell her. Go on. Tell her we know what's good for her, don't we, woman?

MARY: Ye-e-es… Gulama … you've said the truth, but…

GULAMA: Do you hear that? Your mama agrees with me. Now be a proud willing girl and stop whimpering like a dog child. The *Bundo* women are waiting just outside. We don't want them to know that our daughter is a coward.

GINA: Please, Papa I'll die. I have an eight-month old sore on my left leg. It still isn't showing any sign of healing. I have a bad flesh. If I undergo circumcision, the cut won't heal. I'll lose blood and I'm anemic. I'll die.

GULAMA: Don't worry daughter, Chief Jaia, your husband-to-be has engaged the services of an expert nurse from Freetown to attend to you.

GINA: Their services are known to have failed, Papa, and many young girls have died.

GULAMA: (*Pulling her angrily towards front door*) Girl, I've lost my temper. If you don't come with me willingly, I'll pound you like rice in a mortar.

MARY: (*Shuffling nearer to them*) Be careful, Gulama. You'll break her arm.

GRANNY: Gina, will you stop this stubbornness and go along? Don't you have faith in God?

GINA: Grandma, God does not say we should walk to our deaths with eyes open. I don't want to go through circumcision.

GULAMA: Do you hear that, woman? Do you hear your daughter?

MARY: (*Bracing herself*) Gulama, I think we should sit and talk.

☾ Not You Too ☽

GULAMA: About what!

MARY: About Gina and this circumcision business. She is still recovering from her illness; her blood is poor. I don't think she is ready yet for any blood loss.

GULAMA: I ought to have known. Unthinking bull that I am. When a girl gets wayward, don't go out searching for the cause—look under the mother's feet, it is crouching there staring treacherously at you. I ought to have known that this woman is behind her daughter's waywardness.

GRANNY: I hope that proverb is not aimed at me. A man may forget his manners, but doesn't forget the women who carried his wife in her womb for ten months.

GULAMA: No Mama, I don't mean you. I am referring to the mothers of today, like this woman, your daughter, who is encouraging, conniving with her own daughter to disobey me and to go against our sacred customs and traditions. I'm sure Mama is with me - on my side - aren't you, Mama? We want Gina to go to the Bundo bush, right? To perform the sacred rites and customs of her mother and mother's mother and mother's mother's mother before her?

GRANNY: You know I do, but…

GULAMA: No "but" Mama, that's how it should be.

GRANNY: (*Irritably*) Will you control your mouth and let me finish? You may be husband and father in this house, but I'm your aged mother-in-law.

GULAMA: Forgive me, Mama, you may speak.

GRANNY: I was going to say that I'm with you, but Gina must be coaxed. Fear is a terrible sickness. She believes she will be going through an unbearable ordeal. We should let her know it's not so frightening. (*To Gina*) It's a test of womanhood. It's inescapable. You do not want to go about an uncircumcised, half-woman like those shameless girls in the city. And your health is in the hands of God—life and death are matters for God.

GINA: Is it the will of God that we should go to our death with eyes wide open? Why does he forbid suicide? Granny, even if I don't die, there is a lot of terrible things that can happen to me. What if I catch some disease that will ruin me for life?

GRANNY: Your mother didn't catch any, nor did your aunts. I don't know what's gone into your head to talk like that.

GULAMA: Mama, those are not Gina's words, they are words put in her mouth by your daughter. The baby shits out only what its mother feeds it. She has turned my daughter against the pride of womanhood—the very essence of womanhood.

MARY: Gulama, circumcision is something I went through with all its attendant rites and I'm proud of it.

GULAMA: I'm glad to hear that.

MARY: I merely object to the ritual under her current health condition. It is true my sisters and I went through circumcision successfully, but none of us was sickly. Gina is my only child. All I'm asking is that we wait for some other Bundo season when she will have recovered.

GULAMA: A sensible talk. In the mean time what are we going to tell Chief Jaia who is waiting impatiently to take her home as his bride after her graduation from the Bundo Society?

MARY: There will be many graduates from Bundo Society and Chief Jaia may marry as many as he pleases. Why can't he leave my daughter out of this? Gulama, why do you want to throw her life away to that old lecher who marries every two years? Gina is going to get the education I didn't have and the opportunity to marry a husband of her choice and to live a better life.

GULAMA: (*Erupts into a gale of raucous laughter, which startles the others. With one hand firmly gripping Gina's wrist, he raises the other to strike Mary, moving with speed towards her. Mary instinctively moves with matching swiftness to a protective position behind granny who with arms akimbo cocks her head defiantly at Gulama, daring him to strike. Gulama's hand remains hovering above for a few seconds and then falls to his side*) The woman has forgotten the weight of my palms against her face. Thank Grandma, for you would have had a strong reminder just now. (*He swings round and goes out, dragging a screaming Gina behind him with the other two staring after them in silent resignation. The tempo and volume of the drumming and ululation heightens, mingling with and drowning Gina's screams off stage*) Take her away, women, let her be a woman, let her be the first person to go through with it. She's the Chief's future bride. I'll check on you first thing in the morning to know how things are going. (*He returns to the sitting room*) Goodnight, Mama, we shall see in the morning. (*He goes to the door of his bedroom, opens, enters and slams it shut behind him. The women continue to stare after him in silence. Lights fade*)

(*When lights return Gulama is stepping out of his bedroom, stretching and yawning. He stands in the center of the sitting room looking about him as if unsure of what he wants to do*)

GULAMA: Mary, Mary, come out. (*Mary emerges from her bedroom*) What kind of woman is it that allows the sun to expose the wrinkles of her sleepy face in bed?

MARY: I've been up before cockcrow and I've done all my early morning chores. You know I'm not that kind of woman who allows sunrise to creep on her in bed.

GULAMA: After last night I don't know anything any more about you.

MARY: Gulama, it's too early to quarrel—at any rate not when my daughter is being prepared to go through an ordeal.

GULAMA: Ordeal! You! To hear you talk, one would think you're an American or European lady who knows nothing about circumcision. I know what's behind this attitude of yours—your sisters, Kula and Kate, those civilized white imitators, and the great white lady herself, your friend, Christie. They've put madness into your head. I'm going out to find out whether Gina behaved herself.

MARY: That's the duty of the mother.

GULAMA: When the mother doesn't know her duty, the father has no alternative but to do it for her. I want my breakfast ready when I come back.

MARY: You've never found it otherwise.

(*Enter Granny from her room on the left*)

GULAMA: Oh, I'm sorry. I thought perhaps you've neglected that duty as well, Madam Mary. (*To Granny*) Did you sleep well, Mama? (*Exits*)

GRANNY: (*Sits in her settee*) It's true—what your husband said. You've been listening to your sisters, especially your cousin, Kate. They may mean well for you, but they are not helping you by advising you to stand up to your husband. A woman should stoop to her husband, not stand on his head.

MARY: Mama, all they're saying is that it's time I let him know I'm not his bonds woman or domestic animal or tool. I am a free born human being who has a heart.

GRANNY: Do you think your father was any different or any better? But I never talked back to him. And what harm did that do to me? He shall have been in his grave fifteen years come the next rain, while I'm still here, still strong, with you and your sisters all tending to me.

☾ **Not You Too** ☽

MARY: You're lucky, Mama—the lot of the African woman from birth is hardship, suffering misery till she goes to the grave. It's work, work, work, from the house to the farm to the market. It's forced marriage, child bearing, child rearing, premature aging and death. What do our men folk do? How much work compared to us? They make us pregnant, force our children into early marriages and grab whatever is paid as bride price for themselves. They eat and drink and sleep and wake and give orders and beat us.

GRANNY: It's true what your husband said—you sisters have indeed talked to you through their letters. And your white friend Christie too. Those are their words, not yours, but you shouldn't listen to them. Those are foreign ideas. Some of the things you say may be true. But what is new about all this? That is the way it has always been and always will be.

MARY: No, Mama, things are changing. In the white man's country, women are no longer treated like slaves.

GRANNY: That's what Christie tells you. But Africa is not white man's country. The African woman is not a white woman and the African man is not a white man.

MARY: Kula and cousin Kate say if we try hard things will change.

GRANNY: Let me tell you something, my daughter. They have more book learning and more money than you and they have been supporting us financially all these years, but this doesn't mean that they have nothing to complain about in life.

MARY: Mama, they are at least free to do what they think is good for them in any given situation. I would like very much to exchange this slavish life for theirs.

GRANNY: Not all spotlessly ripe bananas are good inside. And it's too late in the day to change, Mary.

MARY: True, Mama, but not for my only child. I'm going to give her an opportunity to live a better life. She's not going ahead with the circumcision.

GRANNY: What?

MARY: Well ... at least not now. If her health improves and the doctor says it's safe for her, she'll do it some other time, otherwise no.

GRANNY: What is this my ears are hearing? Otherwise no? Madness comes in many shapes and forms. Have you ever heard of a Mende girl who does not undergo circumcision before marriage?

MARY: She's not going to get married to Chief Jaia, Mama. She'll continue her education.

GRANNY: And how do you intend to stop the circumcision going on today?

MARY: I'll go to the Bundo bush and get her out.

GRANNY: Eyay! Mary, my ears are burning!

MARY: She's my daughter. They can't stop me. Cousin Kate and Kula are coming today from Freetown. They are to spend Christmas with us and return after New Year's Day, but I'll persuade them to go back tonight and take Gina with them.

GRANNY: My niece and my daughter have been away in England and America for over six years and all that time I've been dying to see them. Since they returned to Freetown they've been unable to visit with us because of the civil war, which has made the roads unsafe for travelling. Now that there is a cease-fire and they are taking the risk to come here to spend at least a week with me, they must go back in less than a day because of the madness they've put into their sister's head.

## ❨ Not You Too ❩

MARY: Mama, now that peace is almost in sight, they'll come to see you as often as you want.

*(Enter Borbor and Gina through the door leading from the back of the house)*

GRANNY: What is this my eyes are seeing? Gina, what are you doing here with this Borbor boy?

GINA: I escaped, Grandma.

GRANNY: You what? My ears are burning! You escaped? Mary, you meant what you said, didn't you? You arranged with your daughter to run away from the Bundo bush. What disgrace do you want to bring to the family?

MARY: Mama, it was my intention to get her out, but I knew nothing about her plans.

GINA: That's true, Grandma. I arranged this with Borbor. He waited for me just outside the Bundo bush and I slipped out just before cockcrow, while the others were still sleeping and then we came right here. We've been hiding at the back of the house.

GRANNY: The spirit of madness is on the prowl here. Someone get Pa Krugba, the medicine man, to drive this spirit away. You escaped from the bush and thought of no other place to come except here. *(They begin to cast furtive glances at the front door)*

MARY: I'm not sure whether you should have brought her here. I was planning to take her to a friend of mine in the outskirts of town.

BORBOR: It's my idea that she should come here, Mama. It's the last place anyone will look for her. As soon as the news of her escape is out, Pa Gulama and Chief Jaia are going to turn this whole town upside down looking for her.

MARY: But where will she hide? She can't hide in any of our rooms. That will be too risky.

BORBOR: She'll hide in the least expected place... under the bed in Pa Gulama's bedroom.

MARY: What?

GRANNY: What?

BORBOR: No one will think of looking for her there. We'll get her out when the whole town is asleep tonight.

MARY: (*After a pause*) Yes, you're right. It's dangerous, but very clever.

GRANNY: Somebody go and call Pa Krugba to come and drive away the spirit of madness from here! Now I begin to respect Gulama for having more sense than I ever imagined. He said the letters from your sisters have brought madness to your head. He also said encouraging any relationship between Gina and Borbor would lead only to trouble. He couldn't have been more correct.

MARY: It's no madness, Mama, and I'm thankful for Borbor's help.

GINA: Grandma, do you want me to go through that painful exercise, sick as I am? Do you want me to die?

GRANNY: Don't you have faith in God's protection?

GINA: And if I do survive, do you want me to be married off to that old lecherous drunkard whom people call chief?

GRANNY: Ask your father that question. It is for him to decide.

MARY: And me too to decide.

BORBOR: Yes, Grandma and Gina too should have a say in the choice of a husband.

GRANNY: I did not invite you to talk. You just want to bring trouble to this family.

## ❪ Not You Too ❫

BORBOR: But Grandma you are aware that I love Gina and she loves me too. And my people have shown interest in her for me.

GRANNY: Don't talk to me about love. How many of your love marriages survive these days? Anyway it is for the father to decide whom she should marry.

MARY: Gina, go in now and wait. When you hear his voice and footsteps, hide quickly under the bed. He should be on his way back now and doubly fast if he has learnt of your escape.

GRANNY: You don't expect me to cover up for you, do you? Or to say I know nothing when I do.

GINA: I swear by God, Grandma, if you let father find me and take me back there, I'll kill myself. I swear I'll do it.

(*They hear the sound of Gulama approaching. Gina rushes to Gulama's bedroom and shuts the door. Gulama storms in, heads straight for Mary and knocks off her headscarf, grabs her by the hair and drags her to Granny. Granny gets off her seat with a quickness that belies her age and bulk and deals Gulama a few blows with her open palms, pushing him away from Mary*)

GRANNY: (*Breathless with the effort*) I'm right! The spirit of madness is on the rampage in this house. We need Pa Krugba to drive it away. Attacking my daughter in front of my eyes? What is the world coming to? Have you no shame? Before you touch my daughter in front of my eyes, you'll beat me first.

GULAMA: I didn't mean to, Mama, but they want to shame us—she and her damned daughter. Mama, Gina has escaped! (*Pauses on seeing Borbor for the first time, then possessed with a renewed burst of anger he lurches forward and takes Borbor by the shirt front and begins to shake him violently*) You are in league with them. My daughter! Where is she? Tell me where she is. I want my daughter. My daughter! (*They struggle as Borbor tries to prevent*

*Gulama from choking him*) I will kill you. Kill you! Tell me where she is. (*The women scream in fear and confusion. Granny hobbles to them, grabs Gulama from behind and tries to pull him away from Borbor. Failing, she starts beating him on the back*)

MARY: (*From a safe distance*) Leave the boy alone! He is not your child. You have no right to attack him.

GRANNY: (*Breathless, barely audible*) Do you want Government trouble?

BORBOR: (*Finally breaks free, gasping for air*) Pa Gulama, you could have killed me!

GULAMA: And you should thank God I didn't.

BORBOR: I wouldn't tolerate such treatment from anyone else but you because I respect your family and love your daughter.

GULAMA: Don't you know she's engaged to Chief Jaia? You are telling me to my face that you love her.

BORBOR: But it's the truth, I do.

GRANNY: Won't you shut your mouth, boy?

MARY: Don't argue with him Borbor; it will only make matters worse.

GULAMA: Yes, he shouldn't argue with a madman. Mama, you are witness to the fact that I have suffered too many insults from your daughter of late. If she goes beyond this, I won't be responsible for my actions.

GRANNY: I'll just leave this house if you people continue like this. I've gone through all my own share of troubles. At my age, I should be living in peace and comfort, not in hell.

GULAMA: There is going to be no peace Mama if I don't find Gina. So tell them. They know about it. Both of

## ☾ Not You Too ☽

them—Mary and Borbor. From the first time I noticed this Borbor boy's interest in Gina, I knew he meant trouble.

BORBOR: Pa Gulama, finding Gina is the least of our problems. There is no hiding place for Gina. I can assure you that we'll help you get her.

GULAMA: Now! I want her now! The rites are about to start and they can't wait for her.

BORBOR: Pa, I promise you I'll help you find her if you listen to me for a few minutes.

GULAMA: You know where she is; so don't tell me you'll help me find her! Just bring her to me!

BORBOR: Well listen to what I have to say. You will not like what I am going to say, but just bear with me until I'm through. You want Gina to go through *Bundo* and immediately after marry her off to Chief Jaia. Pa Gulama, what can Chief Jaia offer Gina and your family that I can't in the near future? Indeed I can offer more. I have a degree in accounting with a good job at the bank, even though I've only just started work. If we allow Gina to go to the university, in four year's time she too will be a graduate. Even without the support of any husband, with a good job she should be able to take care of herself and of you too. Gina's aunt, Kula, has offered to support her through university. I am prepared to give whatever assistance I can towards her education. Afterwards we'll get married and by then I shall have made progress in my job.

GULAMA: You said it was a short talk!

BORBOR: I'll soon finish, Pa. Chief Jaia's favors to you will only last until the day he gets Gina into his house. After that he won't even want to see you. As for Gina, a year or two of marriage and child bearing and Chief Jaia will start looking for someone younger. Is that what you want for Gina?

GULAMA: You said it was a short talk!

BORBOR: One last word. The *Bundo*... Gina would be of no use to either you or Chief Jaia dead. She runs a great risk of dying if she goes through those terrible rites.

GULAMA: Mama, do you hear him? He refers to the sacred rites and customs of our ancestors as terrible.

BORBOR: Sacred rites of our ancestors, our traditional practices and customs! Do we have to blindly follow tradition, whether good or bad?

GULAMA: What is bad about *Bundo*?

BORBOR: Mutilating parts of young girls under unhygienic conditions is barbaric.

GRANNY: My ears are burning! What is this boy doing? Exposing the secrets of womanhood?

GULAMA: That's the madness that comes from too much book learning. He can afford to put his foul mouth into the secrets of his mothers. And (*To Mary*) that old Mama who ought to be teaching her great grand children about the beauty and virtues of those secrets has caught the madness too.

MARY: Borbor, don't say such things, we must respect our customs.

GRANNY: In our day, men don't talk about these things.

BORBOR: I do respect our customs and traditions... those that are good. And if the circumcision must go on, let it be done in a hospital in humane and hygienic conditions under medical supervision.

GRANNY: That's when it becomes mutilation and ceases to be circumcision. Don't talk about things you don't understand.

GULAMA: I have no intention of arguing with him, Granny. Let him just tell me the whereabouts of my daughter as he promised. I've given my word to Chief Jaia and I'm not going to change that.

BORBOR: That's sad, Pa Gulama. But she is your daughter. I must leave. Grandma, Mama Mary, I'm leaving.

GULAMA: (*Barring his way*) Leave where? Not a step until I know the whereabouts of my daughter.

BORBOR: I only said I'll help you find her.

GULAMA: And I say you'll do more than that.

MARY: Let him go, Gulama. Even if he knows, you can't force him to tell you.

GULAMA: But I can force you, and I will. (*To Borbor*) You can go! (*Borbor exits as Christie enters. She is in her mid forties. She wears the uniform of Benevolent Stars, the Relief organization she works for*)

CHRISTIE: Good morning, everyone. Hi Mary. How do you do, Granny Neneh? And you too, Gulama?

GRANNY: We thank the Master above for good health. I must get some rest. I've had enough for this morning. (*Goes off*)

MARY: Christie, I'm so happy to see you. You are a trained and qualified nurse. Please, let my husband know that Gina is anemic and will be endangering her life if she goes through circumcision.

CHRISTIE: Well, I'm not a doctor, but I know that...

GULAMA: Don't waste your voice, white woman. I know you're one of those behind the madness in this house. Where you come from, don't you have your customs and traditions that you respect?

CHRISTIE: Yes we do.

GULAMA: Good! Would you listen to some foreigner who tells you that they are bad and that you should abandon them when you know nothing is wrong with them?

CHRISTIE: I don't see myself as a foreigner any more because…

GULAMA: Are you from this country?

CHRISTIE: No, but…

GULAMA: But nothing. You are a foreigner. I'm leaving now. If you like your friend, tell her that when I come back my daughter must be either here or at the Bundo bush, or else I'm going to find the medicine with which to cure her madness, and she won't like it. I can assure you of that. (*Exits*)

CHRISTIE: Is it this bad?

MARY: Yes. But I'm determined. My daughter will have a better future, just like we've been discussing in the last few days. My sister and cousin are coming today. They are going back with Gina.

CHRISTIE: Will he let you? And the chief too?

MARY: All I need is to keep Gina away from these men until my sisters come, then they'll leave in the middle of the night. If I had seen someone reliable to take her, I would have sent her to Freetown before today.

CHRISTIE: Are you sure you'll be able to weather the storm after you've sent her?

MARY: Christie, I married this man at the age of 16. Since then it has been mainly suffering and hardship. I suffered three miscarriages because of ill treatment and hardship… beatings from him and hard work both at home and on the farm. I've told you, my daughter will not go through that. I have the support of my sister and cousin. Kula will pay for Gina's university education. Cousin Kate will give whatever other assistance is needed. I want my daughter to be like her aunts. They have education. They have independence, materially and socially. Nobody is trampling on their rights or forcing them to do what they don't want or stopping them from doing what they want. That's what every woman wants. If my father had not sold me off to Gulama's father as debt payment, I would have completed my education in Freetown, like Kula and Kate. My aunt and uncle, Cousin Kate's parents, were ready to see us through to university. But father wouldn't let me. He had promised to give my hand in marriage to the son of his friend to settle a debt. And this is the outcome. Christie, how old do you think I am?

CHRISTIE: I don't know. I'm not good at telling people's age.

MARY: Thirty-five! Do I look thirty-five? Gina was born when I was seventeen. I look fifty, don't I? (*Almost in tears*) It's all because of suffering, misery and hardship. I'm only a few years older than Kate and Kula, but you'll think I'm their aunt or mother. I would have been like them. (*Pulls herself together*) We can't cry over a broken calabash, but we can prevent others from breaking. Gina will be saved from this slavery.

CHRISTIE: Well, I wish you well. I hope your plan works. I'm willing to give whatever help I can.

MARY: Thanks, Christie. You are a real friend.

CHRISTIE: Thanks. I must be leaving now. I only called to see how things are going. I'll be back later. I'm eager to meet your sister and cousin.

MARY: They too are looking forward to meeting you. I've told them a lot about you. (*Christie exits*)

*Lights fade*

# ACT TWO

*(It's late afternoon. Kula and Kate have just arrived. Their luggage is still in the center of the room. They are seated in the same settee flanking Granny Neneh. Across the room, in the armchair opposite them, is Mary)*

GRANNY: I thank God you've arrived safely. You will now put out the fire you started from England and America. I'm washing my hands off the whole business. Your sister has turned rebel in broad daylight. She takes on her husband word for word.

KATE: Auntie, Mary has suffered too much in the hands of that stonehearted man.

KULA: All we want is a better future for Gina and we need your support.

GRANNY: Don't put me in it o! The world is not going to sing my name for ending my daughter's marriage. If you encourage Mary to do anything to either stop Gina going through Bundo or marrying Jaia, Gulama is going to leave her.

KATE: No, Mama, he won't. Without Mary, Gulama is like a house without a roof, a tree without roots.

GRANNY: This is the madness you've been putting into her head.

KULA: Mama, it's not madness. It's the truth.

GRANNY: But she can't marry herself, can she? She needs a man at home.

## ☾ Not You Too ☽

KATE: Not at any cost. And not any man.

KULA: He must know her worth… must know she's not his slave. She has the right to back out if things don't work out.

GRANNY: After 19 years of marriage?

KATE: Anyway, Auntie, Mary is not our main problem at the moment. It's Gina. She must be saved.

GRANNY: Saved from what? She is not going through any danger that you two, Mary, and I have not survived.

MARY: It's no use arguing with Mama. She doesn't see our point of view. She's behind Gulama.

GRANNY: Yes it's no use arguing because I don't see how you'll get Gina out of the room at night when Gulama will be in there, sleeping or not.

KATE: I also have a plan in my head. You say she's under the bed? Is she comfortable in there?

MARY: She's not under the bed. She goes under quickly when she hears him coming. You know he never comes in quietly. (*Enter Borbor*)

KATE: Oh Borbor, you've grown so big! (*Borbor shakes hands with Kate and Kula*)

BORBOR: You are both welcome back home. It's been such a long time.

KULA: Long time indeed! Time runs, doesn't it? You've suddenly grown into a man.

KATE: How are your parents?

BORBOR: They're both well. They'll be coming soon to greet you. How's your son, Munda, Auntie Kate?

KATE: He's doing fine in school in Boston.

KULA: Borbor, so you've not only grown into a man behind my back, you are also interested in our daughter Gina. (*Borbor smiles*)

KATE: Do you love her?

BORBOR: Yes, Auntie Kate, I do.

KULA: Very much?

BORBOR: Yes, Auntie Kula, very much.

KATE: Will you wait for her to graduate from university? We want her to go to college.

BORBOR: Yes, I also want her to go to university.

KULA: And after that, you'll marry her and promise to love and to cherish her?

BORBOR: (*Grins*) I will.

KATE: For better or for worse? You men are not to be trusted. You say sweet things to us until we become yours and then it's a different story. For better or for worse?

BORBOR: (*Grin broadens*) Yes, for better or for worse.

GRANNY: God save me from this excess of madness. Now you've brought it live from the city. How can you encourage this boy in such conversation when you know Gulama has already agreed to give his daughter's hand in marriage to the chief, one of the most powerful men in this town?

Kate: Mama, don't worry about Chief and Gulama, we'll handle them. (*Enter Gulama who appears somewhat at a loss for what to do on seeing Kula and Kate. A few seconds of awkward silence follows his entry*)

KATE: Gulama, greet us. We've not seen each other for over six years. Don't behave as if we parted at the backyard an hour ago.

GULAMA: (*Shaking hands with the two women*) Who says you shouldn't greet first? Is that another of the white man's culture you've been injecting Mary with?

KULA: No, it's not. You entered the house to find us here, so you should greet first. That's very African. Besides, we are your sisters-in-law. We gave our sister's hand in marriage to you.

KATE: So you ought to respect us for that.

GULAMA: And for the madness you've put into her head. Mama, have you told them what they've done to their sister?

GRANNY: I've washed my hands off this business. Settle it any way you can.

GULAMA: Well that's unfortunate, Mama, because there is going to be no peace in this house until I get my daughter back.

KULA: And Mary's daughter.

KATE: She carried her in her womb for almost ten months.

KULA: Gina almost killed her at childbirth.

GULAMA: Mama, now you'll believe what Gulama has been telling you. I told you these two are behind that woman's rebellion.

(*Granny purposefully leaves the sitting room and goes to the bedroom*)

KATE: Listen to him! "That woman." She's not "that woman," she's your wife who mothered your child.

KULA: And lawfully married according to our sacred rites and customs.

GULAMA: Rites and customs that you are inciting her to defile. (*Enter Christie*) The other one has come. The gang is complete.

KULA: This is Christie of course. (*Goes over to her and hugs her*) How do you do? We've been hearing so much about you.

CHRISTIE: (*Shaking hands with Kate*) Me too. I've been dying to meet you two.

KATE: It's a pleasure to know you, Christie.

MARY: Borbor, please carry this luggage to Granny's room. Tell her she'll have to transfer to my room so that Kate and Kula will occupy hers. (*Borbor carries their suitcases*)

GULAMA: (*As if seeing Borbor for the first time*) You! I've still not found my daughter. But the matter is in the hands of Chief Jaia now. I told him I suspect strongly that you are behind this. (*As Borbor enters Granny's bedroom, he calls after him*) His men are searching the whole town. If they fail to find her, know that you'll be seeing Chief to answer a few questions. (*Borbor returns for the other things*) You know what that means. The Chief's policemen even went to your bank to question you. You were lucky it was closed to customers and they were not allowed in. (*Borbor goes with the rest of the things*)

KATE: How can they go to his office to harass him when they have no proof that he has anything to do with Gina's disappearance?

GULAMA: I was not talking to you, Kate. You've come back. But this time you won't run my home for me. (*He goes off angrily to his bedroom. Borbor returns with Granny, who goes across to Mary's room. The others keep casting anxious glances in the direction of Gulama's bedroom*)

BORBOR: Don't mind him, Auntie Kate. I anticipated their coming so I told the security guard not to allow any visitors up to my office.

GULAMA: (*From the Bedroom*) Mary! Mary! (*The others exchange worried glances*)

## ❪ Not You Too ❫

BORBOR: Oh no! He's seen her.

GULAMA: Mary! Mama will know that Gulama doesn't find faults with her daughter wrongly. (*Emerges from his room*) Do you know that I did not take breakfast in this house today? (*The others sigh with relief*) Why are you all staring at me so funnily as if I am a snake or something? Do you hear what I say Mary?

MARY: Gulama, it's simple. You forgot to take breakfast this morning because you were angry over Gina's disappearance.

GULAMA: It was your duty to remind me, woman.

MARY: I was also upset, I didn't remember until you had left.

GULAMA: Well, I want it now.

MARY: What, your breakfast?

GULAMA: What else woman?

MARY: The afternoon meal is ready.

GULAMA: My breakfast!

KULA: (*Laughing*) At six o'clock in the evening.

KATE: (*Laughing*) You know. Gulama has no control over his stomach. Gulama treats eating and drinking very seriously. (*The others are infected by the laughter. Even Borbor cannot help laughing. Enter Chief Jaia and two chiefdom policemen*)

GULAMA: (*Fawning over him*) Oh Chief. Welcome to my house. A big visitor and you've just met other big visitors from the city. Take seat, take seat!

CHIEF: Oh what a great honor to this town. Visitors from the city. Kula, Kate, I'm happy to see you. (*Shakes hands with them*) Welcome, welcome. Ah, Christie, our tireless American relief worker. You've been a blessing to this town. With such a large influx of displaced persons, I wonder what we would have done without you and your organisation. Kula, Kate, Christie is a great lady. As you've learnt she now even speaks our language. I keep telling my people, if there is one person for whom heaven is a certainty, its Christie. But of course, you'll have to die first, ha ha ha. That brings to mind that great singer... what's his name? The one who said, "Everyone wants to go to heaven, but nobody wants to die" Ha, ha, ha, that's very clever observation. Kula, how's England, and Kate, how's the United States? I'm so happy you two are back. You'll be able to witness the wedding between me and your daughter, Gina. Kula, I missed the chance of marrying you, but I've got your niece. Ha, ha, ha. Christie, do you know I wanted to marry her? But her aunt, Kate's mother, a very strong woman, may her soul rest in peace, kept her in the city away from me until she graduated from university and then went to England. She doesn't know what she has missed. Thank God Gina won't miss it. (*To Gulama*) Have you seen her yet? I'm disappointed to learn that she's afraid of Bundo. That's not good enough for Chief Jaia's wife. But I'll teach her to be brave. Where's she?

GULAMA: Er...er...Chief, don't worry. We'll soon find her... nothing to worry about... Er... she's all yours... immediately after this er...er...thing. I'm sure she is somewhere...we only have to...to look in the right place...er this boy, Borbor.

CHIEF: Ah, Borbor! I hear that you must know something about Gina's whereabouts.

GULAMA: Exactly, Chief. He must. He's her friend...you know... I mean he used to help her out with her studies for the G.C.E exams. Yes, he must...but he doesn't...

CHIEF: Borbor, is that what university taught you? To interfere with our customs and traditional rites? (*Turning to leave*) Well, come with me. We have a little talking to do. (*The two policemen grab Borbor by both arms and start pulling him away*)

BORBOR: (*Frees himself roughly*) Don't touch me. I'm going. I'm not under arrest. I haven't committed any crime.

CHIEF: Don't touch him, he's coming, he is not under arrest, he hasn't committed any crime. (*Chief and policemen leave with Borbor*)

MARY: I hope they don't hurt him.

KULA: They won't. Chief Jaia enjoys playing around with his power, but he knows its limit. He won't step beyond that.

GULAMA: (*Irritably*) You two city women seem to know a lot more about us in this town than we do. But I want to assure you that you know nothing of Chief Jaia's powers. He is the most powerful man in this town.

KULA: Is that why you can't refuse him your daughter's hand in marriage?

GULAMA: What do you mean?

KATE: Why you're afraid to say no to him?

GULAMA: Afraid? Me afraid? Ha, ha, ha. What are these women talking about?

KATE: Why then are you giving her away to that old womanizer who has no control over the strings of his trousers?

GULAMA: I'm a man of my word. Besides, Chief Jaia has done too much for me already.

KULA: I can't understand you. How can you throw your daughter's future in the dump for material things?

KATE: Don't you want a better life for her than her mother has had?

GULAMA: Gina is my daughter. I'll do what I please with her and you sharp-tongued, bitter-tongued, high-class ladies from the great white civilised world may interpret my actions anyway you please. And if Mary hasn't got a better life, it's because of what you've now put into her head. Life may have been rough for us, but she has borne it like a true African woman.

KATE: It's not true. She's been aware of her suffering and deprivations all along. She has her five senses intact. We can't make her taste the bitter roots where there is honey.

GULAMA: You may fool her because she's become weak-brained, but don't come pretending to me that life has been all milk and honey for you.

KULA: Nobody told you that. It has not been all milk and honey, but we've had the freedom to try to make it better.

GULAMA: Don't tell me that. You're well over thirty years, why are you still unmarried and childless? And you, clever Kate, why did your husbands leave you? Even the white man left you.

KATE: He didn't leave me. We parted.

GULAMA: (*Laughs derisively*) He left you, you parted, you left him—it's all one and the same. It means something is terribly wrong with you. When a woman can't keep her husbands, then something is wrong. When the parents can't be together, the home is broken. There is no control. Both wife and children go astray. Women are like children. If you don't control them, they go astray. This your England and America, why do you think there is so much wickedness and shamelessness in those countries? It's the collapse of the family, which seriously affects the upbringing of the children.

KULA: So, women and daughters should turn slaves just to keep the family intact.

GULAMA: Consider you, the so-called liberated woman and consider your so-called bondswoman. Forget about materials possessions. Which one of you has a happy and more satisfying life? Are you better off emotionally, spiritually?

KATE: You can't put material possessions aside. It goes with independence. To answer your question, yes the liberated woman is better off.

CHRISTIE: I think so too. To be able to hit back or kick against tyranny is more satisfying than slavish submissiveness or resigned acceptance—if I am permitted to join in this argument.

GULAMA: You're not, woman. You're a foreigner. You do not understand our ways. We understand you better than you do us. Why did you leave your beautiful freedom and come to a backward, poverty-stricken war torn country, risking a bullet through your head or being kidnapped by rebels?

CHRISTIE: (*Tremulous voice*) To serve humanity.

GULAMA: (*Cackles and mimics her*) To serve humanity. Is that all? We're not fools. We know why some of you so-called missionaries and philanthropists leave your comfortable homes to suffer hardship with us.

CHRISTIE: Why? If I may ask?

GULAMA: You may. You run away from your frustrations and disappointments. You run from moral filth and depravity to live with us bush men. In short you are here for all your freedom because you're dissatisfied with your lot. So what makes you better that the submissive African woman? There is more dignity in that bondage than there'll ever be in your so-called freedom. You for example are Mrs, married, but you've been here almost four years and have not gone back home since. No doubt, your marriage had collapsed before you came here.

CHRISTIE: But…

GULAMA: No "buts." Divorce, divorce, divorce. Is that the answer?

CHRISTIE: No, it isn't. But until we find something better, it is. Not accepting, fighting back, is a very important step forward.

KATE: Thank you very much, that's the point—not accepting filth.

KULA: Exactly.

GULAMA: Only Mary, who has maggots in her brain, will envy people like you who don't know what they want in life. You're miserable without men, yet you don't do what you should to keep them. As for you, Mary, whether you like it or not Gina will go through the Bundo and be married to Chief Jaia. (*Exits*)

MARY: That's one thing he's good at, to make other people's lives look bad. (*Granny appears in the doorway of Mary's room*)

KULA: There is some kind of logic in the things he says.

CHRISTIE: There is.

KATE: In his own perverse way he sometimes comes up with sound observations.

GRANNY: Have you given food to Gina?

MARY: Yes, Mama, food and water. (*Granny re-enters the bedroom*)

KULA: I've asked myself that question a million times. (*Rather long pause*) I keep asking whether my life is any better than yours Mary. Disappointed by my first love, seduced and made pregnant by a lecturer whom I took as a father, and having destroyed my baby, becoming barren for life with no man willing to marry me after knowing the truth about my barrenness. (*Begins to sob*)

MARY: (*Goes over to Kula and hugs her crying*) Oh Kula, you never mentioned this. I thought life was good for you. How could I be so insensitive to burden you with my own problems?

KULA: It's not your fault. You didn't know.

MARY: Why did you keep it from me?

KULA: What good would telling you have done? You have more than your fair share of troubles. Besides, I've not been able to say this easily to anyone. It's very recently that I told Kate when she visited me in London, even though she had confided all her secrets to me.

KATE: Not all of my secrets, Kula.

KULA: What do you mean?

KATE: I didn't tell you all. The most painful is still locked up here in my heart.

MARY: Oh no, Kate, I can hear the pain in your voice already.

KATE: Kula—and you too Mary in my letters—I told you I couldn't get on with my first husband, Musa, because he felt that because of my PHD… you know we married when we had just obtained our first degrees. He did not go beyond that… he felt that because of my higher degree, I was trying to control his life. We parted and I married Peter, the white man, the perfect gentleman. (*Breaks down*) I told you that I parted with him because things didn't work out. What I didn't say is that I found him in bed with my then sixteen-year-old son.

ALL: What?

CHRISTIE: His own child?

KULA: No, Munda is her son by her first husband.

MARY: Oh Kate, what pain. You who seemed so strong. Here I was, thinking that my two sisters have PhDs, they're independent and happy. What kind of curse is this on the African woman?

CHRISTIE: It's not only the African woman. It's universal, this problem of marriage, the home, children … and there seems to be no simple solution. What I know for now is that we must face the challenge. As I listened to you two I felt your pain, your hurt, your misery. But you're not alone; we've all been through it. I've been through it.

MARY: Oh no, not you too.

CHRISTIE: Yes, me too. For ten years, a hard drinking hot-tempered, violent husband, whom I had the misfortune to love madly, held me captive in marriage. For ten years I was bruised and battered. My children too suffered physical harassment. One day he came home drunk and insisted on stripping me naked in front of my eight-year old daughter and ten year old son. That was the last straw. I took one of his liquor bottles and cracked his skull, took my kids and left him lying in a pool of blood. Miraculously, he didn't die. He dragged himself to the hospital. I succeeded in getting a divorce easily and the custody of my children, since there were many to testify against him. Unfortunately, my son had taken his father as a role model. I caught him smoking at seven. At ten, he started drinking and cursing like his father. He was expelled from two schools for violent behavior. At 18, five years ago, under the influence of crack, he thought himself an aeroplane and flew to his death from the roof of a twenty-storey building.

*(There is a long pause)*

KULA: God! We just need to listen to others to know that we are not special in our misery.

KATE: And where does that leave us all? Women… from the third world to the first world? Black, yellow or white? Simple or sophisticated?

MARY: Nowhere. (*Thoroughly dejected*) What's the use of fighting for Gina?

KULA: No, no, no! Don't say that.

KATE: We have to continue the fight.

MARY: What's the use when all roads lead to misery and disappointment?

KULA: We have to give Gina her own chance.

KATE: We'll join hands to save her.

CHRISTIE: Perhaps the women of the world need to join hands to save ourselves.

(*Lights fade*)

## ACT THREE

◊◆◊

*(Midnight. Lights. The eerie sound of drumming and ululation wafts in from time to time. The four are still seated as in the previous scene, looking as if they represent all suffering women)*

CHRISTIE: Are those sounds coming from the *Bundo* bush?

MARY: Yes. *(Enter Borbor)* Thank God they've released you.

BORBOR: I was hoping that you had left.

KULA: How can we, when we don't know what's going on out there? Up till now Gulama has not returned. We wanted to be sure that Gulama and Chief Jaia and his men are all in bed.

CHRISTIE: What did they do to you, Borbor?

BORBOR: They held me captive for almost five hours, threatening not to release me until I show them Gina's whereabouts. I was released only when I threatened to take Chief Jaia to the Magistrate Court and have his name published in the newspapers. Then he ordered his men to release me. Getting Gina out is going to be far more difficult than I thought at first.

CHRISTIE: Why?

BORBOR: Those two men are desperate. Pa Gulama is under the spell of Chief Jaia. I have a feeling that he'll kill Gina if Chief tells him to do so.

KATE: He'll have to kill us all first.

KULA: He's indeed desperate. He has come in three times to search these other two rooms.

CHRISTIE: Hiding the girl in his room was a brilliant idea. That is simply beyond any stretch of his imagination. But I'm worried about getting her out when he's finally settled down.

MARY: Don't worry. He sleeps like the body of a witch whose soul has gone out hunting.

(*Gulama rushes in, stops short in the middle of the room, looking frantically about him. There is anger and desperation in all his moves*)

GULAMA: (*Shouting uncontrollably*) It is clear now you are hiding your daughter, you shameless woman; you who have no pride, no respect for your tradition and custom. And don't…

MARY: Gulama, it's past midnight. The town has long been silent.

GULAMA: Shut up! And don't tell me you don't know where she is. Don't tell me that … What move have you made to find her since morning? You've not lifted those treacherous feet of yours a step out of this compound. You! You! (*Moves very close to her, his hands hovering as if to strangle her*) If it were not for the law I have a good mind to strangle you. And I may yet do it, if I don't see my daughter.

MARY: (*Stands up defiantly to face him. Christie, Kula and Kate all move towards her protectively*) Don't worry my sisters, let him kill me. I'm past caring. I'm not afraid of him anymore and the little ounce of respect I had for him has vanished today completely. I know that if Gina goes to that bush and dies, he would care less, so long as he has satisfied Chief Jaia. When the chief came earlier this evening you saw him fawning, babbling like some slave trying to please his master.

(*Gulama strikes her, and raises his hand to strike her again, but he is bear hugged from behind by Borbor, while Kate and Kula come between them. Mary picks up one of her slippers and strikes Gulama's forehead over the heads of others)*

KULA: Stop it, Mary, please. Don't fight with him.

KATE: (*Pushing Gulama's head roughly with her fingers*) This man is too brutal.

GULAMA: (*Struggling breathlessly to free himself from Borbor's bear hug*) You see, you see what you've done… allowing these street women to gang up against me. Just make sure I don't get free, because as soon as… I… I'm free, you're dead. (*Kula, Kate and Christie pull Mary away to a safe distance, Gulama continues struggling to break free from Borbor's hold until he becomes completely spent*)

KULA: Borbor, release him, don't let him suffer a heart attack in your hands. He doesn't realize he's no longer young. (*Borbor releases Gulama*)

GULAMA: (*Dashing to his room*) You just wait till I get my cutlass from under my bed.

MARY: Go away, Borbor, go! Don't just stand there.

(*Borbor moves towards exit*)

KULA: Oh God, he is going to find Gina! Borbor go!

(*Gulama lets out a terrified scream, dashes out of the room and makes straight for the front door*)

GULAMA: There's… there's something under my bed, a living thing! I touched hands and feet! (*Exits*)

(*Borbor bursts into uncontrollable laughter. As the truth of what has just happened dawns on the others they too are infected with laughter. Gulama recovers enough from his shock to return to sitting room*)

GULAMA: This is no madness. I touched flesh, warm sweating and trembling… what's funny? What are you all laughing at? Do you think I'm… (*He stops to observe them suspiciously as they try to suppress their laughter. He seems to suddenly realize what's happening. He takes long quick strides to his room and, smiling, he returns seconds later dragging a whimpering Gina behind him*) I must congratulate you on your cleverness. That idea must have come from the city women. It's like what you see in the cinemas. I must admit that I'd never have known. But God is on my side... the side of truth and justice.

KULA: Don't bring God into this please. Is it truth and justice to send your daughter to...?

MARY: Save your breath. He's too drunk with Chief Jaia's gifts to see sense in anything anyone says. (*To Gulama*) All I want you to know is that Gina is not leaving here. (*Plants herself in front of Gulama. She takes off her head scarf, ties it around her waist and puts her hands on her hips defiantly*) I'm ready to die for my daughter's freedom.

GULAMA: Is that so? (*To the others*) Look, tell her, if she doesn't get out of my way I'll use my foot on her to make my passage. (*Again Kula, Kate and Christie come between them*)

CHRISTIE: I think you need to talk this thing over peaceably.

GULAMA: American, this is none of your business.

KULA: Gulama, I agree with Christie. This needs talking over.

GULAMA: Will you all get out of my way! I'll talk with no one... listen to no one!

KATE: (*Cajoling*) You don't have to talk, but we can sit over drinks. I've brought good American rum and fine tobacco. Just listen to what I have to say. If it doesn't go down well with you—Gina is your daughter—you can do what you wish with her. I'll wash my hands off the matter just like Auntie. Gina is right here, so she won't run away. And you've not even given us a chance to show you the gifts we've brought for you and the family from abroad.

GULAMA: How will I when I've been running around all day searching for this ungrateful treacherous girl? And how can I when you yourselves greeted me with fire?

KATE: Kula bring a bottle of rum. In the morning we'll show Gulama his gifts. Let's all sit and talk. Borbor, you can join us.

GULAMA: No! If he is sitting with you, I won't. Let him get his buttocks out of here, before I lose my temper again. All he's brought us is trouble. Get out!

BORBOR: (*Moving to exit*) Yes sir.

GULAMA: Just get out! (*He takes a seat, forcing Gina to sit on the floor by his side*)

KATE: Borbor, please. We'll see in the morning (*Borbor exits*). Kula, go in and get the drink. (*Kula goes to the guest room*)

KATE: While we are waiting for the drink, this is my proposal. Gina will go through the *Bundo* rites.

GULAMA: Nothing is going to stop that!

KATE: I know, but please let me finish.

MARY: That is not true. I'm going to stop it. You surprise me, Kate.

GULAMA: (*Rises and begins pulling Gina away*) I'm not going to listen to any more madness.

KATE: Please wait and be patient. Mary, please let me handle this (*Kula enters with a bottle of rum which she sets on a small center table, goes over to a small cupboard in one corner, and takes out a few wineglasses and some plastic cups and sets them on the table*)

GULAMA: (*Sitting down again with Gina*) One more word from that undisciplined woman and I leave. (*To Kula, who is trying to break the seal of the bottle with her nails*)

Give that to me; don't break your delicate nails. (*He breaks the seal, removes the cap and sniffs*) Doesn't seem strong enough. (*Gives it back to Kula*)

KATE: It's high-class rum. You'll like it. Kula pour a glass for Gulama. (*Kula hands Gulama a glass, which he tilts slightly to one side as if to pour a libation*)

KULA: If that's libation nothing dropped to the ground.

GULAMA: (*Laughs. Drinks slowly*) It doesn't matter. It's the intention that matters. Our forefathers will understand.

KATE: Okay, back to my proposal. We'll coax Gina and take her to the bush.

GULAMA: *You* take her? I don't trust you… none of you. I'll go with her myself and hand her over to the Bundo Women.

KATE: Please, let me finish. That is not a man's job, but it doesn't matter, you can do as you wish. (*Kula hands Kate a glass, offers the other women too*)

CHRISTIE: No, thanks.

MARY: You know I have neither head nor stomach for strong drinks.

KATE: (*To Gulama*) After her circumcision I want her to come home so that Christie can treat her wound.

GULAMA: A foreigner? An American woman to partake in our traditional rites? Indeed you've been away for too long. The Chief has already got a trained and qualified nurse who is an expert in looking after girls who have just gone through *Bundo*.

KATE: Well that's fine. I didn't know.

GULAMA: You never asked, because you took us as monsters—me and Chief Jaia. (*Drains his glass*)

KATE: After that... (*Gets up and refills Gulama's glass and returns to her seat*) After that I want her to spend a week with us in the city to recuperate and then we shall return to talk to Chief Jaia to marry her, but to allow her to go to university first and return to him after her graduation.

GULAMA: (*On his feet*) I credited you with more sense than that. Do you think...?

KATE: Sit down and enjoy your drink. This is merely a proposal. (*He sits*)

KULA: You know that you and Kate get on better than you and I. So at least listen to her. I didn't bring anything for you. All the things you'll get are from Kate— the tobacco, pipe, radio/cassette recorder, the sandals and towels.

KATE: Kula, how can you do that? I wanted it to be a surprise.

GULAMA: (*To Kula*) You've always been the mean one. You're too close-fisted. Anyway, Kate, give me a moment to think about this. (*Walks slowly, thoughtfully, downstage to the apron*) These women are naïve in their cunning. They think I am dumb as they are. If I allow that girl to go to the city with them that will be the end of her marriage to Chief Jaia and he will blame me. But I want the things she sent for me, so I'm not going to say no, I'll play along with them... let them taste their own bitter root. I am...(*Kula and Kate are engaged in whispered conversation*)

KATE: You've caught on to what I'm up to, haven't you?

KULA: Get him drunk, then we escape with Gina to Freetown.

KATE: Right. But I don't intend to just sit by until he gets drunk. He'll soon finish this bottle. I am going to drug the next drink so that he'll stay out for the next three or four hours. Just watch him out there, deep in thought. Right now, his cunning mind is working out how to get his gifts and then go ahead and do exactly as he pleases.

He'll come back to tell us he accepts my proposal and he'll probably let Chief Jaia into his secret telling him to play along with us until Gina goes through the Bundo and then they'll do what they want.

*(Enter Chief Jaia. Gulama pulls him aside and they engage in whispered conversation)*

KATE: Talk of the devil. Just what I said he would do. (*The two men burst out laughing*) See, they think they've got us where they want us. We'll see who gets the last laugh. Get ready to pour Chief Jaia a glass. He's another heavy drinker. (Chief Jaia and Gulama join them) Ah, welcome Chief. Take a seat. You've come in good time. We have imported rum for you.

CHIEF JAIA: (*Sits*) I smelt it from my compound, that's why I came. Gina, why should you run away from *Bundo*? That's not good enough for an African woman. Anyway, Gulama has just told me about your proposal Kate. I think it's a brilliant idea. I always say I have respect for your intelligence. Don't I Gulama?

GULAMA: Yes, Chief, you do, always. You've always said it. (*Kula empties the bottle into a glass and gives it to Chief. Kate hurries away to their room to get another bottle*)

CHIEF: (*Sniffs the drink, gives a satisfied grunt and pours a few drops on the ground*) To you our great ancestors, please keep watch over us. (*He takes a long gulp as Kate reappears with another bottle*) Ah, you city women really know how to celebrate Christmas Day. It's past midnight. (*He drains his glass. Gulama drains his too. Kate refills his glass from the new bottle*) Ah, it's a good thing my feet brought me here. I just decided to check once more to see if my Gina has come back. Now I have been doubly rewarded. Gina is here and cold water is here. Christie, so you're still here. I keep saying that you're one of us. No other foreigner mingles so closely with us.

CHRISTIE: Well, I don't usually stay out so late, but today is kind of special… It's Christmas and Kula and Kate are here.

CHIEF: (*On his feet*) See, isn't she great? Let's raise our glasses to her. (*Gulama and Chief raise their glasses and drink. Lights fade*)

(*Lights. An hour later. Both Chief and Gulama are sprawled in armchairs in drunken oblivion. Three empty bottles are standing on the table. Kula, Kate, Gina, Christie, Mary, and Borbor are all on their feet standing by the luggage in the center of the room. Added to Kula and Kate's luggage are Gina's Mary's and Granny's. Granny is nodding in her settee*)

KATE: Borbor go to No. 2 and wake up the driver. Tell him to be ready with the car in five minutes. (*Borbor exits*)

CHRISTIE: I wonder what he'll do when he wakes up to find his house empty.

KATE: What can he do? He'll be angry no doubt, but with an empty house it will do him good to just calm down and try to think of ways of bringing his wife back.

KULA: He will be too busy trying to calm Chief Jaia to think of his own anger.

KATE: Chief Jaia is not going to pose much of a problem. He'll just ask for his money and wash his hands off. You remember his youngest wife ten years ago… what was her name?

MARY: Massa, the girl from Koribondo, who ran away with her boyfriend to Freetown?

KATE: Yes. He only asked that his money be returned.

KULA: That doesn't solve Gulama's problems. He'll have to cough up money to pay Jaia and he'll still have an empty house.

MARY: This house is going to be empty for a long time. Gulama is going to realise that without me he is nobody. When he does and goes to Freetown and asks me decently to return, I'll come back. I'm glad Mama didn't raise much objection to this last minute modification of our plan.

CHRISTIE: She wants to spend some time with Kula and Kate.

MARY: True, and also she doesn't want to listen to Gulama's complaints when he wakes up to find Gina gone. I think she's fed up with all these quarrels.

KATE: (*Bursts out laughing. The others look at her in surprise*) It's all right. I just wish I could be around when those two wake up. (*Borbor enters*) Is he ready?

BORBOR: The car is waiting on the main road. He wanted to come with me to help carry the luggage but I told him to stay by the car.

KATE: Good. We'll share the luggage among us. Borbor, you and Christie will walk with Auntie. We're about to score one little victory over tyranny.

KULA: Yes, as Christie says, fighting back is the thing.

CHRISTIE: And coming together and sharing.

(*They collect the things and leave with Granny, who is supported by Borbor and Christie. In the background the drumming and ululation continue. Lights fade*)

(*Lights. It's two hours later. Gulama and Chief Jaia are fast asleep, both snoring loudly. Gulama wakes up suddenly. Looks around, realizes what has happened, jumps up and runs towards one of the rooms. He stops suddenly in his tracks as he is hit by a terrible headache. He moves more carefully to look for his family. By the time he gets to the last room, he is almost hysterical*)

GULAMA: Chief! Chief, wake up! Chief, wake up! They have gone!

CHIEF: W...wh...what?

GULAMA: They have gone.

CHIEF JAIA: (*Jumps up momentarily, disoriented*) What? Who?

GULAMA: Gina, Mary...all the women.

CHIEF JAIA: What! (*He is hit by a splitting headache and speaks quietly*) What do you mean? Gone where?

GULAMA: I don't know. I suspect they have gone to the city. Even Mama has gone. What am I going to do Chief? What are you going to do? We must get them back.

(*Chief gets slowly to his feet, stretches out his hand to Gulama and with palm upwards*)

GULAMA: Eh?

CHIEF JAIA: Time to start paying back.

GULAMA: (*Fawning*) Ah Chief, she will come back. I know where they must have gone. Don't worry; I'll get your wife back for you.

CHIEF JAIA: I am not worried. All I want is my money back... all that I have spent on her. In fact, I don't think she will make a good wife. Afraid of *Bundo* and runs away... My friend, just start refunding my investment.

GULAMA: But Chief...

CHIEF JAIA: But nothing. I will give you three days.

GULAMA: To get her back?

CHIEF JAIA: I say I no longer want her for a wife. Three days to start refunding.

GULAMA: Ah Chief...

☾ Not You Too ☽

CHIEF JAIA: Okay, one week. I am off. (*Exits*)

GULAMA: Chief! Chief! (*He collapses on to a chair, his head in his hands*) Oh Mary. That woman. My wife. Where will I find money to pay back that ruthless man? (*Pauses as the gravity of his predicament hits him*) And… how will I cope without that woman, my wife, Mary?

## LIGHTS OUT

# GLOSSARY

◊ ◆ ◊

| | |
|---|---|
| Alpha | A committed Muslim man |
| Barre | A gathering place, usually where the chief holds court |
| Bi wua | Good morning (or have you woken up?) |
| Bi sie | Thank you; hello; or how are you? |
| Bo | Please. It can also be a term of exasperation |
| Bofima | A juju occasionally smeared with human blood |
| Boku Boku | A lot. Plenty |
| Bundu | (Sometimes spelled Bundo) A female secret society |
| Chakabula | A locally made gun |
| Contri cloth | A piece of cloth made out of locally prepared cotton |
| Fritambo | A deer |
| Gbeni | A masked devil associated with the Poro |

| | |
|---|---|
| Gongoli | A comic masked devil |
| Goboi | A masked devil also associated with the Poro |
| Hanging heads | To deliberate or discuss a matter |
| Haram | Something God will disapprove of |
| Hindo | Man; evoking one's manhood |
| Impiari | A greeting: how are you? |
| Jolabete | A vegetable dish made with cassava leaves |
| Jonga | A weapon that is between a sword and a knife |
| Keke | Papa or father |
| Koni | Friend |
| Koto | Brother. Used as a sign of respect and friendship for males |
| Kpako | An elderly person |
| Kurumasaba | It has happened |
| Lai lai | Never |
| Lappa | A large cloth tied around the waist and sometimes over the shoulders |
| Maboye | A female member of the Poro |
| Mampama | Palm wine |
| Na wi… | Is our… |
| Ndake | A fond way of referring to a male of the same age group |
| Ngafo | The act of blowing fire |
| Ngewo | The Supreme Being; God |
| Ngo | A term of respect for a male or a female slightly older than oneself |
| Ndanamba | A poisonous plant |
| Ndumdobai | Another species of poisonous plant |
| Paytaytay | To dance along and stamp the feet while walking |

# Glossary

| | |
|---|---|
| Pekin | A child |
| Poro | A male secret society |
| Sande | A female secret society |
| Shakitomboi | A vegetable dish made with potato leaves |
| Shegureh | A percussive instrument: a calabash or gourd encased in beads |
| Suwui | Bundu Society Head |
| Totogbemui | A diviner or sorcerer |
| Yamama | A masked devil |
| Yeiiyo | Crying out for one's mother |

# PLAYWRIGHTS' BIOGRAPHIES

◊◆◊

**Raymond Caleb Ayodele-Charley (1948–1993)**

A trained certified teacher of Sports education, Dele-Charley (or Dele Charley) was a playwright, poet, drummer, actor, director, choreographer, and athletics coach in soccer, basketball, and volleyball. He is considered the foremost facilitator in the theater community. He is known to have nurtured the founders of almost all the theater groups that sprang up in the 1970s, 80s, and 90s. Julius Spencer, Charlie Haffner, Raymond Desouza George, Clifford Shafume Garber, John Kolosa Kargbo, Tonie French, and Ayo Boye-Fewry are among those actors, directors, and playwrights who passed through some variant of Dele-Charley's tutorship. Dele-Charley founded the Freetown Youth Players in 1968; the group was later renamed Tabule Theatre, which he established with Adeyemi Meheux that same year. Through Tabule, Dele-Charley's award-winning play, *Blood of a Stranger* (1976), was chosen as Sierra Leone's entry play at the Festival for the Arts and Culture (FESTAC) in 1977, in Nigeria. Under Dele-Charley's directorship, the group also took Raymond

Desouza George's *Bohboh Lef* to London International Festival Theatre (LIFT) in 1983. Dele-Charley won a USIS award for a month-long tour of theaters in the US in 1981. In 1984, he achieved a certificate in Miming from Vichy, France. He later earned an MA in Theater Studies from Leeds in 1989. In Sierra Leone, Dele-Charley translated many plays into Krio, including several Shakespearean plays, such as *Macbeth* (*Makuba*) and *The Merchant of Venice* (*Wan Paun Flesh*). He wrote many plays in Krio, such as *Titi Shain Shain*, *Ofori Komot Nah Doe*, and *Pettikot Kohna*. He also wrote a dance drama in both English and Krio titled *Fatmata*. Dele-Charley's plays in English include *The Green Jewel*, written at the age of 12 and performed in London and Nottingham in 1992 and 1993, *The Return of Kindo*, and *Letters*, performed in Leeds, London, and the BBC. Generous with his time, he ran theater workshops in London, and the Gambia, alongside his many community responsibilities in Freetown, where he judged school drama competitions, offered unpaid advice to many theater groups, and did community theater work, such as the dissemination of public health information in partnership with international groups like CARE and UNICEF.

### John Kolosa Kargbo (1954-1992)

Fondly known as JK, his talent for writing was recognized early by his teachers at the Prince of Wales Secondary School, where his skits were performed at major events. By 1970 when he graduated with distinction in English Language and Literature in the General Certificate Examination, he had settled on Wole Soyinka as his role model. That same year, he and a friend co-founded The Revelers Theater Group, which was dissolved shortly after. He then joined Clifford Shafume Garber's Segureh Players but eventually decided to found his own group, the Baranta Actors' Theater, later renamed the Songhai Theatre, and finally African Heritage Workshop. *Let Me Die Alone* (1976) is considered his finest work in English. One of his most popular plays, *Poyotogn Wahala* (1979), critiqued government corruption and human rights abuse. As a result of this play, the government established a Censorship Board that succeeded in silencing many artists. In frustration, JK moved to Nigeria in 1982. After his stint as a freelance broadcaster for Radio Lagos, he pursued a diploma in Theater Arts in 1984. Thereafter, JK worked for several Nigerian magazines as an editor. He went into seclusion after he was diagnosed with tuberculosis in 1991. He died sitting at his typewriter in December 1992. He was buried in Lagos.

## Julius Sonny Spencer (1955- )

Julius Sonny Spencer has an MA and a PhD in Theater Arts from the University of Ibadan. He was also a 1996-1997 Hubert Humphrey Fellow in the School of Communication at Boston University. In the 1980s and 90s, he was a lecturer of theater at the University of Sierra Leone. He became Minister of Information Communication, Tourism and Culture 1998-1999. After the post was renamed Minister of Information and Broadcasting, he served from 1999 to 2001. He then resigned to be the Managing Director of Premier Media Consultancy Ltd, a position he still holds. Spencer has acted in and directed many plays, both in Sierra Leone and Nigeria. He also directed John C. Thorpe's award winning play, *Chap Am So*, in New York City. *Chap Am So* was nominated for 10 Audelco Awards, including Best Director. Spencer's international exposure also includes Europe and Asia. Spencer has written and directed plays for radio, television, and film. He has published essays in journals, such as *African Literature Today*, *New Theatre Quarterly*, and *International Journal of Sierra Leone Studies*.

## Tonie French (1943-1995)

Tonie French was a playwright and an actress. She studied theater at the Royal Scottish Academy of Music and Drama in Glasgow. She worked briefly at the BBC before taking up a position as a newscaster, in both radio and television, at the Sierra Leone Broadcasting Service (SLBS). After twenty years of service at SLBS she retired from the prestigious post as Controller of Production Services. Her return to the theater as an actress in the play, *Iago*, directed by John Thorpe, was, in no small measure a boost for the image of women in theater. Tonie French has written two plays, *What a Life!* (1991) and *The Pool* (1994). She starred in both plays. French's concern for women in Sierra Leone featured significantly in both plays. She was also a member of Forum for African Women Educationalists (FAWE).

## Mohamed Sheriff (1959- )

Mohamed Sheriff has a BA in English and an M. Sc. in Rural Development from the University of Sierra Leone. He is a playwright, director, actor, and short story writer. He has written, produced, and directed numerous plays for both public entertainment and theater for development projects. He is the artistic and executive director of Pampana Communications. Pampana specializes in drama for radio, TV, and community development projects. He has published with Macmillan and Pen Point. His essay on Sierra Leone theater appears in Martin Banham's *A History of Theatre in Africa* (Cambridge, 2004). He won the 2006 BBC African Performance Playwriting Competition for his radio play *Spots of the Leopard*. His feminist play, *Not You Too*, was written in 1996 and first performed in September 2000 by the National Performing Arts Troupe, directed by Julius Spencer.